The Search For Life After Death

Linwood Jackson Jr.

ISBN: 978-1-955622-55-4 (hardcover)
978-1-955622-54-7 (paperback)

Cover art and design by Fatima Azhar

For more information,
email the author at LinwoodJackson@hotmail.com,
or visit linwoodjacksonjr.com

Published by
Fideli Publishing, Inc.

www.FideliPublishing.com

Dedication

This book is first dedicated to me, Linwood Jackson Jr., albeit the 2011 version of my self.

Young man, nine years have passed since we first began writing this series. Since then, I have, both inwardly and philosophically, changed as a human being, but this change would never have occurred if not for you.

Azazel is your creation. *Azazel* is your prophecy. I have published this book in honor of you, my past self, not simply because you are the author, but because I am thankful for your imagination, for your inspiration, for your empathy, for your wisdom, for your concern about us, and for the memory of you continuing to embolden me, each and every day, to reach my highest personal and devotional potential.

I publish this book to say that, with all that I have within me, I love you. Live on, in this series, for ever.

This book is secondly dedicated to my best of friends, and to *Azazel's* number one fan, Bryan Sisson.

Bryan, your hardcore love for *Azazel* has inspired me to publish this book. As this book, in the very beginning, passed through various stages of development, you were there, binder and all, to give ideas and corrections to the book's direction.

I dedicate this book to you because you, more than me, have supported its publishing, seeing absolute and unadulterated treasure within every page. Thank you for your passion, for your support, for your advice, and for your friendship.

Contents

Introduction .... *vii*

1. Origins 1
2. The Deal 7
3. It Is Done 13
4. A Joint Vision 21
5. Ra 29
6. Aepharia 37
7. Expansion 45
8. Seen 58
9. The Writer 68
10. The Judgment 78
11. Recollection 87
12. Hide And Seek 117
13. Into Perspective 124
14. The Trip To And From The Temple 142
15. The Trip To The Underuniverse 166
16. In The Beginning 184
17. Forethought 203
18. The Final Baptism 211
19. A New Past Age 219
20. A Return To Form 227
21. From Whence He Came 239
22. Sight 245
23. Vengeance 258
24. Consolation 265

Note A Zeus' Act Against Azazel 270
Note B The Scars 273
Note C Bune 275
Note D The Wisdom of Bune 277
Note E Bune's Take 279

Introduction

The time came for the Eternal Sovereign to create a new Dimension and to dedicate it to thinking and feeling *beings*. He planned to create a realm, an open void of invisible elements, and to create Creators for doing whatsoever they would with the void and with the invisible elements. Their task would be to create two Universes; one they would call Heaven, and the other they would call the Underuniverse; and to create other thinking and feeling *beings* able to create other realms supporting life within the Universes. This venture was a new and different project for the Eternal who would, instead of doing the work himself, create a class of Creators who would then create a class of Creators to execute the envisioned realm.

Unlike the other realms, the Eternal wanted this realm to cultivate its own character. He didn't want his handprint on it, but wanted the *beings* he would create to act as his handprint, executing the will of his mind through the liberty he imputed to them. Above recognition through what he himself would create, he wanted recognition from within the heart and mind of his Creators and the *beings* descending from them. This new realm was to be an experiment for enlightenment on love and on allegiance. That his brilliance might be regarded due to a respect for the independence given to a new species of transcendental *beings*, he left the realm open to them, his care being only for the realm continuing the constitution he would set within it.

He didn't act alone. Beside him, within the empty void, stood his wife, the Sovereign Empress. Standing not too close together, but face to face, and with their hands clasped, they close their eyes. Soon enough a small orb of light begins to develop within the open space between them. Their presence, radiating a heat from their embrace, is mixing with the cold environment to ignite or cause a certain tension or current within the void. Hovering in nothingness, the two remain hand in hand and meditating on the envisioned realm and its elements for creation.

The orb of light, within that empty pocket between them both, grows. Still silently meditating, the orb begins to develop, within it, intelligence for re-creating the void into a realm supporting life. Now seeing the orb reaching its potential, the Empress removes her right hand from holding her husband's hand and, with her index finger and thumb, reaches into her husband's forehead, pulling out a gem-like object bright in appearance, dropping it into the orb. As soon she returns her right hand to her husband's hand, the Eternal removes his left hand and reaches into his wife's chest. When pulling his hand out, he does so with his palm facing up, a bright mist or smoke resting within his palm. He places the smoking mist into the orb and returns to his wife's hand.

The orb, reaching its ultimate potential, rises above the heads of the Eternal Pair, and then explodes. Invisible elements supporting the structure of the envisioned realm, and of living creatures possessing a version of the character and ability of their Creators, forms from out of the explosion. Soon enough the invisible elements begin to form small star-like flakes. These star-like components are what the Creators will use to construct the two Universes and the *beings* that should begin to populate them.

Again, joining hands, but this time, instead of a clasp, palm to palm, many orbs of light, after their hands begin to develop a bright glow on them, begin to shoot from their forehead and into the newly constructed atmosphere of the open realm. These many little orbs begin to mix with the small star-like flakes around them, forming figures, both male and female, similar to their own. These male and female figures are the Creators of the Architects assigned to generate the realms and the other *beings* inhabiting the two Universes.

The Empress, seeing their lifeless bodies hovering in the open atmosphere of the realm, reaches down her throat and pulls a worm-like creature from out of her mouth. She throws the creature above their lifeless bodies. The creature forms a ring, begins to develop a bright glow, turns into a vapor, divides, and descends into their nostrils, awakening them.

After clothing the Creators, the Eternal Pair informs them of their assignment. Placing them in a circle, and instructing them to hold hands, they tell them that they must section the realm into two parts: the first, Heaven; the second, the Underuniverse.

An orb, similar to the one appearing between the Eternal and the Empress, begins to form. When the orb reaches a certain magnitude, the Eternal and the Empress instruct them all to either reach within the front of their own head, or within their own chest, and to pull out and drop within the orb the gem-like or vapor-like structure that is taken out. They all do as they are told.

Soon enough the orb reaches its maximum capacity. Now ascending over their heads, the orb explodes, the components of the explosion mixing with the star-like bodies of the realm's atmosphere. The realm, once void, being now, due to the Eternal Pair, filled with material for initiating the creation of the Universes, divides, forming two livable planes. The area, in which they all are, the Cosmos, remains undisturbed, being now a small open space where the Eternal and his Empress will set up their invisible Estate. It will become, as with every other realm, visible only to whomever they please.

The two livable planes are now ready to be inhabited. Both have a beauty familiar to the essence of the gem-like or vapor-like characters within their Creators. Still with their Creators, and still within that area of the realm for creation, the Eternal and the Empress tell them their next assignment. They must now create a class of creating *beings* beneath them, and give to that class the assignment of beautifying the Universe and the realms they are assigned to. They must create these *beings* to create the *beings* that will settle in and populate the Universe they are assigned to.

The Empress and the Eternal, after informing them of their next assignment, instruct their Creator to touch the palms of the individual beside them. With the development of a glowing light appearing on their hands, another orb of light forms in their midst. Being close to its magnitude, the Eternal instructs them to break the circle, telling them to put their hands to their sides. Upon doing so, he instructs them to concentrate on the orb and on the figures they would create. Small orbs of light shoot out of his creating assembly's forehead and enter into the growing orb.

Now reaching its magnitude, the orb explodes, its component combining with the star-like matter of the environment to form male and female bodies that are similar to their Creators. But there is a difference. Some *beings* have beautiful wings coming out of and going into their back. Other bodies are similar to the bodies of their Creators, having no wings at all. But then there are others that are created having bodies of animals with heads of men or women, or with bodies similar to men and women while possessing the head of an animal. There are even some that are created with many wings and with multiple heads while possessing bodies of animals or bodies similar to their Creators.

The Eternal and the Empress then inform them of their next two tasks. They must give life to their creation, and within that life, they must encode the power, craft, intelligence, and abilities of those *beings*. The Empress then instructs the Creators to reach into their mouth. She tells them that a worm-like creature will appear rising up from their throat. They must all take that worm-like creature and cast it above their creation.

They all do as they are told. Upon doing so, each one of their worm-like creatures unites, forming a ring above their lifeless creation. When formed, the ring begins to glow brilliantly, and then divides, entering into the nostrils of their creation, awakening them. Upon being clothed and informed about their assignment, the Creators of the Creators are sent into the Universe that they are to occupy. Hereafter they receive instruction from their Creators on how to define their Universe and its realms or sections devoted to certain *beings*, but not before a brief lecture by the Eternal and the Empress, who inform these two classes of Creators of their allegiance to the invisible yet visible throne, of their timeless bloodline, and of their importance to the *beings* under them.

The dawn of a new era and brand of life had come. Having finished their work, the King and his Empress, as they did in all of their other realms, called into existence a kingdom and a royal territory for their throne. This Empire would remain invisible until necessary, or until made visible to whoever should know it. Upon setting up the territory of their throne, they then left the realm, leaving that territory invisible.

And so our story begins. With the Eternal and the Empress giving the realm over to the class of the Creators, and over to the *beings* of the Universes, the experiment began, but with an unexpected twist. One of the Creators created by the Eternal Pair, when engaged in creating the Creators that should labor in the Universes, attached a certain will to one of the created *beings*, encoding the substance creating him with a decree, initiating, through them, a legacy. The will attached to that *being* was a vision of the Eternal Sovereign being overthrown and replaced.

Being a Creator, the power to have materialized or have manifested what is thought is within their ability. Attaching this will to that *being* means its inevitable fulfillment, but in an unknown way.

The Creator, while having the ability to manifest what is thought, is unable to let what is thought take place as imagined. What is thought, while having a fixed result, does not unwind in the expected way, but becomes what it will and in however manner it will. But what is certain is that one *being* will have his way with the Universes, and even with the Mind of the Universes, but how, and to what extent, and in what manner, is unknown.

Origins

The atmosphere gave birth to a god. Hovering in the open field of the Cosmos, the child, silent in behavior and bright in appearance, is alone, without mother and father. Around him are four females, majestic in appearance, their wings encircling him as their voices unite in a hymn. The child, watching and listening to the goddesses, glows brighter with every chord that is struck.

Soon enough the warmth from their voices stirs the child, causing him to cry. One of the goddesses reaches for him and holds him in her arms. After kissing his forehead and having their eyes meet, a tear falls from her face, falling on to her chin, and landing on his forehead. Her fallen teardrop, like as a ripple made by a little pebble in a pond, creates a similar effect throughout his entire body. This effect brings the child back to his silence, and then to sleep.

But this peaceful scene doesn't last forever. A Guard of the Cosmos soon interrupts. He tells the goddesses that this child has violated the laws of the Cosmos by it being there and must be taken to the Council for judgment.

He tries to pry the child from the arms of the goddess, but the other three goddesses rise and form a wall with their wings to protect them both. The Guard, understanding the power and status of the goddesses, tells the goddess holding the child that if she will not let him take the child, that she can present the child to the Council herself. She agrees, and, standing before the Council, makes her case for child's innocence against the law.

Looking down at the goddess from her high seat of judgment, and with a look as if she felt what the woman was feeling, after a long period of deliberation, she says to the woman, "It is a violation for anyone to be in that part of the Cosmos without warrant. The violator, no matter who or what that violator is, must have a sentence of judgment given to them. Just because this is a child, the law still stands."

"So you must punish an innocent baby, an infant not in control of his own life, mind, and body?" says the woman.

"How then," says another member of the Council, "can you justify his innocence? We have no information regarding this child's appearance in the Cosmos other than the word of the Guard, who was told that he received word of it suspended and lingering in the open atmosphere. From the time that it was there and not claimed or observed, its violation was pending."

"So then why not blame the Guard?" says the goddess. "Since when is incompetence overlooked, and especially by you?"

"The child was not present when I last surveyed the area," interrupted the Guard.

"How then," says that same member of the Council to the woman, "do you explain this phenomenon of a child mysteriously appearing out of nothing?"

"The error is my own," says the woman, looking down. "I brought my son into the open radiance of the Cosmos to liquefy certain elements of the air for his bath. Upon being called by my sisters, knowing that my son would be safe right where I left him, I tended to the affair."

"So you left him there?" questioned another member of the Council.

"Yes," she responded.

"And for what reason?" they again asked.

"For matters of Heaven, from which I come. My sisters needed the power of four and not of three."

"Are you sure about all of this?" questioned another member of the Council.

"Why would I lie?" she replied. "I love my son. Despite how this may look, I have done this before. He is newly born. I have taken and washed him in the elements of the Cosmos on many occasions since his birth, even leaving him there to become one with the intelligence within the air."

"And you understand that by do so, even all of those other past times, that you stood in violation of the law?" continues this same member of the Council.

"Of course, I understand," she says. "I want what is best for my child. I will only care for him according to the practices of my father's royal throne. There is a certain way to care for sons of the class of the Creators, and I will not suffer my son to know any *thing* less."

"But you understand that a sentence of judgment must come to the child because of your negligence?" says the same questioning member of the Council.

"I believe you should consider me as the sufferer of the sentence of judgment and not my son," she reasoned. "Whatever the consequences may be, I pray, and even beg of you to let me suffer them, and not my son. I have committed these acts understanding the potential consequences of them, and have been prepared for me, and not for my son, to suffer the sentence of judgment if ever found contrary to the law."

"This woman is not the child's mother," blurted the Guard.

"How do you know this?" asks one of the Council's members to him.

"Her story doesn't make sense. I saw the child, and upon looking at him, I found no resemblance to this woman."

The Council then asks for the child to be given to the mother, that she may hold him, and that a decision about the child's appearance may be made. Upon receiving him, the child possesses a similar appearance to the woman, silencing the claim that he is not the woman's child.

"The child is mine," says the woman, looking down at him, and then looking up. "Let me suffer his sentence of judgment. My son should not have to suffer for my negligence."

"Very well," said another member of the Council. "As a goddess of creation, your ability to create, and to mediate creation, in all aspects, both conscious and unconscious, will be removed."

A small bottle was then presented to her. She was to exhale into the bottle, casting the spirit and intellect of her ability to create into the bottle. After doing so, with the bottle filled with the spirit of her ability to create, it was given to the Council member asking for it.

"The essence of your being is creation. You are hereafter no longer able to create," said the Council member holding the bottle of her essence. "Take your son back to Heaven and amend your negligence with better habits."

Satisfied with the judgment, "Thank you," she says.

Holding the child and looking down at him with a smile, she takes one more look at the members of the Council on their seats of judgment, and then walks out their Court. Waiting for her outside of the Council's Court are her three sisters. She joins them, and with her son in her arms. They all immediately vanish and reappear at their section of Heaven, the only section committed to the society of these goddesses and the families they have chosen to have.

"What do we do now?" she says to her sisters, her son in her arms, who is playing with her locks.

"I don't know," says one.

"We have a son now," says another, wearing a look of dismay.

"Do you think our father would know what to do?" asks the goddess holding the child.

"We can't tell him," says the other sister. "Who knows what his reaction will be."

"He will take him and keep him as his own," says one. "This little boy is so handsome, and so strong, and his brightness is greater than any other newborn child I have ever seen. Our father Anu will take him from you and who knows if you will ever see him again."

"Never mind the fact that he will scold you for having a child and being ignorant of who the father is," says another.

"We don't know what will happen," she says, looking down at her son. "I don't know what to do."

"Why can't we just raise him?" says another sister. "If we are born to create and to protect what is created, should we not be able to care for this child?"

"We only care for our creation from a distance," says the newly crowned mother. "We are never involved with our work to actually guide it."

"So then let us remain indifferent with him," says one. "Let us raise him as our own, but you as his mother. He must only know one of us as his mother."

"And you are his mother," adds the other. "You have sacrificed your life for him. To you belongs this child, but we too, as also his mothers next to you, belong to him."

The sisters then agreed to raise him collectively, with him knowing only one of them as his mother. It is this woman who named him Azazel, saying, "Because I was your scapegoat, so too alleviation for the realms will rest on your shoulders."

But without her sisters knowing, she brought him to their father Anu. He took the child in his arms and inspected him, his omniscience causing him to embrace the child as his own. With his daughter telling him everything that happened, and with him already knowing what happened, he took Azazel and put his hand on his forehead, making his appearance, and also the powers shared with him by his mother, permanent.

The power to create dwelt within this woman's affectionate embrace. Whatever she touched, or whatever she thought about, when moved by very deep thoughts and feelings, would be created. When she found Azazel, he looked like a very different child, but when her tears landed on him, the power and character of her essence was shared with him, not only changing his appearance to resemble hers, but also adding to him the ability to create. With her father therefore being a Supreme creating Mind, within Azazel's veins now flowed the substance of Supreme Minds.

When Anu touched Azazel's forehead, he sealed his mind with the powers that his mother shared with him through her tears, and also made his new appearance permanent. Anu transferred the spirit of the Creating class into Azazel's thoughts and feelings. With him now possessing the beauty of his unknown father and the strength of his unknown mother, having the force of Anu's daughter within him and also the intelligence of Anu's throne flowing through his veins, Azazel is crowned as one of the most powerful gods to ever exist, a status given only to the Supreme Creating Minds.

"You did well to rescue this child," says Anu to his daughter, his wife looking on. "He will overthrow the realms, strengthening our throne, and its reign, without realization. Take him and raise him with your sisters. You are his mother."

The goddess then left her father's kingdom with the child in her arms. Back home, she sits in an open field beside her house, the sound of an active body of water behind her. In her arms rests her son, Azazel.

The Deal

"Sister!" yells one of her three sisters, flying towards her.

"What is wrong?" she asks.

"They want the child," she says.

"Who wants him?" she asks, clutching him tightly.

"One of the members of the Council has secretly sent Guards for Azazel, to take him from you."

"But why?" she says, still sitting with Azazel in her arms. "The issue is resolved. The Council let us go. What more can they want?"

"The baby's brilliance has disturbed one of the members of the Council," she says. "That Guard, the one present with you, has the ear of one of the Council's members and has convinced him to find and kill Azazel."

"I will fly to our mother and father," says the young woman. "Our father will protect us."

"And then have him take Azazel away from you because you can't keep out of trouble? says her sister, annoyingly.

"Well then what do you suggest?"

As she asks her sister this question, two Guards materialize in front of the two sisters. "Give us the child," says one.

"You and I both know that it is the right thing to do," says the other, who is the Guard that spoke against the goddess in Court. "We have an order," he continued.

"No," says the young woman, holding tightly to her son.

This Guard didn't like her answer. After tightening up his face and clinching his fists, he, determined to pry the child from her arms, walks towards the woman. Her sister belches out a scream agitating their mind and bringing them to the ground. The first Guard, fighting the waves of sound grinding against his mind, conjures up enough strength to disappear and then reappear behind the screaming sister, quickly forcing his entire arm through her torso, killing her instantly.

With her sister dead and the screeching sound halted, the other Guard rises to his feet and continues walking towards the goddess and her son. When he gets close enough to them, a light blue shield, like as a bubble, circles the woman and her child, blocking him from reaching them. It is not the goddess doing this, but Azazel.

"You shouldn't be able to do this," he says.

"It is not I," she says, and with a look of apprehension, "but my son."

Suddenly the first Guard began to cough. His coughing then picked up, becoming more intense and frequent. Soon enough he clutches his throat, which was quickly eroding, as if acid had been both poured down his throat and thrown onto his skin. After a moment of struggling, he drops to his knees, his flesh evaporating into the air. The other Guard, the enemy of the goddess and her son, upon watching his comrade pass away, turns his head back on to the mother and her son.

Determined to break the shield, he transforms his two wings into large hammers. As they, in mid air, are about to meet the shield, the same sequence of events occurring to the other Guard's throat happens to his wings. Sensing their fellow Guard's defeat, other Guards show up on the scene. Seeing their brother, just like the former Guard, slowly evaporating, they all begin to rush the shield protecting the mother and her son. Right as they are all around the mother and her son, and are determined to collectively shatter the shield, the goddess and her son disappear through the ground, reappearing in the Underuniverse, and at the dining room table of the child's father.

"That could have been worse," he says, the goddess, still clutching on go her son, which two sit across from him at the other end of the table. "Don't you think?" he continues.

"How did we...?" she says.

"Don't you worry," he interrupts. "He is not the one who brought you here. I brought you two here to me. With you not being able to fully defend the both of you, and with him not able to fully protect you both, someone had to interfere. There is no way I was going to let my son die by the hands of a class not even worth the substance they were created with."

Fighting her shock, "Your son?" she says, astonished. "This is your son?" she says.

"He may look absolutely nothing like his mother now, but the beauty and the brightness attached to his glow, it is mine. I can see through what you did to him, and what your father sealed within him. I can see my son as he is, and I can also feel him. He cried out to me, not verbally, but within himself, and because of his cry, I answered."

"I don't know what to say," says the goddess.

"What is there to say?" he says, slumping back into his seat. "You saved me from having to again war with the Council, although this war would have been about my son and, on another level, completely justified. Because just think about it; imagine the son of the King of the Underuniverse, the Prince of the Amalgamate's throne, put out of existence or worse, having some, as was done to you, amendment disfiguring his intelligence? Can you?"

"Um," she says, unable to put words together.

"Of course not!" he yells, slamming his hand down onto the table. "This would be tragic. It would be tragic because the King of the Underuniverse would not have an heir to not only claim his throne, but also the throne of the kingdoms of the realms, when his father is long gone. And I will not live for ever. Did you know that goddess?"

"I didn't," she says, holding her son even tighter.

"It's true," he says, re-assuming his former slump. "The Sovereign of your realm, the realm of Heaven, will end my life. Even your father, and all of the Creators know that their Sovereign will remove me from life's span, but none of them understand the government of my son. I have started the work. I have strengthened the Underuniverse to match the power, the reputation, and the authority of that Universe you are familiar with. No one knows the legacy that I will have through my son except, well, now you do."

"I don't understand," she says.

"Yes, of course," he says, sitting in a way to where his chin, with his elbow on the table, rests in his palm. "Why are you here? Why didn't I just save my son and let you, the goddess stripped of her strengths, die right then and there? I saved you because I need you."

"But I am useless," she says.

"No you are not," he says, meditatively slumping back down into his chair. "You are not useless. You have become, by encoding my son with your intelligence, and by re-arranging his appearance, and without even giving birth to him, the mother of my child. You have erased his mother and have replaced her. In the eyes of my son and I, you are his mother, and are also in debt to me. You are in debt to me not physically, but mentally, and ecclesiastically, meaning that it is now your responsibility to raise my son in the culture and philosophy of the Underuniverse."

"Are you sure?" she says.

"Of course I'm sure," he confirms. "Would I lie to you? You got yourself into this little situation when you claimed my son. Do you think I had no knowledge about his whereabouts? Just think; how did you and your sisters come to learn about that child?"

"I don't remember."

"Oh you do. How could you forget?"

"I don't remember," she says, trembling.

"Then let me help," he says, getting up from his chair, walking to her, and kneeling close beside her. "You were approached by a very pretty little girl. She told you that she and her friends were playing and found a baby floating in the open and empty order of creation, the Cosmos. All of a sudden you grew concerned and consulted your sisters. You all then immediately flew to the location. Finding the child, you consoled him and, feeling as though this little child deserved an entrance into life that he probably didn't get, you all sung a hymn to him, after which you picked him up and held him, falling in love with him. Now do you remember?"

She sits looking straight, and still trembling, refusing to turn her head to look at him.

"How do you think that little girl found the child you now hold so tightly?" he asks.

He then, placing his hand onto her hand, transforms into the little girl that approached her and, in the voice of the little girl, says, "Do you remember yet?"

Removing her hand from under his, he re-transforms back into his original self, gets up, walks back over to where he sat, and slumps back down into his seat.

"Goddess," he says, "I chose you. I chose you because I know you. I've watched you for your entire life. You are stronger than your sisters, more intelligent, more aware, more of love, more of a mother. I needed someone to train my son in the art of *being*. I, ever since you were born, read your heart, and seeing my love within it, and my passion for creation, when my son needed a mother, you were the first goddess I thought of. You are the law to my philosophy, and I need you to instill that culture of *being*, and of *governing*, into my son, the heir of the Universes."

"What do you want from me?" she said.

"It's not about what I want, but about what your son needs. What do you think Azazel needs? I believe he needs a mother, and I believe that he needs the support of your sisters. Agree to raise my son as I intend and I will not only resurrect your sister from death, but will also restore your ability to you, and with far greater creative strength than before."

"I don't need my abilities restored," she says. "They live on through my son and that is enough."

"Then I will bring your sister back from the dead," he says. "As a matter of fact, I can now hear her looking for you both and worrying about what happened."

"I didn't ask you for that," she says.

"Your eyes did," he replies. "Just don't forget who you are to me and to him. Our son is a King of kingdoms and a Sovereign above the Sovereign. Our son is to inherit the movement and the throne that I have established, overshadowing me, and every other Sovereign Creator, in every way possible."

"I didn't ask for that," she again says.

"Don't be stubborn," he says. "Fulfill your assignment and you will be the Mother of Sovereigns, a Mother to be worshipped. We are finished here."

Moving his hand in a swift manner, he removed her from the Underuniverse, causing her to reappear where she last was, her sister frantically shouting her name.

"Sister!" yells the goddess, who is sobbing while still clutching on to her son, who is now also crying.

Her sister runs to her and drapes her wings around the goddess and her son.

"What happened?" she asks. "I thought I died."

The goddess weeps uncontrollably.

"What happened?" she again asks her sister.

The goddess weeps uncontrollably.

It Is Done

"Am I in trouble?" asks the goddess, her mother holding her son.

"You have done nothing wrong," says her father. "I was hoping the child's father did not threaten my intention. I will not let this child fight for the wrong side. This child is born to rule, and he will rule the Universes by the *name* and spirit of this throne."

"He will have a mind of his own father," says the goddess. "He will do what he is born to do; we cannot tell what that may be."

"What is wrong with you?" he says, sternly looking in to her face. She immediately buries her face into his chest. After a deep sigh, and holding her tightly, "You haven't done anything wrong," he says. "We just have to make sure Azazel knows the light and character within him."

"I'm sorry," she says, crying. "I didn't know."

"You will be a good mother," he says, comforting her. "You will be a good mother and he will be a Warrior of warriors and a King of gods. He will carry on the *name* that has been sealed within him."

"I'm sorry," she says.

"You've given her too much love; that's why she is the way that she is," says her mother. "We will make sure your son knows only the height of his *being*. You did well to become his mother. You are not alone, and neither is he," she says looking down at her grandson, kissing his forehead.

"You are safe here," her father says to her, still holding her in his arms. "No one will harm you or him while you are here at the Royal Estate."

"He will find me father," she says, further burying her face in her father's chest.

"Then let him," says Anu. "Let him war a war that he cannot win."

No sooner than when he finished speaking did the child's father materialize before them. Anu, while confronting him, immediately guides his daughters and his wife behind him."

"Why are you here?" says Anu. "How did you even get in?"

"Like I told the mother of my son," begins the child's father, "when my son calls for me, I will be there."

"No one called you," says Anu. "Leave in peace."

"Leave in peace? How can I leave in peace if I didn't arrive in peace? My son is my peace and I'm here to see him. I felt his call; he called me; I'm here to see my son."

"No one called you," repeats Anu. "Leave in peace."

"What about you?" he says, looking at the goddess. "Do you also wish I was gone?"

"You don't talk to her," says Anu, his eyes developing a flame within them.

"Is that so?" says the father's child. "I bet I can do more than talk to her right now."

As soon as the words left his mouth, time froze, he being the only one admitted to move. Cages of light then began to form around Anu and his daughter. After taking his son from the goddess' mother, a cage of light then formed around her. The cages, moving with the people within them, then formed one large cage. With time now resuming, the father, holding his child, looks at the family within the cage.

Anu then touches the cage and it turns to ashes. The child's father waves his arm in the air, making a hand gesture, and twenty of his Guards appear, forming a line of defense between he and Anu. Anu clenches his fist, touches his heart with his clenched fist, then extends his arm towards their direction, opening up his hand, his fingers open and pointing towards them. A powerful bolt of lightning, coming from his fingertips, strikes the line of defense, killing them.

With one wave of his hand, Anu causes the bodies of the fallen line to vanish. Still with his hand extended out, he, with his mind, calls for the child. The child disappears from his fathers grasp and appears within the arms of his daughter. With this same hand stretched out, the child's father is also made to disappear but then reappear within Anu's hand, his fingers tightly wrapped around his neck, choking him.

"No," whispers the goddess under her breath. Seeing the child's father continue to struggle to find release from Anu, "Stop!" she yells. Now running over, and with her son in her hand, she grabs on to the arm holding the neck of her son's father. "Don't," she says, tears falling from her face while looking into her father's eyes. "Please," she adds.

Giving into his daughter, Anu throws the child's father into a wall, and roughly. The goddess runs over to him, as if checking on him.

"Well done," he whispers to her. Looking beyond her and his son to Anu, "We don't have to be enemies," he says, making it to one knee. "My son belongs to two worlds. His father is the King and *God* of the Underuniverse and his grandfather is a Sovereign *God* of Heaven. Within this child's blood rests the will and the dominion of our families. Let us unite. Let's let this marriage be what it will be, but let us never forget the Union we now have."

"Leave in peace," says Anu.

"We both have intentions for our throne to rule the Universes," continues the child's father. "Instead of fighting for the child, let us raise him together and let us make our throne into one throne. Now the work can easily get done. Now our son can fulfill the will of his family. There is no *God* or Sovereign that can stop Azazel; he only needs the right environment to let him know who he is."

The room is silent. Anu knows what he desires for the Universe of Heaven. He knows that he wants his throne and bloodline to control the Universe and its realms. Anu wants to be the Sovereign Mind of Heaven and of the Creator *Gods*, but he knows he cannot and must overthrow the Eternal Sovereign, who is the Absolute of the Universes and of all the realms. The room is silent is because the child's father is right, and because he is right, there is nothing within them that can excuse his logic.

"You and I want the same thing," says the child's father, rising to his feet and walking towards Anu. "You and I both know that we cannot overthrow the Eternal. But now we can. Can you imagine what we three can do? Can you imagine the *God* of the Underuniverse, and the *Supreme God* of Heaven, and the *God* of Brilliance, Strength, Creation, and *Light*, our son Azazel, coming together? Who can stop us? We would be unstoppable, and after we are gone, our immortality would belong to our son."

The room is still silent. Anu, looking at his daughter holding her son, and then back at his wife and daughters, then looks around his Palace, imagining it, one day, either no longer existing, destroyed by an incompetent Prince, or being overthrown by another from Heaven. The sorrow in his eyes was potent, for his daughter, son in hand, fell once again into her father's arms.

"We can trust him," she says, looking into the eyes of Azazel's father.

"If it were not for my daughter..." says Anu.

"What?" interrupts the child's father. "You would kill me? What if I told you that I, for the sake of gaining your ear through your daughter, let you overpower me? I am only less in power to the Eternal. I was there when you were created."

The room, as the two now look at one another in the eyes, their foreheads almost touching, yet remains silent.

"You have everything to gain," says the child's father.

"Then let us gain," Anu says, swallowing his pride. "From this day forward the Underuniverse, and the portion of Heaven given to the throne and under the authority of Anu, are one. Should this league be broken in any way, may the violator know only death."

"Agreed," says the father's child.

"Then understand," says Anu, "that we are only family through this child. Any violation against our families, or against either one of our thrones by our family, will mean death to the violator. The violator cannot refuse his sentence, or argue against it."

"I agree," he again says.

"You will have none of my daughters as your wife, including the one holding your son. Fidelity and integrity will rule the relationship you two have, keeping you both as nothing more than partners in business," says Anu.

The eyes of the goddess and of the child's father then meet. They are unsure of this one stipulation.

"Cannot, depending on the relation, and on how it is managed, partners in business remain that way with one another, even if their relationship should be looked at as intimate?" says the goddess.

"I will also say," says the child father, "as I previously said to your daughter, that I believe what should be done must be done for the good of the child. Let her and my son stay in Heaven, living as they please, but what may be best for my son might be seeing his mother and father coexisting, as she has said, as, despite the level of intimacy, partners in business. Let that be what it may, but remember my son in whatever you suggest."

The eyes of the goddess and of the child's father did not break as they spoke. Sensing more to their communion than he'd like, "Then let the individual, be it even you, the child's father, harming my grandson's mother in any way, be it light or weighty, accept the sentence of judgment against themselves," says Anu.

"I agree," says the child's father, still looking into the eyes of the goddess.

"Our relationship is business," says Anu. "Your wisdom is an infection this Court doesn't need. We have one goal, and that is the dominion of our joint thrones over the two Universes with their many realms. Let us conquer in the *name* of our unified thoughts."

"I agree," says the child's father who, after taking one last look at the goddess and the son in her arms, vanishes into a portal of smoke appearing behind him.

"It is done," says Anu, looking down at his daughter, who is yet, and still with her son in her arms, buried into his chest. "It is done," he again says, this time with a tone of regret.

"Are you mad at me?" she says, her head under both of his arms, which are wrapped around her and her son.

"I'm not mad at you," he says. "I don't trust him."

"But you can," she says.

Her mother and sisters then give Anu a look due to her naive spirit.

"You aren't alone," says her mother, who joins her husband and daughter in their embrace. "We have just done something very special. All of Heaven and Earth will know and worship you and your son because of the covenant formed between the thrones. I will make sure of it. Earth's energy will assist us in what we plan."

"Do you love me?" asks the goddess, as if hearing nothing her mother has just said.

"We love you," says her mother.

"Do you love me father?" she again asks.

"Of course," he says, sorrowfully looking into his wife's eyes. "I love you."

Anu's wife, being a Sovereign Influence of the earth, confident about the hope secured through the alliance made with the *God* of the Underuniverse, soon after left the Palace for Earth to seal a prayer within the earth for Azazel's future. Understanding the connection between the Earth and the Universes, it was her intention to simultaneously will Azazel into the envisioned promise through human zeal. Gathering additional force through the power of human belief could nurture his character into its expected form, and with all of the Underuniverse, a major portion of Heaven, and all of Earth praying for his reign, the spirit behind time and chance have no choice but to act in his best interest.

She, after appearing to a sect of priests whose fathers had been educated by Azazel's father, taught them the promise of the new future hope through Azazel. Manifesting to the priests through a smoking portal, she taught them the peace the earth should have when once the throne of the Universe has its prophesied King. She taught them about three Sovereign *Figures* found above the heavens, and of a virgin mother living in the same realm, who was the mother of one of the *Figures*. She taught them about this child's resurrection, how his mother saved him from death and how he, through his *Fathers*, should one day manifest to earth, permanently bringing the Royal Kingdom to earth.

She implored them to worship the child of the virgin mother. She told them that this child is the balance between seen and unseen realms, and that the greater his worship, the greater chance for peace on earth.

Peace, she told them, would find appointment for earth because of their service to Anu's throne. Should these priests maintain the *faith* of that throne, they, and their posterity, would have prominent positions on the earth when Azazel, after becoming the one and only King and Sovereign of the Universes, builds his throne on a section of the earth. Should they do this for her, and justly, she would ensure their *name* remains on earth, giving to them *eternal life*.

Upon returning back to the Palace, she informs Anu of the wisdom and ideology she has passed down to the chosen sect. Satisfied for the prayers of the realm, and especially for the hope of the will concerning Azazel, he is, although still concerned for his daughter's wellbeing, and for the safety of his grandson, content. With the earth now joined into covenant with both thrones, the spirit of the prayers uttered on behalf of the hope for the Universes may give what is expected.

Upon finishing their discusion, both Anu and his wife walk over to a window beautifully portraying the beauty and fortune of their portion in Heaven. Looking around, they find their daughter sitting and playing with Azazel on her lap, the two of them happy and smiling. At the same time, the child's father, appearing in the home that the four sisters shared, sits alone in a corner, a piece of clothing belonging to his son's mother in his hands.

A Joint Vision

"Do you think you are a Sovereign?" she asks, siting across from him, on the other side of the room, her arms and feet tied with a rope especially tailored to take away the abilities of whomever it confines.

He says nothing, but looks at her, his eyes showing no care or regard for his actions towards her, or for how their conversation became so tense.

"You are not a Sovereign," she says. "You cannot just do whatever you want. You cannot just react. You are not a Sovereign."

Still sitting and saying nothing, he continues to look at her, his eyes showing no care or regard for her plea that he refrain from harming her father.

"Do you know that we all feel some sort of injustice against ourselves?" she says.

"What do you know about injustice?" he responds. "You know nothing about injustice or its effect."

"I am not your enemy," she says.

"I know," he says.

"Then why am I treated as if I am your enemy? We are on the same side.

"What do you know about injustice?" he again says.

"We all are hurt Azazel," she says, "but we all learn how to get over it if we cannot stop the pain."

"And what do you say of the territory your father desires to conquer? What do you say of him raiding and ruining districts and their families? Do you share the sorrow of these families and those districts?"

"This isn't even your realm Azazel," she says, awkwardly smiling. "What concern is it of yours about what happens in the Underuniverse?"

"And what concern is it of yours to defend your father? You want to talk about injustice, and with me? Do you know the depth of your father's injustice? Do you know the injustice of the throne he serves?"

"What else can I do Azazel?" she questions frustratingly. "What do you expect of me? I am born into the life that I have; I didn't choose it."

"So because you are born into injustice, this means you must accept and support it? Do you even understand the pain I feel for this realm? Can't you see how offensive this government is?"

"You think I cannot?" she says.

"I know, for the love you have for your father, that you will not fully see how belligerent he is."

"You think so?" she says.

"I think so," he says, smugly.

"Have you forgotten why we are even here right now?" she begins. "Why do think the absolute destruction and enslavement of the district has not yet happened? Have you heard of a General taking so long to destroy and enslave a district before? My father has plans to rule an area of the Underuniverse, a pleasure given to him by the Sovereign of the Underuniverse. For what reason does he refuse to act as fast as he will?"

Azazel, watching and listening to her, sits in silence, thinking nothing.

"I do not agree with my father on many things, especially this. He knows that I don't. I actually make life difficult for him in a way.

If it weren't for me, if I wasn't his conscience, he probably would have tried to overthrow the Sovereign of the Underuniverse, losing his life at the same time."

"Then why have you done nothing?" he questions.

"What more can I do?" she says. "What do you expect of me? We are here right now for my last chance to do something."

"What do you expect of yourself?" he angrily responds. "I expect justice. I expect justice to those less in power and in class than you and I. There is no need for you to ignore my regard for and your obligation to the Underuniverse."

"And what is justice?" she asks, as if pleading for him to think about what his feelings are making him say. "Where is the virtue in talking to someone who will not listen? Where is there justice for the hard heart?"

"What is wrong with you?" he replies. "There is justice and virtue in the challenge you run from. You are just and virtuous by your speech. It your speech that commends you and it is your speech that judges you. Wasn't your speech enough to you're your father causing devastation? How much more just would you be if you continued to make sense to your father?"

"You don't get it," she says, "there's no making sense to him."

"So then why do you think we're here?" he says. "He will listen to me. I have taken you, his heart, as would any other criminal looking to gain some *thing* from kidnapping you."

They both then share a moment of silence, after which Azazel falls to one knee clutching his head. He is hearing the screaming voice of her father. The entire scene then changed. Azazel is now in a room alone with her father and, on all fours, her father kicks Azazel in his abdomen repeatedly.

"Who do you think you are?" he says, continuing to kick him in the abdomen. "Why can't you leave me alone?"

Her father then raised nail-like structures from his palm. He directs them to Azazel whose wings shoot out of his back, protecting him from them. Azazel looks back and takes a swing, and then another, and then a swift front kick to her father's chest; he lands them all. Her father then rushes him, tackling him to the ground. He causes his hand to turn into a knife-like weapon and repeatedly stabs Azazel with it, who, while healing instantly from the blows, still feels the fatigue attached to the attack against his body.

Azazel then somehow frees himself from her father, rising to his feet. Upon rising, a light blue beam shoots out of his eyes, hitting her father in his chest. While he is on the floor, Azazel conjures a fire from out of his mouth, pouring it over her father. As it flows out of his mouth, upon meeting her father, the flames then turn to ice, completely freezing him. The only thing not frozen is his head, which Azazel has left unfrozen intentionally.

"How is it that you transformed my reality to harm me, yet it is I, in your own intention, who now have the power to harm you? Maybe it is I who should ask you if you know who I am."

"I will kill you," mutters her father.

"Is that so?" Azazel responds.

Absorbing the frozenness within him, her father, after recovering himself, shoots a flood out of his mouth at Azazel, throwing him through many walls. Teleporting to Azazel after having sent him through many walls by the strong rush of water pouring out of his mouth, he again opens up his mouth, casting another powerful fury of water at Azazel, this time sending him through the ground and down many levels of the old building they fight in.

Teleporting to Azazel once again, he finds him on the ground, soaked, hurt, and lying there, fatigued. Kneeling beside him, he says, "There is no one who can stop me, not even you."

Azazel reaches out his hand and grabs his foot. His leg begins to disintegrate slowly. Panicking, he sits back, grabbing on to his legs, and then on to his torso, as he sees himself slowly eroding.

"Stop!" her father yells.

Azazel, recovering his strength and energy, looks on, saying nothing.

"Stop!" he again yells.

Azazel rises to his feet and kneels beside his head; he waves his hand in a motion and the disintegration of the Captain's body doesn't stop, but slows down. With everything disintegrated from his second to last rib and down to his feet, Azazel calmly sits beside her frantic father.

"You can't win," Azazel says, the Captain desperately pleading for his life. "I'm not like you," he continues. "I'm not like any of you. The question isn't a matter of who I am, but of what I am. Do you know what I am? You and everyone else within the two Universes know who I am, and you're all quite rude about it."

"Stop talking!" yells the man. "Please stop. I'm begging you. Please," he says softly, hoping to change Azazel's mind.

"There'a something I want," Azazel says, the man's disintegration now reaching his neck. "Stop raiding the realms and districts of the Underuniverse. I've decided to make you feel how those families feel and to see what they see when you plunder their villages and cities. As you have erased legacies and have enslaved families, so now you can see your self being erased and being enslaved by one infinitely more powerful than you."

"I get it," her father says. "I get it."

Azazel, looking at the man, his chin, mouth, and nose evaporating, gets up and stands at the top of his head. Kneeling over him once again, Azazel lightly blows down the man's face, reversing the disintegration of his body. Slowly the man's limbs and body returns; it looks as if nothing happened it to him.

"You will not live again next time," Azazel says, rising to his feet. "Understand that your life, that all life, is in my hands. You brought me here, and I humored you, accepting the challenge. Do not ever, for your own gain, or for the gain of the Underuniverse, take life into your hands. Do it again and I will end you."

Her father, who is silent, rises to his feet. He looks Azazel in his face and then vanishes. Azazel also vanishes, re-appearing in the room wherein he and the princess were. As soon as he appears he, with one wave of his hand, releases her hands and her feet.

"Go," he says, apparently frustrated.

"So?" she says.

"He understands," he says.

"It worked?" she says, in a tone of amazement.

"Yes," he says.

"Then what's wrong?" she says, getting up and moving closer to him.

"Why is it that deeds are remembered and not words?"

"What?" she says.

"Why are deeds recorded as a sign of triumph, and not words? By my deeds your father understands my seriousness, but by my words to him, I know I will have to right many more wrongs he will commit. What kind of warrior fights for a fame through deeds and not through words?"

"Words are not so easily understood, but one deed," she says, "because it can alter appearances, it can change much. There is no thought in war. There is strategy in war, but there is no need for words in war. Words come after the war, to the victor; which is how I suppose you got my father's ear. Our strategy worked. You wanted virtue and you got it. Words will only make sense when the importance of the deed is understood."

The princess wasn't content with the decision her father had made to conquer another territory of the Underuniverse. It wasn't the first time he had plundered, enslaved the families of a district, and rebuilt the district in honor of the *God* of the Underuniverse, but she wanted to make sure this next venture would be the last. Secretly having a relationship with Azazel behind her father's back, she turned to Azazel to help her.

She wanted to stage her own kidnapping, and for her father to understand who had done it. While sitting in that room with Azazel, she communicated with her father through her mind. The constraints on her made it difficult to do, so Azazel, while she reached out to her father, held her hand, temporarily breaking the power of the rope.

The two waited, and for a very long time, for her father to act. Knowing as much as she knew about him, she told Azazel to let her father understand their plea for justice, and to do nothing that would end his life. Azazel, knowing that the man cared only about himself, wanted to end his life, but because of his daughter, didn't.

"What's wrong?" she says to him, falling into his arms for a hug.

After a deep sigh, "Nothing," he says. "You should go."

"So should you," you she fires back.

"I will," he says.

After looking at one another in the eyes for some time, she vanishes. Azazel then walks over to a wall, throws his back against it, falls to the floor, sitting down with his back against the wall, and leans over, placing his head into his hands. He sits and thinks about his life, and about how unnecessarily difficult it will be if his legacy is cemented only through deeds.

"Why are you here?" questions a soft voice, rattling him out of his vision.

Azazel's father, still sitting inside of his mother's home, and with a piece of her clothing in his hand, had seen his son in the future. Lifting and turning his head, he sees that it the goddess. While his father was observing his son in vision, she too, without him knowing, saw his thoughts.

"And why were you watching my son?" she added.

"I thought you had no abilities," he responds.

"I no longer have the power or authority to create, but I still have my other abilities."

"Well then," he says, "aren't we lucky.'

"Why are you in my home?" she again asks, this time more sternly.

"Why are you in your home?" he fires back. "Don't you know I'm somewhere out there and can get you at any time."

They both share a smile.

Taking a seat across from him, "I hate being watched. My father is watching me too closely. I needed to get a away for a little."

"Hopefully you remembered not to leave your son in the Cosmos again," he says.

They both again share a smile.

"I'm not a monster, you know," he says. "I'm just tired."

"Tired of what?" she says. "You have everything. Why can't you just be content with what you have?"

"Do you think there is contentment when knowing that what you have is not all that is owed to you?" he says.

"So then just let it happen," she reasons. "If it is owed to you, then it is already yours. Why are you fighting for something that is already yours?"

"If it is mine then why do I not have it? and why am I tired by the uselessness of who possesses what is owed to me?"

"Well if you do not yet have it, then it is not you who is to ultimately claim what is owed, even if it is to be had through you. You are the Sovereign of the Underuniverse. There is no Creator that can match your particular will, power, and vision. Has your need to have what is not yours led you to take what is mine, and to hold on to it as if it is yours?"

They, as he handles the clothing in his hands, again share a smile.

"I may not be able to create anymore, but at least my words can leave an impression with you," she says.

"And what an impression," he says, smirking.

"Isn't it amazing that the young woman you've watched since birth, and for no good intention, has a voice and is someone you can talk with? Would you have ever imagined that she could persuade you to think of anything outside of yourself?"

After a deep sigh and a brief moment of silence, "I don't trust your father," he says. "I don't trust him with my son; I don't trust him with anything."

"Aren't you the one who suggested he remain in Heaven with my family and I?" she says. "Why didn't you just do what you wanted with us? How is it that you will claim what's not even yours, but will not take what is?"

They both pause, looking one another's face up and down.

"I said I didn't trust your father. I didn't say it was wrong to risk giving him my trust."

Ra

"Concentrate!" he says.

"I am!" she yells back.

"No you're not," he says.

"Don't judge me," she says. "I am."

The two are in the Academy library within a realm of Heaven's Universe. Azazel and Anastasia, after learning about teleportation and re-emergence, want to experiment with the process. Upon learning in school about how to control time and space to appear or disappear from any place at any time, Azazel wants to travel to the Underuniverse, to see Ra, and to see the various gods, and the realm, that Ra has created and given birth to. As usual, he turns to Anastasia for joining him in this adventure.

"It says that we have to only imagine where we want to go and then it will happen," he says. "Look at what it says."

Looking down at the textbook, whose words are rifled together with images depicting the expected and studied action, "I can see," she says, looking up at him, annoyed. "Get that book out of my face."

Gently lying the open book down, "Then concentrate. It says to stop thinking," he says.

"How am I supposed to think about where I imagine to be if I can't think about it?" she asks.

"I don't know," he replies, honestly befuddled. "Maybe it just means you have to feel the destination. There isn't any thought in feeling, right?"

Deeply exhaling, "This isn't ever going to happen," she says.

Before Azazel could say anything back, she vanished, a faint and fading scream coming from her.

"Um," says Azazel, looking around the room. "Anastasia?" he calls. Extending his arms to where she last sat, "Anastasia?" he again calls, feeling around. Finding that she was not in the room or in front of him, "Hello?" he says.

Re-appearing behind him, "I saw them!" she shouts, startling Azazel who, surprised, immediately raises his hand, a bright orange beam shooting through his palm. She avoids getting hit by deflecting the beam with her forearm.

"Seriously?" she says.

"What happened to you?" he asks.

"Everything!" she says.

"What do you mean? You left."

"I stopped thinking," she says. "As soon as I stopped thinking about where I wanted to be, and I felt myself already there, I ended up there, kind of like how I didn't have to think when deflecting your attack; I just let go and let it happen."

"I told you," he says.

"Well why haven't you done it yet then?" she fires back.

"Because I spent this whole time trying to get you to relax," he says, taking her by the hand and sitting her back down in front of him. "Let's try this again," he says.

"And, just a word of caution," she says. "You will feel sick after teleporting."

"Whatever," he says. "Focus. Focus on losing focus."

The environment then shifts. Arriving in a very beautiful realm with many buildings, cities, and triangle-shaped temples, the two look around in amazement at the *beings* they see. Upon arrival, Azazel, after feeling in awe of the realm, soon begins to feel his stomach bother him. He leans over and hurls.

"Well," says Anastasia,"I tried to warn you."

Upon lifting his head, Azazel sees *beings* of all different kinds, *beings* walking and appearing as men and women, but with different kinds of wings and animal heads. They stand there and look on, amazed at the creatures they see, and surprised that they can even understand them when they speak.

"We're here," he says. "What do you want to do first?"

Looking around, "I really don't know," says Anastasia. "It's really busy here, and everyone is looking at us weird. I don't think I'm comfortable."

"Put this on," he says, handing her clothes.

"Where did you get this?" she asks.

"Someone gave it to me," he says.

In the distance, there are four creatures running to him. Two of them are leopards that stand as normal men, and the other two have the bodies of men but have heads like a Jaguar. Behind them is the owner of a store, yelling, "Thief! Stop them!" He is a short and bald heavy-set man.

"Are you sure someone gave you these clothes?" she asks,

"We need to blend in, don't we?"

"I mean," she begins," we do, but that's hard to do when chased."

"Make us invisible. Then we can change," he says.

"Do you not understand that we should be running away from the mob that is approaching?" she says.

"Don't worry about it," he says.

As soon as he finished his sentence, and right as they are about to run away, they are both caught by the collar of their shirt and lifted up into the air.

"That's him," says the storeowner.

"Do it now," Azazel says, looking over at Anastasia.

Anastasia takes Azazel's hand. The two then, being invisible, disappear and reappear behind the Officers and the storeowner; they change and run away. Their invisibility, because Anastasia forgot to be mindful of continuing to activate her invisibility, failing, the Officers spot them and again begin to chase them.

Bumping into different people, knocking over tables and making a mess of the area, and loosely saying, "Sorry," the two run as if their life depends on it. Soon enough a royal and alluring looking goddess appears in front of them. They do not see her appear, their heads looking behind them as they run. They bump into her, and, upon looking at her in her face, are frozen.

Every one in the area stops moving and is found prostrating when she appears. Azazel and Anastasia, who are confused about what is going on, look around and try to make sense of the situation. Either someone very important has been recognized, or everyone has so randomly fallen in love with Azazel and Anastasia's apparel that they can do nothing else but worship them for their wise choice in fashion.

Rising from his feet, and walking towards the children, one of the Officers, falling to one knee and with his face towards the ground, says, "My Lord, excuse their ignorance."

"My Lord?" questions Azazel, who chuckles while speaking.

"Hathor," Anastasia, leaning into Azazel and nudging him with her elbow, whispers.

"What?" Azazel whispers beck.

"Hathor!" she again says, this time in a louder whisper and with a harder nudge.

"Who?" he whispers back.

"We learned about her!" she whispers quickly.

Looking her up and down, "How do you know?" he whispers back.

"My Lord," continues the officer, "these two were found stealing clothes from a shop in the market. I will remove them from your presence and see to it they are handled according to the law of the land."

"You will do no such thing," says Hathor.

"My Lord..." continues the officer.

"You will do no such thing," she interrupts. "Rise and move," she, looking down at the officer between she and the young teens, commands. "This is my grandson; I will handle him as I see fit."

"Grandson?" blurts Anastasia.

"Yes," says Hathor, kneeling down to Anastasia and fixing Anastasia's hair. "Azazel is my daughter's son."

"My mother?" says Azazel.

"Come," she says, standing up and taking both Azazel and Anastasia by the hand. "Let us go and I will tell you all about your past."

They then disappear and re-appear in the city of Ra, sitting on the sand of a lake just outside of Ra's Palace.

"I had many children Azazel; some of them were taken away from me. Your mother was taken away from me. My father, Ra, promised one of my daughters to Anu. I was not told why this should happened, but from what I understand, the two had formed and carried out a special agreement. When my father fulfilled his part, and after Anu fulfilled his part, one of my daughters was given to Anu. He had adopted three other little girls from three other special agreements."

"Why should we believe you?" questioned Anastasia.

"That is a good question," she says, smiling. "My daughter, your mother, when she was born, always let me feel her cry before she ever cried. Azazel, as soon as he entered into the Underuniverse just now, and into this realm, gave me the same feeling I once felt from my daughter. I knew you were here," she says, turning to Azazel and lightly touching his face.

"That's how you knew to find us," says Anastasia.

"It is as if he was calling me to him," says Hathor.

"Weird," says Azazel.

"It isn't," Hathor responds. "Where do you think your beautiful skin color comes from? Where do you think your locks come from? Where do you think your handsomeness, strength, intellect, courage, powers, and abilities come from? Why do you think that your thoughts are so different? You have no idea how much of your allure is owed to me," she says, smirking.

"So," begins Azazel, "that means..."

"Yes," she interrupts.

"Ra is your grandfather!" yells Anastasia.

"Ra, like Anu, is your grandfather; the direct spirit of Ra lives within you. As the force of Anu's divine legacy lives within your *being*, so too, Azazel, does the force of Ra's divine legacy. You are connected to both Universes and their realms."

Unable to process what he is hearing, "The what of what is within me?" he says. "All of my life I've read about Ra and I'm only here because I want to see the Sovereign every *being* within and outside of this realm *fears* and worships; I never would have thought that, by coming here, I would be coming home."

"You may not have thought so, but time and chance already knew that you would be here. This is your home Azazel," she says.

"But what about Heaven?" says Anastasia.

"You didn't want me," says Azazel, reflecting. "If you wanted me then I would be here. If you wanted me then I wouldn't need to have you tell me about how wanted I am; I would already feel it."

"There is so much to your life," explains Hathor. "Don't say that you weren't wanted, because you were wanted, but it couldn't happen."

"Why?" says Azazel.

"I don't know," she says. "My father and Anu secretly set up an agreement giving Anu the responsibility of raising you. If I knew what was going on, I would also know why my daughter was given to Anu."

"Then why didn't you ask?" inquires Anastasia. "You are a goddess of revenge. You are supposed to protect."

"Where is there a need for protection when you sense no approaching or intended harm?" she responds. "My father ensured me that my daughter would be treated as if she were here in his city, and I found no reason to be alarmed. What is done among and between the Sovereign Creators cannot be overridden. Not even the statements of a daughter can persuade them to think otherwise."

"So you didn't even ask any questions?" says Azazel.

"Of course I did," she says, lightly touching his chin and smiling, "but that is all I could do, and if got no answers, and if was made to feel that everything would be fine, what more can I do?"

"So you just trusted Anu?" blabs Anastasia.

Smiling, "I had no choice," she says.

"So, what am I?" asks Azazel, looking at his grandmother who looked no more than thirty years old.

"That is for you to discover," she counsels. "Within you is the power and the spirit of the first class of the Creators. Only you can know who and what you are, and most importantly, who and what you are not."

Suddenly landing in front of them from out of the sky, and causing a rattling earthquake from his entrance, "You are born to be a King of *Gods* and the chief Sovereign over every class of *beings*," says Ra. "You are to replace the Eternal."

Anastasia and Azazel rise to their feet, only to fall to both knees, their faces bowed down. Ra then takes them by their chin, lifts up their heads, and stands them on their feet.

"My grandson," he begins, "is it lawful for a Sovereign to prostrate himself before a Sovereign? You are a Sovereign. You don't know it yet, but you control the nature, order, and chemistry of life."

"That speech just means he's happy to see you," says Hathor.

Azazel, pulling Anastasia at the same time, runs into Ra's arms. While Anastasia, being shy, pulls her arm away, Azazel rushes into his grandfather's chest, a very bright light appearing around them.

"He is the one," he says to Hathor.

Anastasia quietly looks on, wondering within herself about who her friend actually is, and why he has no idea about who he is. She can't understand how and why he doesn't know anything about himself. Looking at the embrace between Azazel and Ra, and seeing the affectionate glow appearing at their touch, she begins to care that Azazel receives the love that he deserves. It is at this point that she vows to be for Azazel what that brightness around he and his grandfather represents.

"You love him," says Hathor, snapping her out of her thoughts. "You love him."

"All friends love each other," Anastasia replies.

"True," replies Hathor, "but not all friends love."

Anastasia, looking into Hathor's eyes, understands that her affection for Azazel cannot be hidden. Hathor then leaves Anastasia to join her father and Azazel in the overpowering light. Standing alone, she cannot help but think that Azazel does not belong here, and that this light should have always been there for him. She wants to leave, and to take him with her, but does not want to interrupt Azazel possibly receiving a form of love he has yet to both receive and experience.

Aepharia

Anastasia inevitably returns back to Heaven. After meeting Ra, Azazel spent many millenniums in the realm of Ra, conquering other realms and their districts in the name of Ra. Being trained in the art of war and of his importance to Ra's throne, Ra's Sovereignty flourished through Azazel's bravery and abilities.

One of Azazel's greatest victories came as he conquered Annwn, which was a realm of Heaven given to *beings* found *righteous* by the Sovereign of the realm. Its Sovereign Creator had sent an army into the realm of Ra, crossing over into the Underuniverse to claim Ra's realm and Palace as his own. Azazel and his troop not only defended Ra's realm and Palace, but also carried the battle into Annwn. An agreement was then made that the Sovereign, in order to keep his Sovereignty, should relinquish the realm to Ra, accepting to keep the throne and realm in service to Ra. The Sovereign of Annwn agreed.

Azazel studied the art and the philosophy of war under Ra's chief Officer of war, Montu. Azazel earned Montu's respect upon claiming a divine realm of Heaven and of the Underuniverse for himself.

Hearing, from a member of a divine realm's Palace, that it was raided and that another Sovereign of Heaven enslaved its *beings*,

Azazel, being mindful of the realm's residents who, prior to their invasion, lived in peace without a Sovereign, thought to claim it for himself. He immediately had plans of beautifying the environment, giving to the realm a natural and an eternal beauty it, for the sake of its *beings*, deserved.

Walking in the streets of Ra's realm, amongst the citizens, the sound of someone running towards him alarms him. Acting as if he doesn't hear it, upon the person reaching him, Azazel swiftly catches the runner, throwing him to the ground, transforms his hand and forearm into a sharp sword, and places that sword to the runner's neck.

"My lord," the man says, trembling, "I mean no harm. I'm from the Universe of Heaven, from a realm unaccustomed to conflict and dread. We are suffering. Our people are under the authority of a foreign Sovereign and we need liberation."

Azazel, saying nothing, frustratingly looks at him, his arm still at the man's throat.

"I...I understand this is not the best way to approach," he says, "but we have heard of your spirit in war, how you defend the throne of Ra, and we need your help. I am a member of the realm's Council. We have a Sovereign, but he and his family have not justly handled the realm."

Moving his arm away from the man's neck and re-transforming it back to normal, "You are gods and have abilities of your own; use them," he say, getting up and walking away from the man.

The man, rushing to get to his feet, chases Azazel down.

"My Lord," he begins, "we are a realm of peace and of love. We will not war unless seriously moved to do so."

"I believe the enslavement of your people is enough to move you to war," says Azazel who, in his kingly attire, keeps walking.

Again running up and stopping him, "My Lord," says the man, "if I may have your ear for just a little longer: can you listen to something and then answer it; please?"

"Go on," says Azazel.

"Waters once flooded a world. So long as the waters remained, the world was not able to function or to produce and sustain life. But then the wind blew on the waters, and roughly, giving birth to a dry land. The realm, being thankful for the wind, believing that the wind had judged it as being uninvolved with the flood's character, worshipped the wind, initiating it as the realm's God, dedicating the people of the realm to the wind."

Silent, with his arms folded in a way to where his chin is resting in his palm, Azazel continues to listen.

"But then the waters returned," says the man. "Soon enough the wind and the waters had an argument, resulting in the two settling their difference, causing the dry land to re-appear. The re-appearance of the dry land allowed the realm to once again produce and sustain life for its *beings*. Being now grateful for their newfound fortune, this new generation of people, believing that time had judged them as being uninvolved with the argument between the wind and the water, began to worship time, calling time the realm's new God.

"You see my Lord," continued the man, "there is a way in which life works, and especially for someone like you. Sometimes, it is not the victory attributing praise to the warrior, or even time and chance, but rather the reason behind the campaign's success."

"Yes," says Azazel, "but what can get lost in the reason behind the campaign's success is also the savior, who, in the first story, because of the superstition of the generation in the second story, became forgotten."

"Are you sure of that?" asks the man.

"I am sure," responds Azazel. "If time became the new God of the realm, this means that the labor of the wind, the initial God of the realm, was not noticed."

"But how was the second God discovered?" says the man. "Was it not the wind that highlighted time's justness? Why should you then think that the initial God of the realm was discarded or replaced when, in fact, knowledge of the next God is due to the labor of the first, making all worship given to the second God a service in debt to the first.

"You see, my Lord, what is first revered is never forgotten, but its spirit lives on, and however it lives on, within whatever comes after. This is again something you should concern yourself with, because there can be no immortality, of which you search, without an initial breath of reason behind its campaign."

Azazel understood.

"Return home," he told the man, "to your realm. The waters may linger for yet a little while longer, but the wind is coming."

"Bless you," said the man, as he put both hands on Azazel's shoulders.

After the man disappears, Azazel vanishes and then re-appeares in Ra's Palace, at his throne. He presents his case for leaving the realm to defend that realm of Heaven. Ra, after encouraging Azazel on his campaign, gives him one hundred and fifty of his *beings* created for of war. After gathering the troop together and delivering a speech, the company of soldiers, led by Azazel, teleports from the realm of Ra and into that realm of Heaven called Aepharia.

Upon entering into the realm, Azazel and his troop enter into a war zone. Azazel can remember being in school and reading about the legend of Aepharia's beauty. The world acknowledged for its eternal peace and benevolence now looks completely ruined, its *beings*, if not slaughtered, are mindlessly running around and trying to hide from the gods that are invading.

Azazel's fury boils over. Here rests, now in devastation, a realm that harmed no one. This is a realm serving the *beings* living on it. The sight of this ruined Paradise greatly offends and troubles Azazel, who cares to have such a wise and beautiful realm maintaining its innocence without harm.

Unable to conceal his anger, Azazel falls to one knee and places his hand on the ground. Immediately the ground begins to quake, releasing a thick gold liquid. The liquid begins to rise, swallowing up every one within this world, including Azazel. The liquid is hot, and as it rises, while protecting those meant for the realm, it turns to ash those *beings* causing devastation to it. This magma-type liquid also causes the entire environment to turn to ash.

The liquid rises higher than the realm's clouds, remains for a short time, and then slowly begins to decline. Upon returning into the surface, the liquid unveils a beautiful portrait of nature in supreme serenity; the realm is more divine than before, with cities and districts already built and measured for the people to live in. The *beings* terrorizing the realm are nowhere to be found.

Azazel, when once the magma is completely under the ground, rises to his feet and waves his arm violently in the air, in the motion of a circle. A bright and shining circle appears after he completes the motion, and then expands, forming a seal around the realm. He has secured this world from contrary energies, encoding within the seal a knowledge to only let *beings* into the realm that have labored to belong there.

"My Lord," hesitantly says a member of his troop, "did you even need us here? What can we do to assist you?"

"I needed you for after I made this realm new," he says, walking towards his troop. "If I recognize the unwanted *beings* that were here, then I know you do too. Go to their realm in the Underuniverse and kill every one of them. Leave the realm empty. If, when I enter into that realm, I see it livable, I will kill each and every single one of you. Go into their realm and pulverize it, but whatever Sovereign is there, keep them alive for me."

Upon giving his troop their order, they left. They found that realm in the Underuniverse and annihilated it, leaving no trace of those *beings* behind. They then held the Sovereign of the land hostage, and, being faithful to their orders, remained there with him, waiting for their next order.

Meanwhile, in Arcadia, Azazel is celebrated. The Sovereign and his family meet Azazel, and upon their meeting, Azazel bows to one knee, again placing his hand on the ground. Another quake ensues, but this time it moves and encircles Aepharia's Sovereign God and Creator, and his family. A dark purple ring forms under their feet, and then quickly rises from the ground and shoots into the air. When everyone's eyes return back to the surface, the Sovereign and his family are nowhere to be found; the ring had shot out a vast number of beams, vaporizing them.

Rising to his feet, the people are silent. The members of the Council approach him and thank him for his service to them. In the midst of the uproar, the man who first found him in the city of Ra immediately pulls him aside. Azazel, having no interest to stay, is ready to leave so that he can meet his troop in that part of the Underuniverse they wait for him at.

"My Lord," he begins, "Aepharia thanks you."

Pretending as though he is no rush, "The wind blew," says Azazel, smiling.

"Yes," the man quickly replies, "but the Council has agreed upon something. We care to have you as the Sovereign of this realm, and are prepared to do anything for you to accept."

"You no longer need a Sovereign," Azazel responds. "I have sealed this realm to its character. Only *beings* suitable for the realm will now be able to enter and exit it."

"And we do appreciate this, but we are indebted to you," says the Council's member. "We owe our splendor and our safety to your creating spirit; we will not have this realm exist without its Creator."

Azazel accepted to be the realm's Sovereign Creator, a title and position he thought he'd never attain. Upon agreeing to the role, he created a city above the realm, and a Palace for his residence. He thought to let the realm's Council govern from the Palace, but upon being gifted one daughter from each member of the Council for agreeing to be the realm's Sovereign, he decided to give control of the realm and of the Palace to his *wives*. They were to labor with the Council for ensuring the realm's continued benevolence to its *beings*, and the *being's* continued benevolence to the realm.

"You should know," says Azazel, now in the Court of his Palace, to his realm's Council, "that I love your realm because of its mind and character. I did not create your realm's mind, but upon hearing its disturbance, I, possessing a similar mind, was moved to act for it. In no way did I expect any of this, but I am beyond content with the way things have gone."

"My Lord," says one member of the Council, "we came to you only because we felt as though you pulled us to you. We were persuaded, due to how convincing that pull was, that you were our realm's savior."

"The only Sovereign or Savior is the Eternal," responds Azazel. "I, too, being persuaded by the speech of one of your members, was moved to act, and not for the rationale behind the speech, but for its principle. Both Universes know who I am and believe, concerning me, whatever they may believe, but I am unconvinced of what is said and can care less of what is said," he says, the tone of his voice changing. "I am a Sovereign Creator and the spirit of the creating class is within me. I will, for the failure of both the Creators and of the Eternal to justly bless the realms, conquer both Universes, this divine realm of Aepharia bringing together the two Universes into one."

"My Lord, we are here to serve," says one member of the Council.

After looking each member of his Council up and down, "I can't stand your kind," he says. "I have had no positive experience with any Council and I do not expect to start having positive experiences now, but you all are changing my mind. Know this: I do not trust you and I do not expect you to trust me; I will earn your trust and you will earn mine."

"Yes my Lord," they all say.

"I also accept your daughters as my wives," he next says, "and they will act in my place within this realm's city and Palace. I will also gain their trust, and they will gain mine. I give them liberty to rule as they please, and do expect you to advise them as if your counsel were mine."

The daughters were then called into the room and presented to Azazel. He told them their role to the city, to the Palace, to the Council, to the various *beings* within the realm and under them, to the realm in general, and of their necessary loyalty to him. He then left and returned to the Underuniverse. He met up with his troop, who patiently held the Sovereign Creator of the realm, and his family, for Azazel.

Upon arriving, Azazel angrily disintegrates the realm's Royal Family, falls to one knee, places his palm onto the ground, and renews the realm according to how he had done for his newly acquired realm. After doing so, he next creates inhabitants for the realm, occupying it with different classes of *beings*. He, after sealing this realm with the same seal given to the other realm, gives the responsibility of this new realm to his wives and to his already established Council. He sees the conquering of a realm in the Underuniverse as being key to his plan for unifying the two Universes under him.

After re-establishing this realm, Azazel then leads his grandfather's troop home. Upon reviewing his activity with Ra, a celebration is held in his honor. He then, away from the crowd, shares his venture, and his vision of dominion with the love of his life who, after throwing herself in his arms, looks into his eyes with her red eyes, congratulating him on being one step closer to fulfilling his potential.

Expansion

"I'm happy for you," she says, giving him a kiss.

"I've worked hard over the past millenniums," he says, looking up and into the vast space above them. "It will all be mine."

"I know it will," she says, "but if you keep on conquering for Ra, it will really be for him. When am I going to be the Empress I know I can be?"

"Didn't you hear what my grandfather just said?" he says, hoping to silence her. "I now share the throne with my grandfather. I am the Sovereign not only of this realm, but of all of the realm's I've conquered for the throne."

"Joint-Sovereign," she reminds him.

"That's not how you should look at it," he says.

"But that's what it is. No one believes in you like I do. No one believes in us like I do. You need to realize that, so long as you remain in-debt to your grandfather, so long as you keep conquering for the realm of Ra and not for Aepharia, you are only being used. Aepharia is your realm. The two Universes are to become one through its elevation..."

"Stop," he interrupts. "This will happen," he says, smiling.

"Just like our life and marriage will happen? If you will not, having all power and command, conquer the Universes, should I be surprised that you have not yet married me?"

"What is really wrong?" he says, separating from her.

"You are wasting yourself conquering for Ra," she says. "I'm tired of seeing Ra conquer. Your father is the Sovereign God and Creator of the Underuniverse and you do not even conquer for his throne; do you think to conquer even the Amalgamate for Ra?"

"Ra is my father," he says. "Anu is my father," he continues. "You have no idea what you are talking about and have no right to judge what you cannot fully understand," he says, angrily.

"Then tell me where I am wrong," she says.

Azazel, fighting back a response, remains silent.

"Tell me where I am wrong," she presses.

Observing the couple's tension, Hathor walks over and interrupts by saying, "I'm proud of you Azazel."

"I'm proud of him too," says the princess. "I only wish he knew how much," she adds.

After a brief moment of silence, "Let's get back," she says to them both.

Entering into the main room, "Hail the Sovereign and his future Empress," says Ra out loud. "There is no Creator more proud of his son than I am of mine. You have preserved my throne, you have preserved my name, and you conquer both Universes for me; I am not sorry to now share such a throne with you."

Azazel clutches the princesses' hand, looks around the room respectfully, and then looks at her.

"My meek and humble grandson," continues Ra, "in the presence of everyone, I have something to say," he says, calling Azazel to himself.

"I do this publicly because I want no questions hereafter," says Ra. "I am relinquishing the throne to you, Azazel. I understand that I have made you joint-Sovereign with me, but I believe it best to withdraw."

The room is silent.

"My end has come," he says. "A Creator lives forever only through the next Creator presenting a more suitable and equitable benefit. My grandson has a far superior presence and spirit than I, being the member of a rare class of Creators. I, in fear, do not give him this realm and all of the realms he has conquered for me, but out of honor I will to exist within him, as Anu his grandfather, and as so many others have also elected. This is not the end, but only the beginning."

Ra then turned from facing the crowd to facing Azazel. Looking at Azazel, Ra disintegrates into the form of a mist and enters into Azazel's nose. All are absolutely stunned. Everyone present falls to the ground, as in the manner of worship, with their face to the floor and their eyes closed; his plan has worked.

Azazel, some time before this coronation began, killed Ra, and then created a programmed image of Ra for the celebration. Throughout his conquests, Azazel, while claiming the realm for Ra, established them according to the spirit of Aepharia. Ra, understanding Azazel's goal to eventually overthrow his own realm and throne, repeatedly tried to talk to Azazel about his loyalty to the throne, and that his own throne will eventually have its dominion without force. But Azazel will not listen.

Azazel, over the millenniums, conquered realm after realm for Ra. His strength and his essence is more than Ra, or than any Creator or Sovereign was prepared to face. Ra did not expect that both Azazel's spirit and popularity would be so great, and so tried to manipulate Azazel to direct his energy towards the Underuniverse's throne, the throne of his father.

Sensing Ra's disloyalty, Azazel, with tears falling down his face, on an occasion that Ra asked to meet with him, gently and unsuspectingly took his grandfather by the hand and then disintegrated him, turning him into a pile of ash. Taking one knee, he touched the ash with his fingertips and reconstructed Ra, programming him to call a banquet, and to publicly relinquish the throne to him at that banquet; he wanted to take the throne and the realm, and to possess every realm and throne he conquered for the throne, without drawing any suspicion.

This is not the first time he has done this. He has committed the act of creating a temporary version of a Sovereign with Anu, and with other Sovereign Creators having high affection or regard for him. The silence amongst the crowd, after watching Ra not only relinquish the throne to him, but also become a breath inhaled into nostrils, is due in part to their suspicion of him, as they have all heard the rumors of Sovereigns from both Universes, after disappearing, mysteriously offering both their self and their realm to him.

"It begins," says Azazel, looking at, and at times through the banquet's audience. "I don't care to assume, or to think that I know anything, but I feel as though my time is now. You all know how hard I've worked. You all know how hard I continue to work. I have been a servant while a leader, and this will not stop.

"I will hereafter take every realm I've conquered from the two Universes, combine them, and separate them from Heaven and the Underuniverse, creating a third Universe for us. This is the time for separation. Aepharia will no longer be a realm of realms, but it will become one Universe. From now on, until Aepharia has completely swallowed up the Eternal's dimension, every conquered realm will be taken from either Heaven or the Underuniverse and added to Aepharia.

"Aepharia will be its own Universe," he continues. "All of you, for your allegiance to me, and for your support, and for your continued contribution are, no matter what realm or Universe you currently reside in, citizens and members of Aepharia. This is our Paradise. This is our Empire. There is no one that can stop our conquest. I will be a plague both destroying as a pestilence and regenerating as a blessing to the two Universes from hereon out. The army of Aepharia will elevate its Universe into transcendence.

"I," says Azazel, falling to one knee, his face to the ground, "will be the God we have been missing."

Looking on, and unimpressed by his speech, Hathor, the only one who did not prostrate before Azazel, waits until he is finished speaking and pulls him aside, into a private room of Ra's Palace, from the crowd.

"Have you forgotten Ra's loyalty to you?" she says.

"Ra took advantage of my loyalty," he says. "I became the head of his army. I conquered every realm, both in Heaven and in the Underuniverse, with his own troop. I acted for my grandfather because he never lied to me. I knew only lies in Heaven, and Anu kept too many secrets about me from me, and especially when it came to my mother. I will never be sorry about my desire to know this realm and to see one of the original Creators created by the Eternal, but whether he is my grandfather or not, I will not be used as if I have no mind."

'You are a foolish child,' she responds. "Your whole desire, ever since you got here, was for conquest. Do you not see that you could have your reign and can fulfill your destiny without harming anyone? Do you think that just because the spirit of a Sovereign lives within you that you must act belligerent? Do you understand that you are interfering with a set design?"

"Nothing remains 'set' forever," he fires back. "If what is designed to be 'set' experiences change, then I do believe that the design was never meant to be permanent. Everything that my hands have done is supposed to happen. It is prophesied that the Creator to come, before replacing the Eternal, will uproot every the Sovereign Creator of every realm. I am only fulfilling fate," he says, looking coldly into Hathor's eyes. "If there is anyone that should understand protecting and taking revenge, it is you; I am only defending and executing vengeance for better ensuring what is mine."

"You are your father's child," she says through a tone of disappointment.

"I am nothing like my father. Who is equal to the Eternal and yet remains without the Eternal's throne? If I had my father's power, do you think my life would have turned out like this? I am nothing like my father. My fate is greater than his."

"And you expect respect after your behavior?" she says after a pause. "Do you really expect the people to regard you as they did my father?"

Stepping closer to her, and looking deep into her eyes, "They fear me," she says. "How can I expect or hope for what I already have?"

"You spit in Ra's face by saying such a thing," she again says after a brief moment of reflection. "Your actions and your behavior is treasonous, yet you find excuse because of the fear your image draws."

"I am tired grandmother," he says. "I am tired of being nothing. I am tired of seeing myself advance into second place. I am tired of my potential being manipulated. I am tired of laboring for everyone and not laboring for myself. I am tired of fulfilling the vision you have for me and not the vision I am meant to fulfill without any guidance. I have given my all to this realm and this throne while my own remains without care."

"So why not take your realm and do what you intend to do without harming anyone, separating your realm from the two Universes to exist according to your will?"

"You're missing the point," he says.

"The enlighten me," she demands.

"That is not how it goes," he says.

"And why not?" she says.

"Don't," he quickly interjects. "You know better than I do why I cannot do as you say."

"And what makes you think that you are the *One* prophesied of?" she says, and is afterward, because she knows that he is that *One*, unable to look at him without regret for saying that.

"You are no different than my family in Heaven," he says, a deep sorrow lowering his face. "You, after insulting me, want to talk about me forgetting love and loyalty? Who is it, after I decided to leave Heaven and to permanently live in this realm, that taught me about my special relation to the first class of the Creators? Who is it that, encouraging me to express myself, brought me to Mantu, to train in the art of warfare and of military intelligence? Who is it that never let me forget my destiny, or my mother, and my debt to the realm of Anu and Ra? Grandmother, if you are upset with me about my behavior, if you do not like my actions, you ought to first think about the person supporting it since my youth. You," he says, his eyes deeply piercing into hers, "need to blame yourself for awakening me to who I am."

Saying nothing more, she brushes by Azazel and leaves the room. Standing outside of the room, not too close to the door, is the princess, whose red hair and red eyes make him smile when he sees her enter into the room.

"I heard everything," she says.

"No one understands," he says.

"I do," she says.

"I wish you did," he says.

"It's ok," she says. "Don't let her get to you. You have a vision. You've been given a vision of yourself. Nobody and nothing can stop that vision from coming true; you are doing the right thing."

"I could have done everything she said. I could have just taken my realm and separated it without doing so much. I could have just taken my realm, let it exist as its own Universe, and be happy, but I wouldn't be happy. I would be doing what makes sense, and what would give me peace and contentment, but I wouldn't be fulfilled."

"Be fulfilled," she responds. "You can't keep making them happy while you are not. I share your joy and sorrow for conquest. I see how happy you were to conquer for your grandfathers, but I also see how sad it makes you. It isn't right that you expand districts for thrones while your own receives little to no attention. Listen to no one; the vision given to you of yourself is to be like a *Father* to you.

"I feel no joy when doing what I am doing," he says. "I understand what I'm doing, and I do it because it is right. Who can control where they end up or where they belong? Who, after seeing where they belong, can fail to achieve the vision? There is nothing that can stop what will happen from existing; I'm only fulfilling my place in time."

"Let go of whoever will not understand that Azazel," she says, drawing closer, taking his hand. "Look around at your work. Look around at where you are right now. Look at what you've done. This Palace, the Palace of one of the first Creators created by the Eternal, is yours. We are closer to the government we have talked about since we've known each other."

"Not even you understand," he says disappointingly.

Refusing to let go of him as he walks away, "Don't," she says.

"Let go," he says.

"Don't," she says.

After a deep sigh, he waves his hand in the air, in a certain motion, causing her to disappear and then re-appear in her home within his father's realm and city. Azazel then leaves the Palace and flies outside of the two Universes, where the Eternal's invisible realm sits. While in this open and empty space, he calls the elements of the atmosphere to him.

As a great quantity of elements for creation begins to circle him, he leaves the area and goes into an atmosphere that is just as empty and as full of elements for creation. He gathers the elements taken from the previous area of the Cosmos and somehow forms it into a very large electric ball. With the ball between his two hands, suddenly every realm that he has conquered is taken from its realm in Heaven or in the Underuniverse and is drawn into the ball; forty-six percent of both Heaven and of the Underuniverse is brought into the ball.

After having brought and joined together the conquered realms within the ball, Azazel throws the ball above the two Universes, causing the ball, after combining with the atmosphere's elements for creation, to release and expand. Now, existing in its own plane, yet not without the vision of the Eternal's invisible Palace, is Aepharia.

The realm, upon expansion, is elegant. As he did for his other realms, he creates a seal around the Universe, protecting it, which immediately fails. He is then, after a season of frustration when failing to apply a seal to the Universe, told by one of the members of his Council that the Eternal, while allowing realms to be sealed, did not construct Universes to be sealed off. It is, Azazel believes, a fair regulation.

Azazel, not long after setting up his *world,* brought the princess into it, holding a marriage ceremony, making her his Empress. As the two hover in the air above the entire plane, over one million pairs of eyes look on.

There is a special connection that Azazel shares with his Universe. Everyone present knows that, although making the princess his wife, his first wife is Aepharia. Every *being* that is present is genuinely happy for their Sovereign, understanding the intention he has for separating them from the Universes. He is the first, besides the Eternal, to create a Universe of his own, and the people, while admiring his greatness, are pressed to continue the mission of Aepharia from witnessing their servant-leader's kind behavior.

"You are all from different realms and from different Universes," he says, hovering in the air and holding his gorgeous wife's hand. "Look around and see that you can love and respect one another. Aepharia chose me because I speak her language, and as her *husband*, I will make sure she is within each and every *being* living within and entering into her.

"We were told that the division between the Universes meant that we could not co-exist. We were told that the division between the Universes meant that there could be no peace between the *beings* inhabiting them. My Aepharians, there is no division anymore. There is only one body; as Aepharia has chosen me, choose one another."

No sooner than when finished speaking was Azazel hit and shot out of the sky by a polarizing beam. A radical Sovereign from Heaven claiming to be that believed Sovereign conquering the two Universes, and his army, has entered into Aepharia; chaos ensues.

Recovering from the paralyzing blow, Azazel, with one gesture of his hand, causes the Empress and his *wives* given to him by his Council to disappear and then re-appear within the Palace, which sits in the open Cosmos above Aepharia. Now rising to his feet, he joins his army and Council in war. Looking for the Leader of the enemy army, Azazel finds him, and then violently flies through him, causing him to implode.

"My God!" yells one member of his Council from a distance. "There is more than one Sovereign here."

Azazel then scans the area. It looks like Sovereigns from both Heaven and the Underuniverse have formed an alliance specifically to attack Azazel and Aepharia. Azazel spots four more Sovereigns. After encouraging the army of Aepharia, Azazel begins, one by one, to find and kill the Sovereigns that are present.

But the attack is too much. It seems as though more Sovereigns are entering into the realm with their armies, and that there are Councils from other realms fighting on behalf of their Sovereign. Seeing the turmoil from above, the newly crowned Empress cannot simply sit by and do nothing. She gathers the *wives* given to Azazel by his Council, and also calls together a female troop. The Empress and her army descend from the Palace and into Aepharia to join the battle.

Azazel, in the midst of fighting, sees his Empress beside him in war. He, through his mind to hers, communicates with the Empress; he wants them to keep at least one foreign Council member or one Sovereign alive for questioning.

Getting aggravated with the scene, Azazel commands a bolt of lightning infused with thunder into every trespasser into Aepharia. After the bolt killing most of the trespassers, Azazel takes a shot in the back; a beam has shot right through him, leaving a large hole that one can see through. He falls to the floor, gasping for life, and immediately the hole begins to heal.

Rising back to his feet, he sees that a Sovereign is the one behind the attack. Rushing him, Azazel throws him to the ground, holds the Sovereign's forehead in his palm, removes the life out of him and consumes it through his palm, paralyzing him, leaving him looking very thin and unable to move. With one gesture of his hand, Azazel teleports the living, yet lifeless body of the Sovereign into a room within the Palace; he will deal with him after this invasion.

Returning his attention to the battle, he saves his Empress from an attack, who shortly returns the favor. Both of their armies, although suffering losses, are continuing to ward off the invasion. But Azazel is getting tired of fighting.

His aggravation with this swarm of Sovereigns and their armies reaches its peak, causing him, with his mind, to have every invader elevated into the air. As soon as Azazel clenches his fist, every trespassing *being* suspended in the air explodes. There is now quietness. After finding and checking on his wife, Azazel flies to the Palace, and into the room wherein is the captured Sovereign.

Sitting the Sovereign up on the floor, and resting his back against the wall, Azazel kneels down to him, "Why? Why is all of this happening right now?" he says.

"You are a plague," he says.

"What has happened with the Universes?" he asks.

"You are a plague to us all," he says.

Resting his hand on the man's shoulder, Azazel causes a beam from his palm to shoot inside of the man's arm. Soon enough his arm disappears, the beam eroding it from within. The Sovereign, paralyzed and unable to move or feel anything, wears a look of sheer terror.

"Talk," Azazel says.

"You are, by your actions, saying that you are the Eternal," he says. "You have created a Universe and have made yourself its King. All realms of both Universes are upset and will not let you disrespect the Eternal like this."

"Since when have the realms cared to honor the Eternal? Since when have the realms even remembered the Eternal? There is no one more aware of the Eternal's Majesty, and of the Empress' Sovereignty than me. If anything, I have created this Universe as a Son of the Eternal, keeping a mindful watch over the serenity of my *beings*."

"You have lost your mind," the Sovereign says. "All Creators of all classes will not sit back and watch you disrespect the Eternal. You are becoming more than a God and a Sovereign to the realms, even a lie to our faces and to your own self. Before you bring the Universes down with your selfish appetite, they will kill you to ensure less damage than expected occurs."

"The Universes misunderstand my intention," he says. "The Eternal divided the Universes, signaling to us a division of realms. I have advanced their design. There is no division in Aepharia. The line that the Eternal drew is no longer a challenge; I have removed the line and established unity. It is your class that has forwarded the Eternal's disunity. It is your class that must no longer exist."

"You are the one creating division Azazel," mutters the Sovereign. "This new Universe is what has created a line of division."

"Can you not see?" says Azazel, rising to his feet and looking down at him. "Can you all not see my sacrifice? Can you all not see the reason? The Eternal created the realms with the intention of subtly invoking division. These two realms were established as an experiment to put us against one another, to see if we would either argue or unite: so long as those two Universes exist, their realms will never unite. The very existence of a divided plane encourages thoughts of separation, and the Eternal knows what he is doing, he knows what he envisions, he knows that he sees unity as being impossible so long as a subtle example of disunity exists. Heaven and the Underuniverse exist only to make sure disunity continues and that the *beings* of their realms never realize it."

"You are creating chaos Azazel," he says. "Your Universe, if what you are saying is true, is furthering the Eternal's intention. If disunity for unity is his plan, then if you think that the disunity of the Universes means unity within one Universe, then you are being used to bring in unity through your chaos. If you think that you are right to create unity, and if you think that the two Universes are chaotic, then by creating what you imagine to be unity, you are creating a new type of disunity, causing the two Universes to unify. This means that you are wrong, that you are not acting for good, but that good is using you as its actor; your disunity means your overthrow, and this means that you are not that prophesied Sovereign. That is why we now attack; we can see that you are a pawn to usher into existence the One we look for."

His temper rising at what he has just heard, he kneels down and picks up the Sovereign. Carrying him, he walks outside of the Palace, throws him into the air and disintegrates him with two dark red beams shooting out of his eyes. Shrugging off the Sovereign's words, he then stands still with his eyes closed. Stretching out his right arm and opening his hand, an electric ball forms over his palm, which rises from his palm, goes into the open atmosphere over Aepharia, falls to the ground, and spreads out under its surface.

Aepharia is receiving every realm of every Sovereign killed in the invasion. Spreading out into the land, new territories spring up and are added to the realm. Aepharia is growing. Forty-six percent of Heaven and of the Underuniverse once resided in Aepharia; Aepharia now has fifty-three percent of Heaven and of the Underuniverse within her.

Flying into the air, above his Palace, and looking down at his Universe, Azazel sees his realm expanding and is content. He is close to doing what he believes the Eternal has created him for, which is for uniting the two realms under one ruling *family*. Azazel can only think that he will fulfill this vision, uniting the two Universes under Aepharia, annihilating the code of hate subtly set up by the Eternal. Looking down at Aepharia, he therefore sees the future, where an Aepharian ideology has him, after overthrowing the current Eternal Sovereign, as the Eternal Sovereign of the Universe.

Seen

"I'm starting to dislike living in my grandfather's Palace and realm," he says, the two of them laying by, in the Underuniverse, a lake of lave-like fluid having the color of blueberries.

"There is nothing wrong with Anu or with his realm," says the young princess.

"You think so?" he quickly replies. "You have no idea."

"Oh of course, I'm so sorry," she says, sarcastically, "forgive me for misunderstanding life in one of the most gorgeous realms and Palaces in both of the Universes. Your easy life must be so difficult; forgive me for not understanding."

"Are you serious?" he says.

"Are you serious?" she fires back. "Do you even know what it took for me just to meet you here? You can go and do as you please, but I'm watched. I can't just do whatever I want and I'm told what to do every day."

"Yeah well, you're the daughter of a Captain; you father directly works for the Amalgamate; what do you expect?"

"And you are the son of a Sovereign Creator's daughter; where is your security?" she says.

"So you're mad at me now?"

"A little bit!" she shouts, sarcasm directing her tone.

"I think we should have a little fun then," Azazel says, a devilish grin germinating on his face.

"How?" she asks, looking puzzled.

"Do you ever get tired of it all?" he asks, moving on.

"What?" she asks, confused about the direction of their conversation.

The two are by a lake in a forest within the Underuniverse. They find comfort in one another, believing the presence of the other to be what their life is missing. Meeting at their favorite place, they have scheduled a time to talk, and to let in to their life, in feeling, in conversation, in affection, in energy, in love, what has been missing since they last saw one another.

"Do you think that we have a point?" he asks.

"Everyone knows who you are Azazel," she says.

"I don't mean it like that. I mean, do you think that we, who we are, who were aren't, serves a purpose?"

"We know the science of life."

"I'm not talking about that," he rebuts. "Ok, so let's talk about that then. What's the point?"

"We have both learned this in school Azazel."

"Well then talk to me like I don't know. Why are we here? How come we aren't happy?"

"Life isn't for us to live," she says, "but is for the essence within us, the character within us. Life isn't for us; we aren't the ones to benefit from life. There is an essence within us: that essence chose to live and so a body was given to it. We are not that essence; that essence is not us; we are to experience life through it, and then it is to experience life through us."

"So we don't matter then?" he says.

"I don't know," she says.

"So we don't matter? All that matters is that what is within may live and experience life?"

"I don't know," she says, growing frustrated. "Why are you even talking about this? You know that creation isn't about the body, but is about the essence that is entered into the body. You even told me about the time you saw Anu creating more *beings* for his realm. You told me all of the strange things your grandfather did; pulling from the Cosmos elements, combining those elements for those elements to have thoughts and feelings, creating a body for those thoughts and feelings by using other elements from the Cosmos. Nothing is about us; everything is about what is within us, or is about who is within us."

"I saw him create and it scarred me. We learn these things in school, but my grandfather is a Sovereign Creator. I saw him create a *brain* for the brain within bodies. I saw him put sense into every essence and then I saw the essence re-direct its energy into forming a physical body. It is as if my grandfather put some assignment within every essence developing a body of its own, for that body to carry out the purpose of its essence."

"You told me this already," she says.

"I did but it's wrong!" he yells. "It's wrong! It's not right! The *beings* would awake and would not know anything that took place before they even took their first breath. I saw them awake to life and not even know that their nature is and would be manipulated by a *mind* living within them. As they looked at me and I looked at them, I thought I would feel the joy my grandfather felt, but I only felt sorrow, sorrow for them not knowing they exist for the pleasure of an essence within them, and sorrow for wondering about who will get to live: will the essence live, or will the *being*, being ignorant of that essence, never know about it and live, killing the essence by it living and it failing to fully live without knowing what is within it?"

"You're not making any sense right now," she says. "You're not your grandfather Azazel," she adds, not knowing what else to say.

"Do you know what seeing something like that can do to you?" he says. "If what I am doesn't even matter, but that the essence within is all that matters, what does that even mean for me? Who am I? If what I am doesn't matter, but that what is within must be fulfilled, then what happens to me when I fulfill what is within?"

"Nothing happens to you," she affirms. "If you fulfill what has to be fulfilled, then you can never die, because what is within is alive. When you are living through your essence, the only thing that should happen should be your immortality; we only *die* when what is within isn't fulfilled."

"And that's what I've been debating," he says. "Lately, I've been feeling as though I've been sacrificing myself for what is within, and it hasn't made me happy."

"Why should happiness matter when all you're doing is fulfilling your vision?"

"My grandfather only wants me training for war and learning the sciences of creation. He is constantly forcing upon me the prophecy of who I am to be, and I can see that much of what he says is right, and I can feel that I am to fulfill the vision he talks about, but how can I do anything if only preparing for everything? Why am I forcing myself to be something I am already destined to be?"

"Anu has good intentions," she says. "We don't know the power you have over whatever is to happen, but maybe he does."

"So then if I have whatever power I have, can containing and shaping it mean any more or any less of the power that it is? What if all of this security is actually harming me? What if I lose *me* on my conquest?"

"That's not possible," she says. "Successfully completing your conquest means successfully finding *you*."

"And what if I don't want to find who I am supposed to be?"

"What are you saying?" she asks.

Scratching his head, "I can't be myself in the Universe of Heaven," he says.

"And what makes the Underuniverse any different?" she asks. "We live the same kind of life in this Universe, except its just handled a bit differently."

"Exactly," he says. "The culture of the Underuniverse suits me. The more success I have, the greater the tension I feel between my grandfather and I."

"Maybe he is just trying to live through you," she says. "You know how parents are. Maybe he knows that you will one day conquer him and wants to share your journey with you."

"Or maybe he is against me somehow," he vents.

"Where is that coming from?" she asks.

"Remember earlier, when I said we should have some fun?" he says, a smile taking over his face. "Lay down flat on your back."

"No," she says, unconsciously folding her arms.

"Just do it," he says.

"No," she says. "Why?"

"You're so annoying."

"So are you," she says.

"We are just going to switch bodies," he says.

"I'm sorry?"

"Just lay down and you will see."

"This isn't sounding fun," she says.

Gesturing with a wave of his hand, he forces her to lie on her back.

"You'll see," he says, smiling. "Now close your eyes."

They both, while on their back, release a vapor-like substance from their nostrils. With the two vapors flying into the air, and then descending into the other person, entering through their mouth and into their lungs, the two have officially switched bodies. Frantically getting up, the princess, while Azazel is calm within her body, paces back and forth in disbelief while in Azazel's body.

"Get a hold of yourself," he says.

"Get what?" she says, stopping and channeling her anxiety in his direction. "I don't like this."

"Now let's live as though we were the other," he says, ignoring her.

"I don't know if I can,: says the princess, still in disbelief, reaching out to touch her own face with Azazel's hands.

Feistily hitting her hand away, "Just go," says Azazel, who disappears wearing her body and re-appears in the Palace of the

Underuniverse's Sovereign, which Soverign is Azazel's father. The Sovereign and the princess' father are in a discussion.

"Are you alright?" asks her father after seeing he stumble into the room. "How did you even get past the Guards at home? Is everything alright?"

"I'm fine," she says, walking closer to the Sovereign and then standing close in front of him, eyeballing him.

"You've seen the *Lord* before," says her father. "Is your mother alright?"

"Yes, I've seen him before," she says, "like, before, but there's something on his face."

Reaching up to the Sovereign's face, he catches her by the wrist before she makes contact with his face. He then studies her eyes.

"My Lord," says her father, hoping to disrupt the trance they both seem to be in. "My Lord," he again cries.

"Leave us," he says to her father.

"My Lord," says her father.

The Sovereign, with one wave of his hand, teleports her father out of the Palace. Slowly bringing the girl's hand down to her side, he lets go of her wrist, puts his hand on her head and brings out the immaterial *body* of Azazel. With her body now lying on the ground, the ghostly or phantom-like image of Azazel now stands before him.

"What are you doing?" asks the Sovereign.

Looking back at the princess' body on the ground, and then at his father, "I don't belong there," he says.

"So what did you think? Did you think to live within this girl forever? This is how you would belong?"

"I needed to see you," he says, his head down.

"You're not supposed to be here," says the Sovereign. "Anu is what is best for you. You have to know more about who you are before you can come here."

"And how much more must I know about myself if the other part of me is still unknown? Where do I belong if you don't want me and if I don't want to be where you say I belong?"

"Azazel," says his father, "you can't just use people like that."

"I can't? I suppose you are one to talk?"

"That was different."

"Are you sure? What seems similar is the personal gain we both desire from using women," says Azazel.

"Go home," says his father.

"It is because of you that I have hate," says Azazel.

"Go home!" yells his father.

"All I wanted to do was to see you and to know if I can come home."

"I know," says his father. "I can understand how you feel."

"No you can't," says Azazel.

"One day you will understand."

"Is that the day I've so sacrificed myself to fulfill your vision that I no longer know who I am?" he says.

Azazel's immaterial figure then begins to slowly fade, loosing more and more of its tone with every second. Soon enough Azazel vanishes and the princess awakes. In Heaven, in the realm of Anu, Anu's wife, finding Azazel's behavior to be odd, drew out a confess from the princess occupying his body. Promising to not tell Anu about their switching bodies, she forces the two to retain their own bodies.

"Get up," says the Sovereign to the princess. "Go home," he adds, after watching her stumble to her feet.

She removes herself from the Sovereign's Palace, disappearing and then re-appearing at home, within her room at her father's castle. In Heaven, Azazel, slowly waking up, finds Anastasia next to his bed.

"Are you in there?" says a young Anastasia.

"Anastasia?" he says, his vision beyond blurry and his head aching him.

"Your grandmother told me what happened."

"Whatever," he says, sitting up in bed.

"Why do you want to leave here so badly? You have everything here."

"It's not about having everything," he says, both palms of his hands covering his face. "It's about having everything when starting from nothing."

"You will have your legacy Azazel."

"It's hard to have a legacy when everyone keeps taking it for their own," he says.

"You have to let go."

"Anastasia," he says, still holding his face, "please."

"No," she says. "I never see you. We go to the same Academy and even then I rarely see you. You're always with HER..."

"Don't do it," he says, cutting her off.

"No," she again says. "I don't like her and I never will. Not even your grandmother likes her."

"My grandmother doesn't even like me," he says.

"This isn't about you," she fires back. "Every time you're with her, something bad happens, and every time you're with her, you end up having to jeopardize your life to please her."

Azazel, with one gesture of his hand, causes her to disappear; he lies back down on his bed, taking a deep breath. But she re-appears.

"If you do that again, I will hurt you," she says. "If you didn't avoid me then it wouldn't all just come out at once like this."

Azazel, again with one gesture of his hand, causes her to disappear. But she soon re-appears, snatching him by the top of his shirt, disappearing with him, and then re-appearing in the combat training section of their Academy.

"Stop!" he yells while on his back, her hand on his neck with one knee jammed into his side.

"Fight me," she says.

"What?" he quickly replies.

"Fight me," she says.

"I will not."

"You would fight her," she says. "You would even take over her body just so you could fight yourself."

"What?" he says.

Disappearing from him and then re-appearing in the distance, she creates an earthquake, causing the ground underneath Azazel to become weak; he falls far into and within the ground. Walking over to see into the hole that now looks like a very deep well, Azazel appears behind her and pushes her into the hole.

Smiling as he looks down into the pit, Anastasia, like a bolt of lightning, shoots up from the earth and takes Azazel into the air with her. At a certain point, and at a very great altitude, she lifts Azazel above her head and then forcefully throws him down into the ground.

Hovering above him, she shoots beams of a blue fire from her palm at him. Azazel, moving swiftly out of the way and dodging every attack, disappears from the ground and re-appears behind her, throwing her beyond the altitude that she brought him to and then violently holding her down as he, with all of his weight on her, crashes with her into the ground. He then picks her up and, with his palm, strikes her in her chest, roughly sending her through a very large wall of stone.

"Are we done yet?" he asks.

Upon asking his question, Anastasia, again like a bolt of lightning, shoots out from the wall and into Azazel, almost as if to cut him in half. She, carrying him on her shoulder, shoots into the sky and again drops down onto the earth with him still on her shoulder, creating a very large crater in the ground.

"Are we done yet?" he barely manages to say.

Falling on top of him and hysterically laughing, "Maybe?" she says.

"Let's just be here for a minute," he says.

"And I thought they trained you," she says, falling limp on him.

"Did you really have to do all of this just to tell me that you miss me?" he says.

"Nobody can tell you anything," she says. "You have to be shown."

"Well I see," he says, "now get off me."

"I can't," she says. "And if you make me, I'll just come right back."

Mustering up his arms and wrapping them around her, "I hate you," he says, but not before a sigh.

"Why can't you see that I love you Azazel?" she says, slightly lifting her head from his chest to look into his eyes.

Moving her hair from out of her face, "I only pretend like I can't," he says.

"Don't erase me," she says.

"Don't what?" he replies.

"The Underuniverse appeals to you, and it should, but don't erase me from your life."

"Hard to ease you from a life that isn't even mine," he says.

"I see you, Azazel. I can see you," she says. "This is all that anyone can ask for: to be seen."

The Writer

“He said what?” says the Empress to Azazel, the Council and his other wives also present.

“He said I have created unbalance by separating Aepharia as its own Universe. He said I’ve jeopardized my own life by doing so.”

“That doesn’t make sense,” she says. “How can there be unbalance when we are restoring balance?”

“Perhaps the satisfaction you seek isn’t the satisfaction that is wanted,” says one of the Council members.

“That is impossible,” says Azazel. “I have spent my entire life hearing about the hate between the Universes, and the rumored revolutions of one conquering the other. I have created the peace that has been desired.”

“We have thought about this for millenniums,” says the Empress looking at Azazel. “We feel the Universes and their beings,” she says, directing her speech towards the Council. “There is nothing more right than what we are doing.”

“Perhaps,” says another member of the Council, “but you cannot deny the fact that a third Universe disrupts the Eternal’s original intention. Three Universes were not planned.”

“If I have done it then it was planned,” says Azazel.

“Then if planned,” continues the same Council member, “then the backlash against you is also planned.”

"It is an examination," says one of his wives.

"The Eternal arranged this discontent since the beginning," says another one of his wives.

"If I am now here and Aepharia now reigns," says Azazel, "and if there is confusion, I am not the creator of it. I am to build a third Universe no matter what, and the discontent is to happen no matter what; we need to strengthen the Universe's defense."

"Or what if we removed the cause of the confusion from the scripted discontent?" says the Empress.

"What are you saying?" says Azazel.

"If the cause of the confusion was removed, we could re-write the script," she states. "The script of actions belongs to the Eternal, who is the author of all of this. If we could remove the author and possess his writer, we could re-write the record of events."

"Empress," says one member of the Council, "while it is true that the Eternal has a writer for his ventures in creation, it is not possible to detain him."

"The Eternal manages his agenda through his writer," says another member of the Council. "What is to occur is to transpire according to how the writer interprets the Eternal's spirit. Before any venture, his writer must write what the Eternal's spirit is feeling and what his spirit sees; what is written then afterwards combines with the Eternal's creative authority over the Cosmos to create whatever should be created."

"We know this," says another member of the Council, "but it is far too risky to achieve. There is nothing that is created without the Eternal's writer. Everything that is created, that should be created, that would be created, is created through his writer. To get to his writer involves going through the Eternal Himself; I do not see this as being achievable."

"And let's pretend that we did have the Eternal's writer," adds another member of the Council, "what then? What do you propose the next action to be when possessing his writer?"

"We get him to write the Eternal out of the script," says the Empress.

"Get the Eternal's writer to write him out of his own creation?" says Azazel. "You're insane."

"Am I?" she says. "The writer only knows to write; he has only one function: to write; he cannot do anything but write. His writer knows only to write; if we can possess him, he can become our writer."

"And I'm sure he only recognizes the Eternal's spirit," says Azazel. "How are we going to get his writer to write without the Eternal's spirit? I may be able to transform into the Eternal, but I cannot possess the Eternal's spirit."

"It shouldn't matter," she says.

"I do believe the Empress may be right," says one of the Council members. "His writer is a writer, meaning that, given the situation, he can be used. Possessing the Eternal's spirit does not matter, but what matters is that the same kind of feeling given to the writer by the Eternal is given to the writer through you."

"What are you saying?" asks Azazel.

"He's saying," says another member of the Council, "that the Eternal's writer does not respect the person or spirit of any *being*, but will write when prompted by the disposition it is familiar with. Should you, my God, match the Eternal's spirit as Creator, his writer will *write* any thing you want."

"There is nothing that can exist without his writer," says another member of the Council. "Everything that is made is still available, and every element that is born for creation works and maintains life because of the breath his writer put into it. It doesn't matter who is moving the writer to write, but rather what is moving the writer to write. He is creation's gift, and with your will to re-create the dimension, my God, the writer will fulfill your vision accordingly."

After a brief pause, "So then if this is what must be done for order, then it must be done," says Azazel.

"But how?" asks one member of the Council.

"The Eternal lives within his Palace in the Cosmos, and it will not become visible unless induced, or unless it wills," adds a member of the Council.

No longer interested in speculation, Azazel, beckoning every one to remain behind, leaves the Palace and Universe of Aepharia for the Eternal's Royal Estate. Not quite knowing its location, Azazel, flying into the Cosmos, deeply scans the open nothingness from which all things are created for the Eternal's Paradise. After looking around for a very short time, the Palace, to his surprise, appears in the distance. Stepping, out of the starry nothingness around it, onto the ground of the floating kingdom, Azazel walks up the Palace's very long entrance and up to the front door; the Eternal's writer greets him.

"Please," says the writer, "come in. I just happened to be coming up as you approached."

"I thought this place could never be seen," Azazel says. "I didn't expect to find it so easy."

"The *house* can sense and feel," says the writer, whose form, due to his loosely fitting hooded garment, Azazel is not quit able to make out. "The *house* is seen by whoever it wants inside of it," he adds.

"So it knows why I'm here?" asks Azazel.

"It does," he says, walking back down from where he arose.

"Do you know why I'm here?" Azazel says while walking behind him and trying to keep up.

"I do not know why you are here, but I'm sure I will soon find out," he sarcastically says.

"And why are you alone? Where is everyone?"

"The Eternal has an invisible kingdom in every one of his created dimensions. He is never at one for a period of time, but travels to them while reviewing the dimension he is in. He is not here, nor the Empress or their Assembly; I don't know when they will return."

"And you?" Azazel inquisitively asks. "Why are you here?"

"I belong here," he says. "The better question is why are you here?"

"There is disorder," Azazel begins. "I was told that I am the cause of it and I believe that this is not true. I believe that many Sovereigns are jealous of me, and want me overthrown."

"That is a bold claim," says the writer, still walking in front of Azazel through a now very narrow walkway.

"You don't understand," Azazel says.

"Then make me understand," he says.

"Tension, ever since I was born, existed between the two Universes."

"I'm sorry," the man says, laughing, "but you'll have to be more clear. There are many dimensions with many Universes that the Eternal has created."

"I am from a dimension where there are two Universes: Heaven and the Underuniverse," he says, entering into a very large and luxurious room with only a table and a chair behind it.

"Sit," says the man who, after gesturing with his hand, causes a chair to appear out of smoke.

Taking a seat, "Ever since I was born, discord has existed between my two Universes," says Azazel.

"YOUR Universes? You are from them both?"

"My mother is from one and my father is from the other," he says. "When I was born, there was hate between them both, a kind of hate that was so potent that it's feeling is engraved upon my heart. And of course, being a child, I could do nothing about it, but after learning more about myself, I found myself training for both of my families in both Universes. The more I saw, and the more I spent listening to the *beings* of both realms, the more I realized that something isn't right."

"And then you wanted to do something about," interjects the man.

"Absolutely not," says Azazel. "I didn't care, and to be honest, I still don't care, but as I listened to the *beings* of both realms, and as I saw that no one cared to challenge the Eternal, to question his agenda, then I began to care to do something not just for the *beings* of the Universes, but for the Universes. These Universes have been suffering under a creed of hate since I was born and I, having gotten to know the two Universes and coming to love them, want them under one *Mind* and *Constitution*. And I've begun to do this, creating a third Universe; a Universe bringing the two Universes to form one new dimension."

"And what do you hope to achieve by this oneness?" the man asks, as if becoming interested.

"The Eternal created the Universes to experiment with discord," says Azazel.

"Are you sure about that?"

"I am," affirms Azazel. "If discord was not his intention, why not simply create one Universe? Why divide the dimension into two?"

"Well, why divide the two dimensions into a third? Are not the two Universes, in reality, one Universe?" says the writer.

"If the two are one, then why seal the whole with a division?"

"You have two eyes," says the writer. "When you see, or when you look at something, do you see two different things with both eyes, or do both eyes share the same vision?"

"Both do share the same sight."

"How, then, can you say that there is a division between two Universes within one dimension? There is no divide between them both, unless the division exists in how it is believed to exist," says the writer. "Division is never the Eternal's intention. Division exists because whatever is created is liable to develop, apart from the Eternal, its own thoughts and feelings."

"So then you understand my complaint," says Azazel excitedly. "My concern is for the dimension, and for the Universes within it. I understand that the dimensions are not created for any malicious reason, but the liberty given to the dimension by the Eternal has sparked a possible experiment of discord, to where it looks as though one Universe must conquer the other for universal wellbeing. My concern is for returning to the dimension its lost wholeness, the innocent unity it was created in but due to liberty given to it by the Eternal, has become lost. This is why I have separated a Universe from the two Universes; I will recapture the lost innocence of the dimension within my Universe."

"And what will happen to the other two Universes?"

"They will cease to exist and will not be remembered; my Universe will erase their memory."

"And you cannot understand why there is now discord? Your actions and intentions have thrown off the balance of the Universes."

"I do not think so," says Azazel confidently. "The dimension was given the liberty to embrace an uneven balance of love and hate the moment the Eternal created it. The shift towards one above the other came as *beings* entered into it, altering its liberty to suit a liberty of their own. That more suitable liberty is a liberty of division and of competition where, although the two may share some form of love, the fear of one overtaking the other has become greater than that love, causing a form of hate to flourish. I have known only this form of hate between the two Universes all my life and do vow to bring it to an end through my Universe."

"And how do you expect to reverse that hate without again violating the liberty of the dimension?"

"I will let the spirit of the dimension guide the Universe," he says.

"But if the Eternal created an uneven balance of love and hate within the dimension, how do you expect to reverse, or to even put in a new or better operating system within the dimension?" says the writer.

"I think that this is where you come in," says Azazel. "Do you have any involvement with creation at all?"

"Creation cannot happen without me," he says.

"I mean, when it comes to creating, do you understand the intention of what is to be created, and why it is to be created?"

"I only guide the elements of creation by my writing. I translate the Eternal's feelings inro writing, and from what is written, those feelings influence the actions of the elements in creation. I don't create, but I assist in creation. I don't have any power over what is created and why it is created or how it is created; I give power to the movement of the elements doing the work of creation."

"So, you hear the Eternal's ideas for what he wants, write down what he says, and then the elements of creation act?"

"Not quite," the writer says, meditatively. "As the Eternal is engaged in the act of creating, I am connected to his thoughts and feelings. This connection places me at the location for creation with him, even though I am not physically there. I write what I feel from him at this time of creation. The moment I put his feelings into words, liveliness enters into the creating elements, causing them to do what they believe the Eternal thinks it should do. It is in this sense that I am connected to creation and that nothing can be created without me. If I never translated the Eternal's feelings into words, and then, as he is in the act of creating sent those words into the creating elements, nothing would be created."

"Then this is the only way to restore balance to the dimension," says Azazel, "by you channeling my thoughts and feelings for the dimension as you do for the Eternal."

"You speak as if I've already agreed to this. What you are talking about isn't simply creation, but a re-writing of creation, a renewing of what has already been perfectly created."

"Perfect how?" says Azazel, surprised at the writer using the term "perfect" to describe what he only sees as flawed.

"It is perfect because there is no appointed direction towards love and hate. An imperfect appointment, which is what it seems you desire, is an appointed direction towards either love or hate. The perfectness in the dimension is in it being given the liberty to have its *beings* choose either love or hate, not to have it chosen for them. You see the inhabitants consenting to the liberty given to the dimension as being insulting to the dimension when choosing hate over love, and by wanting to re-write the dimension's *Constitution*, you will create an imperfect Universe, where the harmony you seek will not be developed through a persevering and conscious effort, but by the force of a re-written liberty. This is why there is animosity against you, which has nothing to do with jealousy, but with the Universes understanding the dimension's wholeness, through you, is come under attack."

"You are wrong," says Azazel.

"I am wrong and I am right," he says. "I am right; your intentions disrupts the spirit of the dimension; but the Eternal created the *Constitution* in a very fractured and incomplete way, as if leaving the invisible document within the dimension open for editing. Who is to say that you are not completely wrong or completely right? Your issue, being not for yourself but for the dimension holding the Universes together is an honorable concern, because it not only sorts out the dimension's fracture, but it has the potential to add peace to the *beings* within it, and in a way the Eternal did not think of. But a greater evil can come from re-writing the dimension's *Spirit*, an evil that can cause the entire dimension to cease existing."

"And what is the risk?" says Azazel. "If the *beings* of the dimension have persuaded the dimension to let discord and disunity govern it, what can be worse than what has already taken place? The regeneration of the dimension is the only possible outcome; it ceasing to exist is no worse than it living in and failing to correct its defect in character."

Lightly sighing, "I can feel you," he says. "I feel your sorrow, I feel your regret, and I feel your care for the dimension. I have no care for creation. I have no concern for outcome; my burden is for the feeling behind or within the Creator. I am persuaded not by the act of creation, but by the will, and I will for your will.

"This *house* is seen, or reveals its self for a reason known only to it; it, and I, rarely becomes visible to anyone. Know," he says, his now voice taking on an infinitely more serious tone, "that the *house* has a mind and an eye of its own, and the visibility of the *house* means that you are, and have been, watched."

"Then watch!" he screams, wearing a smile and looking around, as if talking to a ghost. "Watch as I do what your Lord cannot do."

"For the sake of your intention, because, although you are coarse, the expression of your wisdom, being beyond your years of millenniums, is moving, I am, for wisdom, and for a wise intention, despite its success, impartial and indifferent."

"You will not regret anything," says Azazel.

"It is never I, young God, that suffers regret," says the writer. "My lack of an investment in the project preserves my sanity. As for what is created, and for its Creator, that is another story."

Upon finishing his sentence, both he and the *house* disappear, leaving Azazel hovering in the Cosmos. Returning back to the Palace at Aepharia, and telling the Empress, his Council, and his wives about the writer consenting to the assignment, they all look at him in disbelief, wondering why the writer agreed to assist them. But Azazel doesn't question it. He sees the future, and envisioning that *world* to come, can only see greater endeavors within other dimensions carrying his *name*.

The Judgment

"You need to leave," she disappointingly says, waking him from his trance-like state.

Still sitting within the main quarters of the house, the child's father is still at her former home. She has awoken him from the vision he was having of Azazel's life.

"There is nothing for you here," she continues.

"Are you sure?" he says.

"I understand that you've been observing your sons life. I also, as you were watching, saw what you saw. But it does no good for you to be here and doing that if you will not help me make Azazel's life easier."

"Aren't you curious?" he says, adjusting his posture.

"No," she says.

"Why not? My son will do what I, and what no other being is able to do."

"You need to leave," she demands.

"Do you have an issue with knowing?" he asks. "Is there something wrong with knowing? I wish someone had knowledge about the direction of my life. Don't you? Now we can correctly guide him."

"You will do no such thing to my son," she says. "Life is sacred. Just because you have the power to oversee a suspicion does not give you the right to transform it into something certain."

"Yes it does," he says, "especially if the goal is charitable. My intention is self-sacrificing: I am willing to commit the greatest sacrifice so that my son may reach his highest potential for the dimension. Aren't you willing to do the same?"

"Your sacrifice is not a sacrifice of self, but is a magnification of self. You will manipulate for the benefit and outcome that you want, but what about my son? Do you think it is fair for him to have his life guided in a way that will hurt him?"

"Yes," he says sarcastically, "belittle the one whose intention is to forward a vision of his son's dominion."

"You will not harm my son," she says, coldly looking at him.

As soon as she finishes her statement, a female messenger, from out of a portal of smoke, appears.

"Goddess," she begins, "they have taken him."

"What are you saying?" replies the goddess. "Who has been taken?"

"The child," she says. "Your father's realm and Palace is destroyed; invaders appeared looking for the child and, when they found him, after troubling the kingdom, they took him and left."

Looking at Azazel's father in shock, "I know," he says, "it's happening."

"We must act," suggests the messenger. "We must act fast; you are in danger my Lord," she says, looking at the goddess.

"I don't understand," says Azazel's father.

"She is the mother of the child believed to be the future Eternal Sovereign," says the messenger. "This belief makes her body valuable."

After a moment of silence and of meditating on the figure of the goddess, the look on the face of Azazel's father drastically changes. Disgusted at the thought of her body being seen, by *beings* of all classes, as a commodity, "No one will touch you," he says, looking at her. “Do you have any idea who is behind this?” he says, looking at the messenger.

“I do not,” she says, “but, from what I understand, they are from the Universe of Heaven.”

“Then so be it: There will be war in Heaven,” he says, looking at the messenger. Turning to the goddess, “You will stay in the Underuniverse.”

“I will do no such thing,” she says. “I will not leave my family and our realm when they need me the most.”

“We have no idea if or when they will come back. I will not put you at risk.”

Looking at him with a look of disdain, the goddess disappears, her mind determined to materialize at her family’s Palace. But Azazel’s father brings her back into his presence within her former home.”

“Do you think you own me?” she says.

“We have no idea if or when they will come back. You do not need to be there.”

Coldly staring at him, she again disappears, re-appearing inside of Anu’s Palace. But once again, Azazel’s father brings her back into his presence within her former home, wherein also the messenger is present.

“What is wrong with you?” she says.

“We have no idea...”

“I understand,” says the goddess, cutting him off. “I’m aware.”

“You will not go back there,” he says.

“May I suggest my responsibility to the goddess?” says the messenger.

Disregarding the messenger, with one wave of his hand, Azazel’s father causes her to disappear.

“Do you see me as some little helpless thing?” says the goddess.

“I cannot risk losing you,” he says. “You are far too important. You will stay within my Palace and under my watch until Anu collects himself.”

“I will not,” she says.

Azazel's father, with one wave of his hand, removes the goddess from the scene and sends her to his Palace, where eight Guards are waiting for her.

"You are safe here," says, upon her arrival, the Captain of the Guards, stepping out from the group.

Escorting her to the Palace's main parts, the Captain, to get to where Azazel's father would prefer her to be, takes her through a number of rooms. One of the rooms stands out to her. This room has a large number of adolescent girls dressed in hooded robes and quietly sitting in a circle, a lead mistress found sitting in a chair at the center of the circle. A little girl, whose red hair slightly peeks out of the bottom of her hood, catches her attention.

"One of the many schools of purification for our girls," says the Guard who, now standing still and no longer walking because of the goddess, senses her curiosity.

"I'm familiar," she says, staring at the children.

"Of course," says the Captain, pressing his hand into her lower back for encouraging her to continue walking.

Back at the goddess' former home, Azazel summons a large army. With this army he visits different realms of Heaven, ruining them for the sake of his son and killing whoever does not have enough information about his whereabouts.

But then something happens. After ravaging a number of realms and Palaces, Azazel's father begins to feel his son calling to him. His son's call could have been stronger if not using Azazel as an excuse to plunder. Now observing the feeling given to him by his son, he gathers his troops and moves into its direction.

Azazel's father is led into the realm of a Sovereigness. Materializing within her Palace, he and his army rush into the room of her throne to find his son in her arms.

"You're welcome," she says, peacefully handing over the child to his father. "Hopefully you remember your promise."

The men of his army, because of the opening conversation between he and the Sovereigness, are wearing looks of bewilderment. Because it appears as though he and the Sovereigness know one another, and have previously entered into covenant, there is a murmur among the army. And they are right to speculate, because he and the Sovereigness, in secret, came to an agreement about helping Azazel's father retain the child.

The conquests, the plundering, the rushing into and out of different realms, it was all staged, and even, after she and her army sacked the realm and Palace of Anu, the scene of his son in the arms of the Sovereigness. She, according to their pact, perfectly fulfilled her part of giving Azazel's father a reason to keep his son and the goddess in the Underuniverse and at his Palace.

To properly return the favor to the Sovereigness, Azazel's father had promised to plunder realms and to kill Sovereigns she felt suspicious of. He wonderfully fulfilled his side of the agreement, annihilating her suspected enemies and claiming those realms with their thrones for her.

The idea was the goddess'. Understanding the need for her son to experience his father's Universe, and her father's strictness against such an experience, even though she did not want to leave her family, she had to do what she felt was best for her son's wellbeing.

Being in the Underuniverse, having its smell in his nose, its feeling within his self, its landscape in his vision, its accent on his tongue, its sentiment on his mind, she felt as though the environment of the Underuniverse, coupled with the feeling of her father's environment, would leave an impression upon her son to influence his later years. She then, after finding Azazel's father sitting in her former home and appearing to be in deep meditation, knew that she had convinced him of her plan's brilliance.

"Don't doubt me," he says to the Sovereigness after receiving his son from her.

Azazel's father, after securing Azazel in his right arm, holds out his left arm and, turning his hand upwards, opens up his palm. Nine green, blue, purple, and charcoal colored orbs appear from out of his palm; they are the realms that he has conquered for her. After the orbs rise above the Sovereigness' head, Azazel, his father, and the army vanish, re-appearing at the Palace within the Underuniverse.

"It worked," says the goddess who, seeing Azazel in his father's arms, runs over to collect him.

"But at the expense of many, including your father," he says.

"It had to be done," she says. "You knew it would be better for Azazel and I to be here. You wanted us with you but you did not act on the thought."

"It is better if he has Heaven's atmosphere and your father's resources; he needs to understand that he does not belong there, and when he can think for himself, he needs to understand that he does not belong here."

"He needs to have no one determining his conscience for him," says the goddess. "If I stay with my father or anywhere in the Universe of Heaven, my father will rule his life and I will have no say; if he stays with you, you will influence him. He is better with me here in the Underuniverse and not in Heaven; at least I know my word concerning Azazel will be honored here."

After quietly looking at her and waiting for her to finish speaking, "You and Azazel are going back as soon as your father has recovered himself."

"I don't think so," she says through a sarcastic laugh.

"Your father will want revenge on the troops and the Sovereign pillaging his Palace and his Palace's city," says Azazel's father. "After he gets his revenge, you and Azazel are going back. I trust that this experience has moved your father to think higher of you and Azazel, and, seeing that his domain is not infallible, to think about raising Azazel differently."

"Of course he will," she says. "Now he will keep stricter watch over Azazel and I; I cannot go back. Azazel and I lost our liberty to normalcy the moment the Sovereigness invaded my father's Palace."

"This is not a discussion," he says. "After your father gets revenge for the intrusion, and after a period of stillness, you and Azazel will return. I'm going to see Anu and tell him about the conditions of your return," he says as she walks out of the room while he talks, his words hitting her back.

Upon arriving at Anu's Palace, and after a period of time, which appeared, along with the city surrounding it, to be recovering, Azazel's father, stating the conditions of the goddess' return to the Palace, is surprised by the request Anu presents to him. Anu, greatly humbling himself before Azazel's father, asks him to join him on a conquest to find and to annihilate the Palace's invaders. Azazel's father states that he will agree to the conquest on one condition: upon revealing that he has retrieved Azazel and has safely delivered him to his daughter, he asks that the goddess remains with him until his city and Palace are completely safe.

Anu, desperate to use the knowledge Azazel's father has on the invading Sovereign, agrees to the condition. After agreeing, both Anu and Azazel's father call their armies together and depart for the realm and Palace of the Sovereigness. Upon arriving, as if expecting them, the Sovereigness is prepared for war, and with four other Sovereigns and their armies on her side.

The grueling battle causes loss on both sides. Anu and Azazel's father suffer a higher percentage of loss than the Sovereigness and her team, but, nevertheless, the two recover themselves, defeat the enemy armies and maraud her Palace, claiming for Anu's throne not only the realms, thrones, and constitutions of the presently defeated adversaries, but also the constitutions and thrones of the realms Azazel's father had claimed and secured for the Sovereigness.

The secret plan of Azazel's parents to assist in the goddess' exodus from her father's supervision was a success. After their victory, Anu and Azazel's father separate, returning to their thrones. Upon returning home, Azazel's father finds the goddess in a room lying on the ground with his son next to her; the two are asleep. Looking at them, he can only think about his son's future, how he has just, due to him assisting Anu in conquering many thrones in one battle, helped gather to his son, after Azazel will conquer and replace Anu, the very same thrones he has assisted in getting for Anu.

"Did you see my father?" the goddess calmly asks, her voice as tranquil as the scene of her and her son lying on the floor and asleep together.

"Yeah," he says, walking over to her and sitting down next to her feet, his back and head resting against the wall. "Everything will be as I have said."

No sooner than when finished uttering this sentence did he find himself in vision. It is a vision of Azazel at the center of the Cosmos. With his wings covering his body, and his eyes closed and head bent down, he is communicating with the Eternal's writer for solidifying the character he would re-write into the dimension holding the Universes of Heaven and the Underuniverse together. Being connected to Azazel's disposition, the writer writes:

"And so it was that, after the prophesied Champion understood the reason for his birth, his spirit was directed to charitably look after the dimension created by the Eternal. Taking it upon himself to insert into the dimension a new and living awareness of its strengths and weaknesses, and of its ability to refrain from consenting to the drive or zeal of its being's characters, the Champion, the dimension's new Eternal Sovereign, decrees and places within the dimension's conscience a revised attitude."

Azazel, while the writer is writing, Is finding himself surrounded by many bright orbs. These are the orbs of creation that, when activated and given their assignment, will refresh the dimension's constitution, placing Azazel's intention within it.

With his wings now no longer sprawled about his body but stretched out, the many orbs begin to congregate and to form an open scroll. Written on the scroll is the dimension's new creed, which scroll Azazel takes and holds while it is magically written on my an invisible hand.

"With the character of the dimension belonging to the prophesied Champion," writes the writer, "the judgment against any and all anticipated Eternal Sovereigns, as is stipulated by the Council of the Eternals, is hereafter performed. The dimension suffering the Champion's decree, as is stated by the Council of the Eternals, cannot accept that

Champion's will until they have proven their gravitation to the dignity of Eternal prominence. Should the Champion, successfully overcoming the administered judgment, prove their distinction, the dimension will hold their decree for it. The Champion will then replace the dimension's former creator and receive recognition as its Eternal Sovereign God and Creator, giving them the opportunity to claim the rank of the less than few."

Azazel, knowing nothing of the writer's office and of what is inspiring his hand, places the scroll before his face into the dimension's thoughts and feelings. Upon doing so, the Eternal immediately appears and removes both he and Azazel from that scene and into his Royal Estate. On both knees before the Eternal and his Empress, Azazel, completely bewildered as to what is going on, is told by the pair that, although piecing into the dimension his will for it, the dimension will not be what he intends for it to be without him suffering a loss; the loss he is to suffer, up until this point, is a loss of the memory of his life.

The Eternal tells Azazel that, if he would replace him, he must somehow, after having his memory removed from him, find himself back in the present state of mind to take the dignity owed to him. The Eternal tells Azazal that he saw his disturbance, and so Azazel's silence is a way to re-claim the original paradigm created for the Universes. Azazel is told that Aepharia will suffer attack and will experience loss without him, and that if he is to fulfill the prophecy, he must regain the memory of his conquest to claim the Eternal's seat as his own. Still trying to understand why all of this is happening, Azazel is speechless, and before he knows it, he is cast in a domain and awakening from a great sleep without any memory of what took place prior.

Recollection

The search feels like forever. The days are long and the nights are longer. The sun, while the moon has turned blood red, has darkened; there are no stars, for they had fallen centuries ago. The air is both hot and cold, but not warm. It feels as though all heat is trapped behind the darkness of the sun, but then it escapes, teasingly brushing over my frigid skin.

I do not know how long I have been walking in this barren *land* — years must have surely passed. I have very little memory — all that remains are flashbacks of what must have once meant something to me. As I look around I see nothing but a flat land and a few holes in the earth. The sky looks angry and the weather feels aggravated; something makes me feel like I am the cause of it all. If so, then it is the reason I am down here.

Armageddon took place not so long ago — perhaps a millennium or two ago. The memory of it seems so fresh that time means nothing. I cannot do anything about that. I can, however, do something about my memory, and what I remember is leaving both Heaven and the Underuniverse. I can't quite recall what I was doing in Heaven; I despise that place and its God, and though I question my place in Heaven, I cannot remember why I fled the Underuniverse. I have vague memories of both worlds, but I cannot seem to piece it all together.

When I do think back on the Underuniverse, all I have are memories that are like scenes that skip. Though the more I think about them, the more things start to become clear. From time-to-time, as I walk, I have flashbacks of where I am someone in command, someone of high rank situated in a *dark* world; could I be a commander of many and the ruler of a universe? It makes no sense to me.

One memory replaying constantly is on my disappearance — my last night in the Underuniverse. I keep playing the memory over in my head, trying to make sense of it. It always starts with me in a room smelling of a thousand corpses and I am pacing back and forth. Then out of nowhere, either one of my soldiers or commanders, someone who is an advisor to me, interrupts me. His presence does not stop my pacing as we converse.

"My lord, stop this at once. We need you levelheaded."

"What are we to do now?" I ask.

"We must collect ourselves and free him," he calmly says.

Still pacing I say, "I must run this universe on my own and the weak-hearted souls defeated by the Sovereign God of Heaven."

"This is true, but you must not cast fake ideals upon your people. You have run the Underuniverse before, why is it a problem only now?"

"The problem is I served under the Amalgamate; I took orders from my father and so I never truly commanded on my own."

"Do not doubt yourself," the advisor says.

"And why should I?" I say. "I am more powerful than any *being* that may step forth and challenge me. How my father became confined to the bottomless pit I do not know. Now he sits, a Sovereign caged for an eternity."

"Until you release him," he quickly interjects.

"Yes, yes," I nod, speaking quietly to myself. "But I must do this alone."

"You do not need to — you have an army that will will fight by your side."

"I feel I have lost my mind, and not just recently," I say, letting the words of the soldiers bounce off of me as I continue pacing back and forth. “I have gone to the three witches and my fate has been told to me.”

“My Lord, why would you do this? You know there is nothing to foretell in your future.”

“Apparently there is. I have been told I will be a God, have a an Empress, and reign as the Eternal Sovereign.”

“This is great news my Lord!”

“Yes, but with this, I will be eternally shadowed by death and disappointment,” I assert. “I refuse to be reduced to the same fate as these other lowly *beings*.”

“This is impossible Azazel, you are immortal. I do not understand.”

“Those *fallen* ones dwelling on the Earth need to be found and rescued,” I say, briefly standing still to urge my point across.

“Yes, my Lord,” he says, lowering his head.

“I am fretting day and night because of what that God has done to me, to us. I must exact revenge.”

“All that you say will happen.”

“I have also been feeling misunderstood,” I confess, starting to pace once more.

“My Lord, we have already discussed there is nothing for you to concern yourself about.”

“I am starting to think differently; I do not know if I can do this.”

“Do not ever think that way,” says my advisor frantically. “You are the son of the Brilliant; you are strong Azazel.”

“But I will for more!” I cry out.

“What more can a king such as yourself want?”

“Peace.”

“Peace?” he laughs.

“I need this for the dimension.”

“Peace between the Universe? Was it not you who stood in front of your army and said that peace is nothing but a solution for the weak?”

“This is true,” I say, as I come to a rest.

“Then why do you seek such a thing?”

"It is not peace between the Universes, as I once thought, but rather peace within the dimension holding the Universes together."

"You need to stop with this foolishness and take your father's throne as you rightfully deserve it. Do you know what will happen if you leave us?" He says, taking a few steps closer to me.

"I do not care."

"Your people will be led by Apep. Do you wish this injustice upon them?"

"Apep is my father's general, he will make a fine leader."

"Do not be so foolish!" my advisor yells. "You must stop these trifling thoughts and command as you were born to! Lead the dimension into the peace you envision."

"You are right," I say. "Maybe I am just upset at my father's capture."

"That is simply all it is," he strongly agrees.

"I will do as you say and seek the revenge that will unite the Amalgamate once again. Please," I say, "leave me to my thoughts."

"I will do as you ask of me."

It is always after the advisor leaves the room that the scene begins to fade and I begin to picture myself flying up to Heaven. I then just as suddenly see myself falling to Earth and walking amongst the *souls* put out of the Universe by God.

The memory is ghastly and troubles me. What I have pieced together from my reflections is that I am not entirely deviant. I have only done what comes natural and whether that is of a good or a bad nature, I simply carry out what feels best. I believe through this journey I seek awareness. I already have a mind of my own and so I merely need to match right and wrong in my head.

My understanding of good and evil is chaotic because my mother is Metis — the first woman Zeus, my father, took to marry. I do not know how it happened, only that my *father* seduced her into having a night of passion with him. Metis could not hold on to this lie and so she confessed all to Zeus. I was then thrown into the Cosmos by an angry and betrayed god.[1] I am born from all that is evil and all that is *godly*; this is why I stood between two *worlds* and desired peace.

Though I walk this barren world in search for a new state of mind, I do not walk it alone. This land is indeed completely empty — all that lives on it turns to ash, but through the ashes, I have made a beast.

In the final chapter of this world's legacy, everything ceased to exist; every structure reduced to the invisible element from which it came. To comfort myself on this journey, I have created an animal of my own; this animal is a new breed, the mix of something between a black panther and a lion. My beast has beautiful black fur with light green eyes; its claws take on an off-white color. Its wings are most peculiar. With feathers of a bronze tint, this nine-foot-tall beast looks out for me just as much as I look out for it. My Panthon is my life and that is why I made a beast in my *image* — because I can only trust myself.

I am eleven-feet of pure muscle. Black wings thrust from out of my back. Scars lay over my arms and back and one that runs down the left side of my face.[2] My body has been through many wars and yet I feel as powerful as can be.

I like to believe I am the only one on this planet, but I am wrong. What lives here with me are fallen *beings*, residing in another realm along with the physical body of estranged minds living within their bodily forms. I know this because I have captured and questioned many of them. Often I mate with their females for pleasure, but mainly I kill them, disposing of them when they are no longer needed. Of course, I never experience hunger but I know the feeling, so I eat for fun.

I do not have any weapons, instead I use, as is given to me from my mother, my speed, wisdom, and strength. Once I catch one, I

---

1 See Note A

2 See Note B

then tie them up and bring them back to my resting area for experimentation. I first began to study these creatures to understand what exactly it was that ran around as I walked, but I soon discovered that they too had a reason for being here.

One day, I caught one and brought it back with me.

"Got another one," I said to Panthon as he sat.

Usually, to cut them open for whatever I want to do to them, I have to knock them out so they stop screaming. This time I wanted to try something different; I wanted to talk to this one to see what was happening. I made sure its hands and feet were tied down and then began to speak to it.

"Who are you?" I asked.

He said nothing.

"What is your business here?"

"I cannot escape," he says, trying to shake free.

"Were you sent here?"

"I am to dwell on Earth until the Palace falls upon it."

"I do not understand."

"We are here to remind you of your cowardice."

"What are you saying?"

"You left us and so we suffer because of you. You are not worthy to be born of your father."

"Why did I leave?"

"That is for you to answer is it not?"

"How many more of you are there?"

He momentarily stops shaking and says, "Thousands."

"I don't understand why you suffer because of me."

"Because you are a fool," he said. "You do not even know who you are, for that memory has been taken from you — and more than once."

"What do you mean?" I asked.

"You are nothing Azazel, nothing," he finished.

The *being* then began to choke, so I cut its throat and set it on fire by touching its forehead. I sat on my knees trying to piece together what had been said to me, but none of it made sense. It made me think of Anastasia — I could not even remember the last time I saw her.

Anastasia was my closest friend in Heaven, the only bright spot in that encroaching place. Anastasia would always be the one to look out for me; I remember that she was always slightly older than me. Age is quite different in different spheres, but time in Heaven feels so nonexistent that you never feel yourself growing older. Everything moves so slow that one does not pay attention — you are not supposed to. One time I questioned why Heaven was so different from Earth and one of the Gods questioned me back, asking, "What is it to you?" I stayed quiet.

Of course, the Council would always have me in the center of their palm, but Anastasia was not the Council, and to have her there with me meant something, or maybe even everything. Our friendship is one that has a history, and through that history, we share a bond.

Heaven has an accelerated time zone, meaning that three or four days in Heaven are akin to three or four years on Earth. Sneaking down to Earth to speak with its people made me forget, momentarily, that I existed in Heaven. Eventually, I would make friends and lovers on Earth, but they would age so fast that it became hard to keep up with them.

I will never forget the first time I went down to Earth. I told Anastasia and, of course, she tried to persuade me not to go to Earth, but in the end, I convinced her to go down with me. She has such a good conscience that it required much effort, though I was glad she agreed to accompany me. I remember her reading in her quarters as I barged in to disrupt her with my plans.

"Anastasia, what are you reading?" I asked.

"Well, that's a dumb question," she said, annoyed.

"Yes the *holy* writings, I see. What a good read," I said sarcastically.

"What's with you?" she sighed.

"Nothing," I replied.

"Well, the only time you ever come to my room is to preach a new adventure to me. A new and probably dangerous adventure might I add," she says, closing the book.

Our last trip ended in chaos. When I read about Agdistis in our history books, I wanted to see if she really had two genders. We waited outside her room for some time until we saw her naked. When Anastasia saw both female and male body parts, she screamed and Agdistis saw us looking. She told us to come in and gave us a lecture about how wrong we were to spy on someone.

After the lecture, she touched Anastasia's head, a bright electrical ball of energy appearing through her palm, and, because she could see how well-hearted she was, gave Anastasia a new power over nature. All I got was, "Take her and yourself back to where you came from and don't show your shadow here unless your motivation is for good intentions." Anastasia was mad at me when we got back, but her temper eventually settled.

"What if Agdistis wasn't a healing goddess? We could have been in some serious trouble," she continued. "We got lucky she wasn't mad and killed us, or even worse, cursed us."

"Anastasia, relax. You have a new power to add to your list; you share the power of nature with many gods. Isn't that something to take pride in?" I said, trying to calm her down.

"Well..."

"Exactly," I interrupted. "Whether you learn to see it or not, I am good for you and we make a good team. Think you'd have better luck with anyone else?"

Immediately after I said this, Anastasia formed a cloud over my head and rain cascaded over me.

"Very lady-like Anastasia, very lady-like," I said, wiping the rain from my face.

A voice from below yelled out, "What is going on up there? Who lets water fall without care?"

Just as fast as the rain and cloud came, it went.

"You are not clever, Azazel," said Anastasia, folding her arms.

"And when did I ever say I was?"

"You are not smart either."

"I don't have to be smart, I'm powerful. Aren't they the same thing?"

"And you know the rule about boasting!" she stormed on. "Let that tone in your voice die down before it is killed for you," she warned.

"Whatever, Anastasia. Anyway..." I trailed, attempting to change the topic of conversation. "I came to see you because I want to go down to Earth."

"What?" she said.

"Yes," I confirmed.

"No."

"No?" I questioned.

"Yes," she countered.

"Anastasia!" I cried out in exasperation.

"You know the consequences of going to Earth if you are not a member of the Guard."

"If we go, I will guard and fight for you if anything should happen," I said.

"This is a bad idea. I want no part of this."

We then quickly scurry from the scene, making it to her quarters, where I move on to her bed and sit down next to her. I then take her hand into mine.

"Your hands feel so good," I said.

"What do you know about hands?" she questioned.

"Look, Anastasia, I need you with me. You're my partner; I can't go without you. You give me the courage to be brave and strong. I need you," I pleaded.

"I'm not going," she said, snatching her hand away.

"Fine, I'll go alone," I retorted.

"You just said you needed me."

"I lied."

"If you lied then why isn't God talking to you right now?"

"I don't know."

"When we tell an honest lie, He always calls us. You're telling the truth because you do need me," she smiled.

"And, so what if I do?"

"I don't think you've ever said that to me," she said, tilting her head in a way that suggested she demanded an answer.

"Quit with all of this Anastasia. Are you coming or not? Even though I do need you, I will go alone."

After a moment of deliberation, she looked up at me and finally said, "I will go."

"Excellent," I said with a gigantic smile, and then flew over to hug her.

"Why can't you be this nice when you have no plans plotted in that head of yours and need none of my assistance?" she asked.

"Simple, since I'm plotting adventures, I don't have time to be nice until a new idea comes to me."

"Of course," she said. "It is only natural."

Shrugging off her sarcasm, I announced, "We will leave tonight."

"Are you sure flying at night will be safe?"

"It will be more than safe Anastasia. Maybe we can get back before anyone notices we're gone?"

"If you say so," she said, trying to convince herself.

"That's the spirit Anastasia," I rose from the bed and headed toward the door. I looked back. "Have a good study," I said, and I left.

Immediately after I left Anastasia's room, a giant hand wrapped around me and I was taken to the temple in a flash. I stood before the Council. They knew what I was going to do and they tried to get me to confess to my plans. Unable to get an answer from me, they send me to see the Eternal.

"Azazel," he says.

"Yes, Father?"

"Tonight you will do something, breaking the trust of not only myself, but also of the Council and of your fellow peers."

"What is this unworthiness?" I asked.

"Not only will you suffer the threshold, but you have also managed to bring Anastasia down with you yet again."

"I am still unaware of this accusation you place upon me."

"You know what your spirit commands of you — don't stand there as if you are being honest."

"My God, I have not told any lies."

"Why do you do this, Azazel?"

"I am who I am," I stated.

"You are nothing but trouble. But you are my son, nonetheless."

"There is much debate on the subject of who my father is."

"You are truly brave, but I know and see your character. You have fooled no one but yourself and you will see how action matched with bravery can cancel out intelligence when there is none."

"Once again, my God, you speak to me as if I've told you a trifling deed will be committed. I have not once stated my honest ways to be atrocious. May I leave now?"

"You may. Be safe." I stood there and nodded, then made my exit.

~ ~ ~

Soon after Azazel left them, the Council spoke amongst themselves about the foreseen struggles that plagued Azazel. They desperately want him to come to his senses and see the wrongful ways of his thinking, but they know it will take time.

"He is nothing nice," says one of the Council members.

"Nothing nice at all."

"But he is our son."

"Yes, he is."

"Love is something that can never be separated from him."

"He is confused, a youth who is lost and needs hard lessons to find himself."

"He is nothing but eight millenniums and believes he can travel to earth; who else commands this presence at his age?"

"I can think of one..."

"His father was a hopeless case."

"One must not judge the past of a man to determine the future of his seed. He is to be nurtured, cared for, and then we will see him turn a new light."

"There must be a means whereby light is given."

"He is hollow."

"We are that light and he will see where he belongs."

"Eventually."

~ ~ ~

After I left the Eternal, I went to Zeus' Kingdom, which rests within the western part of the Universe of Heaven. Sometimes, I would get so sick and tired of the realm and city of Anu that I would go to Mount Olympus and see my friend, Hercules.

At this time, Hercules was just like me in being a little runt — he wasn't so famous yet. But Hercules and I connected in more ways than one because we shared something innovative: we were created from two different worlds. Hercules was a demigod, and as we got older, he would call me a demigod too, but I never would accept the name or title.

"At least you were made from love," I would say to him.

"So what, Azazel? Embrace what you are and grow from and with it," he would respond.

I was never big on Zeus and since Hercules and Zeus were always close, there was really no way to avoid him. Nobody on Olympus knew how I came about except Zeus and he wouldn't tell anyone. But even though he told no one, they would always wonder why he treated me so badly. I tried my best to avoid him at all costs, but it just couldn't be done; I was in Olympus to see my friend.

"Azazel," Zeus said.

"Zeus," I chimed back.

"Hera, why is he at our table?"

"He's with me," Hercules replied.

"I understand that Hercules, but why is he at our table to eat."

Lightening echoed through the sky and everyone stood still, except Hera.

"Don't mind him Azazel, that's what hunger can do to one who is the god of all," he whispered in my ear.

"Or one who is made to believe he is the god of all," I said, looking at Zeus.

"It's fine," Hercules said. He turned to Zeus, who began to look at me in disgust, "it's really fine."

I spent that whole time eating silently with my head down, afraid to look up. Every time I did, I would see Zeus with his white beard eying me. It was very quiet for a while until Hera started to get the conversation flowing. When it was time for dessert, I hauled off for the exit, but Hercules cut me off.

"I don't know what it is about you that gets to him," he said.

"Maybe it's my wings?" I questioned.

"Everyone has wings here. I wish I could help you out on this one. I'd like for you to just come here and play around and be happy."

"It's really nothing — I've learned to deal with it. But anyways, guess what?" I say.

"What?"

"I'm going down to earth tonight," I said with a wide smile.

"Why would you do that? They're so small down there."

"I need to see what it's like, it's calling me."

"Whatever, just get back quickly so you can tell me about it."

"It will be a fantastic trip and I'm sure I will have a lot to talk about."

"If it's really that good, maybe you can bring me down with you some time?"

"I promise," I said as we grabbed on to each other's forearms to say goodbye.

With those last words, I flew back up to Heaven in the appropriate time to complete my journey. I've always just watched from a distance and so going to Earth meant something dear to me. The moment I arrived, I ran to Anastasia's room but found it empty. She wasn't there. I looked everywhere for her in that spacious room but she was nowhere to be found. I left her room in disappointment and searched another area close to her quarters. I had begun to worry, but then I found her standing by the temple gates. My face instantly began to glow at the sight of my partner — she hadn't failed me.

"Well, it took you forever, where were you?" she asked.

"It's not my fault, I was with Hercules."

"You two really need to separate from one another for at least a millennium, maybe a century," she advised.

"Who else would I have?"

"You always have me," she said quietly, lowering her head.

"No time for that now Anastasia, the Earth awaits!" I expected her to join me in my excitement but she simply looked crestfallen. "What's wrong?" I asked.

"Nothing," she said, sounding disappointed.

"You're still with me, right?"

"Yes," she confirmed.

"Did I say something wrong?"

"If it wasn't wrong to you, then I guess not."

"All smiles Anastasia, please. I will protect you."

The flight from Heaven to Earth was not quite what I expected. Just as it does from Earth, from Heaven the stars also look small. I can now say that the stars are not small at all. Stars actually became an obstacle because there are so many of them and some are so gigantic you have to go to great lengths to avoid them. I accidentally flew through a star and blew it to pieces because I was going so fast and trying to avoid everything else in the sky. I wasn't sure how Anastasia was doing, but I knew I was growing tired easily.

Back then, my wings didn't yet have the kind of strength to travel these distances or speeds, but after a long while, we made it. I'm not quite sure where we landed, but wherever it was, I caused a lot of damage. Eventually, believing I could manage a good landing, I stopped flying and just let my weight and speed pull me down. I was going so fast that flames began to wrap around my body, so when I hit the Earth, I hit with the force of a comet. I dug a deep and wide hole into the earth but I didn't feel any pain, I just laid there and collected myself. I didn't see or hear Anastasia, so I thought she must have had a good landing; either that or she exploded, like that star back there.

So there I was, in a huge hole in the dirt and Anastasia was looking down at me and in a loud whisper said to me, "You are an idiot and we will be obliterated for your ignorance."

Dusting off as I rose, "Yes Anastasia, I get it. Look, this hole, it's not even that big and I'm sure I didn't make that much noise." I said. We looked around and saw that not only had I created a huge dent in the earth's surface, the ground was also shaking violently. "Maybe I'm wrong," I said. "Use your nature...thing — heal the land," I said.

"You are an idiot," she said with a blank face.

"I know, just...fix it...please?"

Anastasia put her hand on the ground and then the earth began to come together. In a matter of seconds, everything was back to normal. "See, good as new," I said, but she didn't seem to care for my forced smile.

"Whatever," she said. "We came and saw, now let's go."

"Go? But we haven't even seen Earth yet! We haven't seen them living; we haven't done anything. It's not even their morning yet."

"Azazel look — we have wings. We are different from these creatures. It would not be good if they were to see us," she reasoned.

"We learned how to blend, right? Just blend in, suck in your wings."

"No," she said.

"Anastasia."

"No."

"Please," I begged.

"The textbook said doing that would hurt."

"What's a little pain?"

"No."

"Look..." I reasoned.

I sucked my wings into my back. I could feel them run down both sides of my spine. I shrieked out in pain and dropped to my knees, but it was all done. For a youth, I was very gallant. After I did mine, she took a deep breath and hid her wings too.

"I can't believe what I'm doing," she said.

"Our wings are gone, but we have the same abilities, nothing's gone but our wings. It's okay."

"We need to find clothes, you know, to look like them," she pointed out.

We walked around until we saw a house. I walked through the walls to see if there were kids our age in there, and when I saw that there were, I called Anastasia in. We went into their closet and took some clothes. Although they were kind of big, they fit well; clothes are clothes after all. After we changed, we walked back outside, ceased our angel form and took the human one.

"We are going to be in so much trouble," she said.

"It's okay Anastasia, we will be fine."

When we got to Earth, the sun was just rising so we decided to walk until we saw something interesting.

"It's strange down here," Anastasia said.

"I know." I looked around.

"It smells...unhealthy," she said, wrinkling her face. "And this air, it's so strange. It's taking me a while to get used to it, to breathing."

"I know, I was scared to actually breathe too," I agreed.

"Where are we?" she asked.

"I don't know."

"That looks like a farm," she pointed.

"A *what*?" I asked, having never heard the word before.

"A farm, where people grow food and keep animals. Then they kill the animals for food, or sell them."

"And how do you know this?"

"They teach it to us. You never know who you might have to protect one day, the Masters always say."

"So we protect the farm?"

"No we...never mind, you'll see what it's all about," she said, dragging me by the arm.

We ventured into the farm and found all sorts of animals, fruits, vegetables, and machines. While Anastasia was in the field, I sat on one of the machines, hoping to use it. I pulled myself up the steps and pushed and stepped every place I could think of, but the machine wouldn't turn on. I found a keyhole but no key, so I made my finger into the shape of one. I put it in the hole and formed the correct key that would work based on how the inside felt. After a few failed turns, I had it going and then drove right through the little house it was in. I jumped out in fear and ran to find Anastasia to let her know what happened, but when I found her she was flat on her back with a mouth full of fruit.

"What happened to you?" I asked.

"I don't want to leave," she said, barely able to speak.

"What are you eating?"

"I'm eating very delicious fruit," she smiled.

"Don't act like you've never eaten fruit before."

"Not human fruit. Their fruit is so...so *different*," she said as she squinted her eyes and gazed into the sky.

"Well, we have to go...I sort of...destroyed something."

"Why do you always have to do something horrible? Can't you do something good like me and eat fruit?" Before she could barely finish her sentence a voice in the distance shouted, "Who the hell are you out there? Get out!"

"They curse down here?" I asked.

"They do everything and more down here, now let's go," she said as we ran away.

We ran as fast as we could, but to make an even hastier escape, we decided to fly to a different territory. Once we landed and hid our wings again, we stepped back out into the open. A vehicle was stopped in the middle of a road — the perfect getaway vehicle.

"We will be safe in here," I assured Anastasia.

We hid in the back on the grimy floor littered with human trash and sucked in a breath as the driver got back into his car and started it. His entrance was unattractive but I wanted more of it. The driver let out a belch so loud it made me jump. He threw whatever he was drinking on to the back seat. I peered out from my hiding spot briefly and read, "Bud Light," on the thrown object. The smell was horrible.

"Are you sure about this, Azazel?" Anastasia whispered.

"Yes Anastasia, go to sleep. We will reach our destination in no time."

She placed her head on my lap and used the jacket I was wearing as a blanket. She was out like a light in a matter of seconds.

It seemed like forever, but the car finally stopped and we reached our destination. I waited until the driver got out to wake Anastasia because I had to be sure this was the final stop. But before I had the chance to wake her, the driver opened the back of his big vehicle and, no longer able to hide under my jacket, found us in the back.

"What the hell are you two doing?" he questioned.

All the noise woke Anastasia up and we both sat quiet, looking at him fearfully.

"Damn kids, how did you get here?"

"You left everything unlocked," Anastasia said feebly.

"Two little smart mouths," the driver said, trying to physically remove us from the vehicle. Out of self-defense and in a panic, I breathed fire in his eyes.

"Azazel!" Anastasia yelled.

The driver backed out of the area, clutching his face. We took the opportunity to run for it. We ran and ran until we came across some people walking down a street.

"Excuse me, miss, where are we?" I asked a woman walking with her husband and two children.

"This is Saint Petersburg," she said. Anastasia and I looked at one another in confusion.

"Oh," Anastasia said holding my hand.

"Well, thank you," I replied.

"Where are your parents?" the man asked us.

"Our parents? Oh yes!" I said, quickly trying to cover my confusion. "Our parents, they...they're somewhere...where we are not," I replied confidently. "But we're going to go now. Thank you!"

We left as soon as possible but then Anastasia looked back at the family and yelled out, "We don't have parents!" I shot her a look.

"Why did you just say that?" I whispered.

"They look nice," she said.

"Humans look nice but they're all evil."

"Not all, not them," she stated.

"Did you just say you had no parents?" the mother called out.

"Yes," I said reluctantly from a distance.

"Come on back," said the husband. "You can stay with us I guess, until we get more information on you."

"Really?" I said. "Thank you."

"Why do you want to take us with you? What are your intentions, personal gains?" Anastasia asked.

"Personal gains?" the husband said. "Who are these kids?"

"We're just Christian people; it's the right thing to do," the mother said.

"Oh," I said.

"Told you," Anastasia whispered.

"Mommy always says to be nice to everyone because you never know who is an angel and who isn't," one of the children offered.

"How did you know?" Anastasia asked.

I punched her arm lightly, chiding her honest question.

"What?" the woman asked, confused.

"Nothing, we're just hungry," I mention.

"Well come on with us, my name is Susan; this is my husband Earl and our two kids Emily and Jason."

In Heaven, they always say kids can tell who is and who isn't an angel — they have the innocence to connect with us in that way. I never thought it was true until those kids saw us. They looked at us as if they knew, as if they could feel our presence. They must have felt something because they hid behind their parents whenever we were around.

Once we arrived at their house, they told us that we would have our own room to sleep in.

"You will share the guest room until we figure out what to do with you," Susan explained. "Most likely we will let the police know of your whereabouts."

"Police?" I asked.

"You're minors walking around and saying you have no parents?" Susan said. "I'm sure they'll sort all this out."

Anastasia and I looked at each other confused. We didn't know what *police* was.

"Dinner will be ready soon," she then quickly added.

"Okay, now what?" Anastasia said to me after Susan had left us alone.

"I don't quite know yet," I said, thinking of a plan.

"What do you mean *yet*? This was your adventure — remember the dangerous part I mentioned to you? Well, this is it."

"This isn't dangerous at all."

"Yes it is; we're in a home with people we don't know and we're too scared to go back to Heaven because of the trouble we'll face."

"First of all, nobody is scared to go back to Heaven."

"Really, Azazel?" She stared at me incredulously.

"Okay maybe a little scared, but we're fine. We can leave at any time," I said confidently.

"That's what you think, but then where would we go? If we expose ourselves to these creatures, we will surely face harsh consequences"; I could see Anastasia was starting to panic.

"Anastasia, listen to me," I said, placing my hands on her face. "We will be fine." Little did we know the door was cracked and the two kids were listening to us.

"You're from heaven?" Emily asked.

Anastasia said "no" and I said "yes" at exactly the same time.

"So are you or aren't you?" Jason asked.

"We are," I said.

"How come you're here?" Emily asked.

"Curiosity," I said.

"I want to go to heaven," Emily said. "Mommy says it's pretty and that's where grandma went. Have you seen my grandma?"

"No," I replied. "Nobody goes to Heaven after they die."

After the awkward silence, Anastasia said softly, "You two don't tell anyone, okay?"

They both nodded.

"You can fly?" asked Emily.

Once again, we both uttered two different answers of yes and no.

"We fly," I said. Their faces lit up with such happiness. "Want a ride?" I offered.

Anastasia pulled me aside. "What exactly do you think you're doing?" she whispered.

"Having fun," I responded.

"No."

"It's okay."

"No it isn't, we are to be hidden, blend in," she said.

"I promise it will be fine."

"I want a ride," Jason said.

"I'm too scared," Emily confessed.

"Well, we'll just go to your backyard. I'll just say we're going to play, not a lie, right?"

I looked back at Anastasia kindly and flashed a crooked smile. She just turned her nose up at me.

After telling Susan and Earl we would be playing out back, they gave us a fifteen-minute time limit to be back inside for dinner. I was not familiar with their way of time; I should have bargained for a little more. We got outside and I told Anastasia and Emily to keep watch so their parents wouldn't see. As soon as it was clear, I released my wings. It felt so good to let them go free. Jason stood there looking at me with his mouth open, his action figure slipping out of his hands and to the ground.

"Can I touch them?"

"Sure," I said.

"Ow!" I yelled after he tried to bend my wings. "Hey, watch it," I said.

"Sorry," Jason said.

After he observed my wings, I told him to get on my back and hold on tight. Within seconds we were up in the air. After a few minutes of ducking, swaying and floating, Jason threw up on the back of my head. That didn't stop him from screaming in excitement though. I took him so high into the sky that we flew inside of a pack of birds and then beside an eagle.

"It's nice here, on Earth," I said.

"Stay with me forever," Jason pleaded.

"I wish I could."

"We can be friends; you can be my brother," he bargained.

"Then let's be brothers," I said.

"Okay," Jason said.

After some time, I flew back to his home. In the backyard, I horrifyingly saw his parents with Emily and Anastasia.

"Where are they?" I heard Earl say.

In split-second thinking, I landed us on the roof.

"Mom, dad!" Jason yelled.

"Jason?" Susan called.

"How did you two get up there?" Earl said. "Don't move an inch — I'll be right back with my ladder."

"Okay!" I yelled

"Your wings," Jason reminded me.

I cried out in excruciating pain while sucking my wings into my back. "What's going on up there?" Susan questioned.

"Nothing," I said. "Just having some last-minute fun," I said, swallowing the pain.

"Okay," Earl said, climbing up the ladder to us.

As soon as I hit the ground, Anastasia pulled me aside to whisper yet again in my ear, "You know you're an idiot, right?"

"Whatever," I said.

Dinner went well, but Anastasia and I decided to leave after everyone had fallen asleep. They were a nice family, a good group of people, but my image of Earth still needed more color. Earth called to me for a reason — one I had to discover. I couldn't' be satisfied that my experience of Earth was complete with this one family because humans are all different. I needed to see more.

After the family said their goodnights to us and to one another, we laid in the guest bed pretending to sleep. Anastasia held on to my hand as we lay there but I didn't get up immediately because I liked how it felt. She quickly dropped off to sleep beside me. I liked how she looked as she slept, as if she was at peace with our situation, and that made me feel happy. But this moment didn't last. Our plan had already gone wrong. I woke her up kind of rough because I wasn't sure how heavy she was sleeping; she looked unconscious.

"Stop pushing me!" she whispered loudly. "You're so annoying."

"You're sounding more and more human, you blend in very well."

"That's what you woke me up for, to talk about blending in?" she said, slamming her head back onto the pillow.

"We were supposed to leave an hour ago but you fell asleep."

"Why didn't you wake me sooner?"

"You will need your rest."

"I don't need it, we need to get back to Heaven as soon as possible."

"Trust me, Anastasia, if it was horrible getting here then you better believe it will be horrible getting back."

"Then let's just go," she said.

"Be quiet," I hushed.

"Don't tell me to be quiet, you're the loud one," she challenged.

"Shh," I said as we opened the bedroom door and slid out.

"I have to use the bathroom," I said.

"How do you know?" In Heaven we never experience bodily functions.

"I don't know but when I press down on my belly it hurts," I said.

"Okay go, but be quick and make no noise," she advised.

We separated and Anastasia waited by the front door of the house while I journeyed to the bathroom. To get there, I had to walk past the parents' room and as I passed I heard voices. These voices were not normal, but ones that could lure anyone into any trap through seduction. I stood by the door and listened. It was very tempting to listen out for the sound of evil.

"The boy is here," the male voice said.

"He is with another," said the female voice.

"We will sacrifice him like our lord says," he continued.

"We will be seated at the throne of Leviathan," the female voice said.

"He must not live because he is the one."

"And the girl, she must be taken care of also. She is in the way. She is powerful and needs to die before she grows into her strengths."

Just then, the door creaked and the two looked back. I moved quickly out of the way and stood silent. The two then continued talking.

"Come, young ones, you must give blood to Leviathan, for he is our Sovereign."

I looked in through the crack of the door and saw a shrine with an inverted cross on the wall. Underneath this cross, two ill-looking *beings* were kneeling with their hands outstretched. The voices finally matched their image. Their skin looked elastic, slimy and rotted. They looked and smelled like a corpse but the magnitude of their power could be felt. I looked farther into the room and saw the two little children walking towards them; they all transmitted the same energy and carried the same mutated appearance. The adult *beings* picked up one child each and ate it.

"We must act accordingly," the male said to the female.

"Yes," she agreed.

I ran back to Anastasia and found her nearly asleep in the living room.

"Wake up, wake up!" I yelled.

"Well it took you long enough, did you have to defecate?" she asked.

"I don't even know what that means, but we have to go, and right now!"

"Well, I'm glad you've decided going back is the right thing," Anastasia said, smiling.

"It's not that...look, these people are NOT OKAY, get it? They want to kill us. We have to go, NOW!" I said in a hurried whisper, trying hard to keep my voice down. Anastasia finally got the message and we hurried toward the door. I began fumbling with the locks on the outside door.

"The door won't unlock," I said in desperation after battling with them for a while.

"Melt them," she said.

"What?"

"Melt them, with your fire thing you did on that guy."

"You said not do anything to give ourselves away."

"The one time I ask you to do something and you don't," she said frustrated.

"I don't know how," I said.

"What do you mean you don't know how?" she asked, confused.

"Yeah, I don't know how, I was scared when I did it before and it was to protect you."

"Listen to me; I will die if you do not do this," she said to get a rise out of me.

I closed my eyes and fire came out of my nose and mouth as I blew out. The locks melted like butter. Anastasia yanked the door open but just at that moment the adults came out of their room and threw hot sticky lava from their mouths, sealing the door shut; I couldn't open it.

"He knows," the female said.

They got closer to us. Anastasia put her fingertips to her forehead and suddenly lightning came crashing through the house, striking them. It didn't seem to do much damage because they got right back up and began to spit acid at us. The acid ate through everything, including the door, which created an opening, but I didn't want to leave just yet.

"Come on!" Anastasia yelled.

"No!" I yelled back.

I felt so much anger that my whole body caught fire and when I stuck my hand out, the female demon flew to my palm like a magnet. I had her neck in my hand. My right hand held her and with my left, I sent a fireball into the male's chest, shooting threw him. Once he was down, I stuck my index and middle finger through the female's eyes and I concentrated so hard on what I was doing that her head exploded.

"Stop, stop!" the male pleaded.

"Why did you do this to us?" I asked.

"Leviathan, our god, he is the one who commanded this."

"How did you know of my whereabouts?" I asked.

"Let's go," Anastasia pleaded.

"We will find you wherever you go. You must die before the prophecy is fulfilled."

Through my anger and confusion, I let out a yell so loud the ground shook. I stuck out my left hand, organized my fingers in specific ways and in each way they moved, so did the male's body. I took his body and folded him up into a ball. I then opened the ground up and dropped him into the hole now gaping below us, along with the house. Soon after, my flames died down and I looked at Anastasia.

"Are you okay?" I asked.

"Yes," she said.

"Nobody will hurt you," I said.

"Thank you," she said softly.

I walked over to her and hugged her. I formed a bubble around us, shot us into the air and we reappeared in a forest, where we would settle for the time being.

"What was that back at the house, Azazel?" she asked.

"I don't know," I said, cutting down tree branches for a fire with my hand I had shaped into a saw. "Something took over my mind."

"You're not like me," she said.

"No, I'm not," I agreed.

"My attacks did nothing."

"They made them weak enough for my attack," I said, flashing a smile.

"They wanted to kill you," she said, looking at me as if I was deformed.

"Yes, I heard that."

"Why?"

"I don't know," I said.

"They said you were the 'one'. What does that mean?"

"What one?" I asked, placing the chopped wood in a pile and breathing fire on it for heat.

"I don't know either, you're just the 'one'."

"See Anastasia, this is why I need to be here."

"And your abilities," she said.

"I need to know more."

"You have so much strength and you gain it so easily," she said, still looking at me as if I had six heads.

"I belong here," I admitted.

"I'm scared," she said.

"Don't be, you're with me."

"I know, but you weren't you just now, you were something else."

"I don't know how I did that." I looked into the flames of my fire.

"You concentrated, you learned quickly on how to control yourself."

"I guess so, I mean, how did you know how to do that lightning thing?" I asked.

"I don't know, it just came to me I guess," she shrugged.

"There's something we aren't being told Anastasia. Why are we so different, why can you just acquire new powers and why do I have so many hidden ones?"

"We must not question our Father," she said.

"He's not mine," I said spitefully.

"Don't say that, Azazel."

"Why not? It's plain to see I don't belong in Heaven."

"Then where do I belong?" she questioned.

"You belong there because you are good Anastasia, I'm not."

"You are good!" she cried out.

"There is nothing good about me, I can see it."

"There's *something* good about you."

"What?"

"You care," she said, looking up at the sky.

Right then, something came at me out of nowhere and at a fast speed, picked me up into the air and took me below the ground. I looked and saw that something had taken me through the sky and dropped with me through to the Underuniverse. I could hear Anastasia yelling my name but it was no use. I brought my wings out and tried to fly away on my own but all that happened was a struggle that I lost. The next thing I knew, I was in this dark land on my back, trying to figure out where I was.

"Lucifer awaits," the creature said.

"Lucifer?" I questioned, but it was too late — he had vanished.

I gathered myself and began walking in this strange terrain. I immediately knew where I was because there these unpleasant looking *beings* everywhere, but they didn't attack me. Some would point, some would stare, and some, while others cursed at me, bowed.

I was just walking, not paying attention to where I was, and then I stumbled upon a forest. This forest had burnt trees, magma flowing through its banks like water through a stream, and three and four-headed animals. As I walked into this mystery, I noticed a female who looked to be about my age or slightly older; I recognized her.

She was the most beautiful *creature* I had ever laid eyes on; even as a youth I had wanted to be with her. She had long silky blood red hair, petite arms and wonderful legs. Her beauty was so seductive and elegant that I began to think of the foulest thoughts I knew; at that time, I had only known a few.

Her eyes were soft. She stood wearing a dress detailing her *young* frame. Her body already bore the curves of a woman, which is why I probably went to speak with her. She sat brushing a two-headed beast, waving her fingers through the hot stream of fire that flowed beside her.

"Hello," I said, causing her to jump in fright.

"Oh," she said, circling me, trying to understand who I was.

"I've never been here before. I was brought here," I said, looking around.

"Oh," she smiled.

"What?" I asked.

"It's you."

"Me?"

"Yes, Azazel," she said as her hands caressed my face.

"I don't know what's going on," I say, enthralled by her touch.

"You must get out of here before they find you," she informed me.

"Who is Leviathan?" I asked.

"The Amalgamate," she corrected.

"Where am I and what's going on?"

"The Amalgamate, it is the form they take when his four selves combine."

"I see," though I really didn't.

"He wants you," she exclaimed.

"What did I do?"

"You were born," she said.

"I can't control that."

"No one can control their birth, but you are the one conceived in spite and more powerful than all."

"I don't understand," I say, looking into her eyes.

"It's fine; I'm here," she openly welcomed.

"What's your name?" I asked.

"Jahzara," she answered.

That name sounded sweet to my ears.

"Thank you, Jahzara."

"Thank you for blessing me with your presence," she said.

"I can't lie, this is really strange," I said awkwardly.

"You are a prince. You have abilities way beyond any *being*, probably even way beyond this dimension," she said, latching onto my arm.

"Are you sure?" I said, taking a deep breath.

"Do not fear it, Azazel. Cope and train so that you can control it. Let it no longer control you."

"I need to know more."

"In time, you will know all you need to."

She let go of my arm.

"Thank you," I said.

"You're welcome."

"Can I just say something to you, Jahzara?"

"Yes?"

"We better meet again."

"I have a feeling we will, now go." In the background, I heard many heavy footsteps along with many wings fluttering. "Leave now," she commanded.

"I don't know how."

"Just fly up and lose consciousness."

"What?"

"Do it, you will get used to it."

"Goodbye, but not forever," I said.

"Be safe," she advised.

I took off so hard that I dented the ground below my feet. Below me the *beings* gave chase. I dodged left and right, all sorts of aerial attacks, and then I finally made it to the Earth's surface. I was far from Anastasia, but I could smell her and so I flew towards the smell. When I got there she was gone — what remained were the clothes she was wearing. My limbs then began to fade and I felt a force pulling me towards the sky at a rapid speed. Before I knew it, I was standing in front of the Council and there stood Anastasia next to me with her head down.

Hide And Seek

"I believe we are looking at another member of our collection," says a member of the Council for the Eternals.

"He will revive and return," says one.

"He will understand," says another.

"This will determine eligibility," says one more.

"He will succeed," says a fifth. "I refuse to believe he will not return to finish his work."

Azazel labors through a barren wasteland. He has encounters in this land that are but semblances of a reality that he once knew. As he, in this see-through cryotherapeutic-type chamber, is observed, while lifeless in body, his mind is fully active, greatly anticipating its return to life.

The moment the dimension's Eternal gave Azazel his judgment, his mind was transferred into a realm without his body. Azazel, although not entirely, is alive within this other realm. While his environment appears real, while it appears as though he is in control, his existence is an illusion made up of fragments and suppositions from former thoughts and feelings.

Will he look beyond the beliefs that his new environment imposes on him to finally awake and return to his work? He is not the first to receive a vision of prophesied rule, and he is not the first to have that vision overthrown by the illusory realm. It is rare that one prophesied to replace the then Eternal has the will to claim the position.

Upon his disappearance, Aepharia suffered a plague, killing most of its inhabitants. The sickness began because Azazel, being the current of the Universe's life and intelligence, was taken away. His departure brought a contagion into the environment, which affected the spirit of the inhabitants, causing violence within the Universe to rise.

The plague, and the violence caused by it, moved the Council of Aepharia to separate Azazel's Estate from the rest of Aepharia. With the inhabitants of Aepharia killing and sabotaging one another, and with many failed attempts on Aepharia's throne, and especially on Azazel's wives and Empress, a division became necessary, which division further enraged the realm's *beings*.

"How long can we live like this?" says the Empress. "Where has my husband gone?"

"That is not for us to know," says one of the members of the Council, "and I doubt if it can be known."

"I can't live without him," she says. "Nothing can happen without him."

"The longer he stays away," says another member of the Council, "the greater the scourge against Aepharia."

"We should think about how to stop whatever is affecting our *beings*," says one of Azazel's wives.

"You heard my father," says another one of Azazel's wives. "In order for things to be normal, he has to come back."

"Then I will get him," says the Empress.

"From where?" says a member of the Council. "His whereabouts are unknown."

"I will go to the Eternal's writer," she, rising to her feet, confidently states.

"And what makes you think that this is where the answer will be found?" asks the same Council member.

"The Eternal's writer is the last one to have contact with Azazel," she says. "If he will not tell me what I want to hear, I will make him."

Despite the advice from the Council, the Empress, and with three of Azazel's wives, leaves to have a word with the Eternal's writer. Upon entering into that hollow yet abundant part of the Cosmos, the Eternal's Abode soon appears.

"It is revealed to whomever it would reveal itself to," says one his wives.

Approaching the door of the Estate, it utters a light creak, which, to them, suggests their desired entrance. Upon entering, they are met by the Eternal's writer who, after looking at them for a short while, turns around and begins to slowly walk away.

"Follow me," he says.

He leads them to the fifth floor of the Estate, and into a room. The Council of the Eternals are in this room and, in a tank-like chamber filled with a light-purple liquid, rests Azazel in their midst.

The Council does not see them. As a matter of fact, the writer and his guests are walking through their bodies. The events that are being shown are not actually taking place in that room, but are a hologram of events that are occurring in another place.

The Eternal's writer has led the Estate's guests into a room portraying what is happening to Azazel. They can hear the Council of the Eternals talking. They can see them moving around. They can see Azazel, who is lifeless and unaware of what is going on, in that chamber-like structure. But they cannot interact with them, or with anything in that room.

"There is nothing you can do," says the writer.

"Where is he?" asks the Empress.

"I am only the writer," he says. "I do not control what happens, but how things happen."

"Then control how he is released," says one of Azazel's wives.

"Write about his release," says another wife.

"I cannot do that," says the writer.

"Where is he?" says the Empress. "I will write what happens next, and how it happens, if you just tell me where he is."

"Do you think that, after rain falls, the sky tells the rain where it should land and how? The rain simply falls, and however it will fall, that is how it will fall. It is the same with my pen. I cannot change a vision after it is fallen, nor can I re-write how it will fall, but I am given power over the spirit of its manifestation. I cannot control what happens after," says the writer, "or how it will manifest."

"He cannot tell us the location because he does not know," says one of Azazel's wives.

"That is correct," he says.

"But you do not need location in order to work," says another one of his wives.

"That is correct," he says.

"So we need to rephrase our question," says another wife.

"That is correct," he says.

"I don't have time for this," says the Empress.

"Time is of a character whose existence is between two doors," says the writer. "The opening and the closing of those doors mean the how and the when of what is within them."

"He is between dimensions," says one of Azazel's wives.

"What if the Eternal's writer cannot work outside of the dimension he is in," says another one of his wives. "What if each dimension has its own writer."

"Then we have wasted our time," says the Empress.

"That is correct," says the writer.

"We are speaking to the wrong writer," says another of his wives.

"You are correct," says the writer.

"This will not be easy," says the Empress.

"You will find him," says the writer, "if you stop looking. His return doesn't depend upon you, but is entirely dependent upon him. He is born for claiming the Eternal's position, to become the dimension's Eternal. Because a great responsibility is conferred upon him, he must prove himself worthy of the position."

"We have to let Azazel go," says one of his wives.

"I cannot," says the Empress, "and neither will you. We can neither ruin nor help what is going on with him by bringing him back; we need him."

The four women leave the Estate. They return back into the empty Cosmos looking for a possible entrance not into another realm, but into a dimension. If they can find that door, maybe they can enter into it and rescue Azazel.

The emptiness of the Cosmos is discouraging, yet, being an environment used by Sovereign Creators for creating, they are hopeful to discover something. Every potential crack in the atmosphere, every strange looking glimmer of light, every hunch given through the stillness of the domain's blackness, is investigated, and with a curiosity watering their desire for uncovering the hidden portal.

"I think I've found something," says on of his wives.

The women then come together to observe a slit in the atmosphere, a slit bearing a resemblance to a piece of clothing that has been cut down the center with a knife. The Empress, stepping forward, kneels down, lightly touches the slit, and with both hands, rips it open. An entirely new world is on the other side.

Looking at one another one, they seem to have the same thought: "Once we cross, how do we get back?" Nevertheless, they walk through the portal and into the dimension, fearing nothing. Entering, the environment is green, being a beautiful portrait of nature. In the distance is a building at the center of the landscape; it appears to be made out of crystal.

"The legend is true," says one of Azazel's wives.

"The Estate of the Eternals," says the Empress in awe.

"We are here," says another one of his wives.

"Do you really think he is in there?" says the third wife.

"He has to be in there," says the Empress.

"If we can find the writer, and if we can persuade him, we can get Azazel back," says one wife.

"I can care less to persuade anyone," says the Empress. "They have taken my husband, and without me knowing."

"Imagine what will happen to us if we are caught," says another one of his wives. "If we are caught, they will surely kill us."

"Azazel will not let us die," says one wife. "If we can free him, he will save us."

The women walk forward and, passing through the walls of the building, enter into the Estate. Traveling down many flights of stairs, they enter onto a floor of many rooms. Each room has someone in a tank-like structure floating in a light-purple fluid. Each floor thereafter has a similar scene.

"These are Sovereign Creators," says one wife. "What are they doing here?"

"They're just here," says another wife. "They are just here, in these chambers."

Startled by the movement of one Creator, "Did you see that?" says the third. "He just moved."

"They're alive," says the Empress. "How long do you think they've been here?" she asks, her hand on a tank and her eyes looking around within it.

"What is this?" says another wife.

"I've heard about this, but I didn't think it was true," says one wife. "It is the holding place for Eternal Sovereigns. They say that many Sovereigns are kept in the Estate of the Eternals, but I've never heard why."

"They don't want to be replaced," says the Empress. "It is almost as if they are collecting their competition and holding them here as trophies."

"And Azazel is next," says the third wife.

"Should we also set them free?" asks one wife.

"No," says the Empress. "If it is true that they are all Sovereign Creators, their release means war. There is no way they will awake and not want to claim their prophesied position. Their time has already come and gone, but Azazel's time is now. Azazel will know what to do once he is back."

The women continue traveling into the Estate of the Eternals. Entering onto the final floor, they look through every room to find the same collection of Creators in tank-like structures. Either they have not looked closely enough at the rooms of the Estate for the true version of the holographic scene showed to them, or Azazel is not there.

"Maybe this is literally only an Estate of the Eternals," says one wife in frustration.

"So this only a Mansion keeping Creators in chambers?" says the third wife.

"It's only a house of trophies," says the Empress. "I don't think he is here."

"Then that's good!" shouts one wife. "Right? If he isn't here, that means he's not part of the collection."

"At least not yet," says the Empress. "But it doesn't make sense. That scene we saw, he should be here. Either that, or the writer has us looking for something to divert our attention."

"Or maybe he guided us here for a reason," says another wife.

Into Perspective

The Council is disappointed in us.

"You two sacrificed your existence, for what?" they said.

"For nothing," says Anastasia.

"For understanding," I said.

"And with this understanding, I hope you acquired useful knowledge."

"Yes," I said.

"You defy our rules and compete with our love and trust."

"I apologize," Anastasia said.

"It is exactly how I believed it would be," I said.

"Are you satisfied with yourselves?" they asked.

"I will never disobey you again my Lords," Anastasia cried out.

"I will be going from universe to universe until I find out exactly who I am, my Lords," I sternly said.

"In time you will see your heart change," said one member of the Council.

"He will," said Anastasia.

"Don't speak for me," I said to her.

"I'm not speaking for you, I'm just helping."

"I do not need yours or anyone else's help," I threw back.

"Enough!" roared one member of the Council. "Azazel, you will learn who you are and in time you will be faced with the option to choose who you want to be. It's no surprise you two happen to care for one another because you have similar ties. We look at you two in shame now, but we love you with everything within our strength. We created this universe out of love and yet our first Heaven has become monstrous. We, Azazel, found you in the second Heaven among the stars and planets. Your birth is one that shook all natural and godlike creations; special is not the word for you. You, Anastasia, will hear more of your birth; it is not your time to hear as yet."

"Earth, the Underuniverse, these are the places where I belong, my Lord," I said.

"You do not know enough to make that decision."

"We will look out for one another," Anastasia said. "May we go?"

"You may go and I expect no more trouble from you."

"No more," said Anastasia.

"We will see," I said.

"To your quarters," the Gods commanded.

"Yes," Anastasia said.

I decided to walk Anastasia back to her room and then either stay in Heaven or go back to the Underuniverse. I shouldn't have spoken to Anastasia about it.

"What do you mean, you're thinking about going to the Underuniverse?" She said, angry and confused.

"I met someone down there who I think can help me."

"Whoever it is, they are not worth the wrath of the Council."

"You will never understand, Anastasia."

"I don't wish to, but I do not care to see you hurt. You need to stay here and live. Think about it more and make the right decision," she pleaded.

"I'm dying without this knowledge," I tried to explain.

"Well, I'll die if I never see you again."

When we got to her room, she leaned into me and kissed me on the cheek. "Stay," she said, before wishing me goodnight and shutting her door.

~ ~ ~

Now that I think back on it, those were the best times of my life. Should those days return, I would make different choices. That was my first trip to Earth and I forgot it was also my first unwanted trip to the Underuniverse. After these events, I periodically returned to the Underuniverse, and always in hopes of bumping into Jahzara again, who, since Lucifer was captured, sat by her father's side on the throne.

Here on *Earth*, it is just my Panthon and I. I reside in creation's former original location but travel to nearby areas in search of *beings* I believe are able to best assist me in recollecting my memory. I'm still looking for answers as to why I'm constantly marked for death.

But Jahzara — I would love to see her again. Often, I get flashbacks — more like fantasies — of the life we both share together. I've only seen her that one time I was dragged to the Underuniverse, and yet my fantasies feel so real. I also miss Anastasia.

This Earth is barren, but I know that more secrets to my strengths lie in its depths. Though destroyed, what remains on this planet are blood-filled bodies of water. With the darkening of the sun, and with the moon turning blood red, I spend my time meditating on possible situations, adventures, solutions, myths, truths, everything mentally possible to conceive.

I live in peace here in this *wasteland* and yet I feel I am always disturbed by something. What's interesting is that the sun still rises and falls but the moon is forever placed in the sky. I lie down to sleep, not knowing if I should be awake or not. Either way, I enter into an unconscious meditation that leaves me refreshed for the next day; there's always something new to learn.

Soon after I fall asleep, I am awoken by a violent quake beneath me. My Panthon is standing above me more alert than ever and so I have to maneuver my way from his protection.

"Out of the way, boy," I say to him softly.

In the distance, I can see the ground open and a figure floating up from between the cracks. My wings spread and I place my left hand in the air with the palm facing out. I close my eyes and my left eye rolls down my neck, onto my left arm, then into the center of my open palm. I scan the area until I come across the foreign figure. It is a male who wears a trench coat and carries two voltaic orbs in each hand. He hurls both at me quickly. I shut my palm, sending my eye back up my arm and into my head. I catch the force of its energy with my hands, throwing one roughly onto the ground, extinguishing it, and squeezing the other so hard in my hand that it disintegrates.

"Why have you come?" I yell.

"For you," he says.

He swiftly disappears and reappears a few feet from me.

"And why is your presence necessary?" I ask, not letting his presence bemuse me.

"Justice."

"Justice for what?"

"Our Lord is captured and is caged in Heaven."

"And?"

"We need you to return."

"Who is 'we'?"

"The army of Aepharia sectioned within the Underuniverse."

"The army of the Underuniverse serves Apep," I reply.

"This is true, but we serve you, and from the army of Aepharia laboring under the army of the Underuniverse."

I look at him with a confused look. He speaks nothing but nonsense to me. How could I have led something I wasn't a part of?

"And so now you want to rescue the one you fear?"

"We do not fear him, but rather respect him — and you."

"I am not your helper."

"You are a Sovereign Creator. You are of the bloodline of the Eternals. You are the ultimate *being*, my Lord."

"I am no such thing and I will not be used as a pawn."

"Then I see a coward," the *being* says.

"You see something heartless and who will eat the ashes of what it burns."

"I am Purah, fallen *Lord* of the dead, and if you do not agree with our movement then we can handle this differently."

An abundance of corpses appears around us, each glowing with power.

"So you need many to defeat one?" I say.

"I need many to defeat the Eternal."

I raise my hand and then a tornado of fire emits from the center of my palm. I take the tornado and with my right hand I cover my left, which bears the power. I then point both hands to the ground. Fire travels in every direction, picking up each vile corpse and throwing them into the sky, destroying them instantly. Once again, it was Purah and I.

"I am Azazel," I say.

Purah began to mock me by clapping. I close my eyes and pick Purah up with my mind. He throws electric heat waves at me but it does no good. He is in the air where I quickly paralyze him.

"You are nothing but a traitor, Azazel," he struggles to say. "You do not remember? Is it true? You do not remember anything, do you? You are a coward."

"I have a message you can take back to wherever you came from," I say.

I fly beside him and touch his forehead. He turns to marble and drops to the ground. I then raise my hand to the sky and drop it. Immediately comets crash down upon him. His figure is pushed through the Earth and into the Underuniverse.

"Can you believe that?" I say to Panthon. "I apparently have a history. See, Panthon," I say as I collect myself, "there's always something new to learn."

~ ~ ~

Panthon and I leave our area and travel until we believe we have come across new life. Around forty-five days into the trip, I stop to collect my thoughts and try to make sense of everything. I have kept that *being's* electric orb handy so that when I can find a place to rest, I can analyze it.

Our resting point marks the time for a new case study. I take out the orb and give it a closer look. It is like nothing I've ever seen before; I need to find more like it. There is so much energy and overlapping anxiety within this one weapon that if I were weak, I would have died from one blast.

As the days continue, I walk on with a hope that I can possibly gain more knowledge my former life. There is just so much more to learn about myself and my past, abilities, and strengths, but it feels like there is a block stopping me from reaching those memories. Maybe there are no memories and maybe there is nothing to block, but I need answers. I'm wanted for something but I don't know what for or why. All of this thinking is bound to wear even the greatest thinker down, so I put everything aside and lie beside Panthon.

But once again I am disturbed. The atmosphere within the sky begins to quake; what comes out of its surface surprises me. As its vortex shakes and separates, a female figure appears. Panthon lies beside me as this figure descends, and as the ground furiously shakes, Panthon rises and stands defensively.

"Azazel?" the warm voice cries. "It's me."

I get up and make my way closer to her, quickly realizing it is Jahzara. I can't believe my eyes! I have thought on the day we should meet again. She still looks like how I remember her, except more mature.

"Jahzara," I say in sentimental excitement. "It's good to see you."

"I've missed you, Azazel."

"Missed me? I haven't gone anywhere. I've been here."

"I was forbidden to see or to speak with you."

"Why?"

"You don't know the chaos you've caused in the dimension, do you?"

"What chaos?"

"You were once present in the Underuniverse, but then you left and never returned."

"What?"

"I saved you, Azazel."

"Why?" I ask.

"Because I've been waiting for you; I've been waiting for you to save me, to save us."

"I don't understand."

"Your father has been captured," she says.

"Yes."

"Satan, Belial, Leviathan, they are missing their fourth part, who is Lucifer, your father."

"I still don't see how I'm involved with this."

"With all four combined, they form the Amalgamate, the unstoppable legion. Few can stop them."

"Few?"

"Those few are the remaining Sovereign Creators...and you."

"I have nothing to do with this."

"You are the son of Lucifer, Azazel — you must free him, kill the Amalgamate, and then destroy both Heaven and the Underuniverse. You are the dimension's Eternal, and Aepharia is to be the only Universe of the dimension."

"Aepharia? This makes no sense."

"I've been waiting to see you again, that's why it took me so long. My father, Apep, rules the Underuniverse, manipulated the Council of Aepharia, and desires nothing more than to kill and replace you. It took me centuries before I had enough courage to venture out and find you."

With those words, she slides close to me and lays her head on my chest. Her smell and touch remind me of home, but her words bring fury to my eyes.

"I cannot do all that you say," I reply.

"You can; you must."

"Maybe I am not who you think I am."

"You are to free us Azazel. Remember me as your woman, as your spouse, as you queen, as your sister. We will rule the dimension; can't you see it? Imagine the power and the control you desire," she says, sliding up to my ear and whispering, "it is all to be yours." She gently bites the bottom of my ear and kisses my cheek. "Your children," she says, moving to my backside, "your children will be royalty, powerful royalty at that. We are to rule."

"You're very convincing, and your beauty weakens me, but things will happen my way."

"Is that so?" she says, surprised.

"Yes, this is so. I remember when we first met; the tension we both felt. I wanted you then and I want you now, but I must contemplate how today unfolds at my own pace."

"You truly only remember me from that very ancient encounter? Then as you wish, but don't forget who you and I were," she says, vanishing.

"What's happening to me?" I say to Panthon. Hereafter as we move from one territory to another, I go in search of any female *being* to release my *tension* out on.

As Panthon and I are walking, we come across some little footprints. The footprints appear to be that of a little child, so my curiosity begins to rise. We set up a site for what we would call home and then I set out alone on our journey.

"Watch over our stuff," I say to Panthon. He just plops his body down onto the ground and goes to sleep; it is his way of saying, "Get out of my face."

As I follow the footsteps I hear little children singing a lullaby in the distance: "Take me, take me, spin me up and take me. Lilith lives in lovely lands; her hands will touch and kill me." As I draw closer to the song, I see around one thousand little children surrounded by another five hundred *souls* holding hands, turning in circles and chanting.

At the side of the children, I see a woman. She wears ugly, worn-out garments and a physical appearance to match. Her skin is rotten and her toenails and fingernails have grown to gross lengths. Her face has part slimy rubber skin while the other half is bone, but she moves as if she is young. I accidentally stand on a stick, snapping it in half due to my weight. The chanting stops and within seconds, the woman is peering into my face and is as curious as ever. She looks me up and down, pokes and prods her way around me until she finally speaks.

"Who are you and why have you entered my land?"

"I am Azazel. What is going on here?

"Azazel," she wonders. "It can't be; we thought you would never come back to us."

"Who are you?"

"I am Lilith, one of the many *beings* serving your father. While Earth existed, I searched for and killed any *child* I could get my hands on. I captured certain human minds to accomplish my will and I must say, the fruit of my work has developed beautifully. Wouldn't you say so, my Lord?"

My heart fills with so much rage that I yell "Be free!" to the children, but they just stand there watching me. Their eyes look like Lilith's — cold, lost, angry, and yet within them I can see they also desire freedom.

"Say what you like, but they are mine," she says.

I grab her neck and she spits acid that melts my face, but my face heals itself immediately.

"You are just as powerful as I remember," she says.

Concentrating on my anger, I reach into her back and pull her spine out. I then take out her dry intestines and wrap them around her neck. I tighten them and squeeze her neck with her own inwards until from out of her mouth, eyes, and ears, a thick dark green liquid oozes out. When I look back into the open field, all the little *beings* ascend into the sky; I wonder if they are ascending to the Aepharia I've been hearing about.

It is a good walk back to Panthon. Not wanting to disturb him with an aerial call, Azazel walks in silence, meditating on his thoughts. Frustrated with his endless thoughts, to ease his mind, once back to his site, he decides to bathe in a nearby river whose waters take on the color of blood. Soon enough, to his surprise, Jahzara joins him as he, after bathing, takes a seat by the river.

"I'm sorry," she says.

"For what?"

"I've been approaching you the wrong way," she says.

"It's no an issue," I say with a smile.

Jahzara, looking down, smiles at my response. In the background, Panthon lets out a roar.

"He's awake and is hungry," I say.

"I've just been wanting you to remember us," she sighs. "Life is different with you like this."

"With me like what?" I ask.

"I should go," she says.

"No, you shouldn't."

"Why not? I have to."

"Because we are in love, remember?" I say, as if hoping to convince myself.

She lies back down on my chest. I take my hand and place it over the dirt, making food bloom from the dirt for Panthon. I make five small lifeless animals, one on top of the other, and throw them in Panthon's direction with a gust of wind.

"You really care for him," she says.

"I do, he's all I have."

"You know Azazel, what has happened to you is unfair."

"Why talk about something neither one of us can control?"

"Because I'm not lying."

"Well, I'll never know until I get the answers I'm looking for, but I believe you."

"Who do you think you first made love with? Do you believe you have the mind and courage to lie with anything just because?"

"Well I never thought about it, I just did."

"The Eternal erased me from your memory every time you came to the Underuniverse to see me. How do I know this?" she adds, after seeing my hesitation. "Because after every time we met, you didn't know who I was or where you were. You probably don't even know anything about yourself because the Eternal has taken it upon himself to rob you of your character. Why we kept meeting, I don't know, but every time we spoke, I grew to love you all over again."

"I'm sorry," I say.

"It's not your fault, Azazel — it isn't. But the Council of the Eternals wants you dead and for reasons that I don't know. You were born before you think you were and I think we really did something to them."

"I don't understand; why do they want me dead?"

"I don't know, but every time you would come to the Underuniverse, they would find you, catch you, and take you away."

"I still don't understand anything."

"You need to understand and to harness your powers more. You need to better remember who you were before all of this."

"That's what I've been doing!" I say in aggravation. "Why are you talking like this?"

"Maybe I haven't been natural with you, but this is who we naturally are. Please believe that."

"What do you mean?"

"My father wants me to seduce you into a trap."

On hearing these words I sit up and force her off me.

"What?" I say.

"I'm sorry."

"You do not love me at all."

"I'm not like them," she says. "Since they changed you and sent you away, our Empire has been crumbling and I've been searching for who I am. I only know how to be me with you."

"So you are here to kill me?"

"No, I am here for my survival, but I can't hurt you; I'm sorry."

"No, you're not," I say.

"Look," she says, lightly touching my hand with her palm; immediately I am sent to our past, to the past I cannot remember. Passing by so many conversations, so many laughs, so many tears, so many arguments, and to even fragments of our Royal Estate, I am speechless.

"See," her voice echoes through the hollow memory. "I tell you no lies; I love you."

There we were, in the same place where we met for the first time, barely remembering her, yet she still gave me her honest affection. But then I began to feel upset; I don't know what to think or believe.

"I'm so confused," I say.

"Don't be," she instructs.

"How can I not? You are here to kill me, yet you would kill for me."

"I know it's hard, but just imagine what I've been feeling. I've been with no other but you because I've been waiting for you to remember our conquest. I am good Azazel, I'm not like them."

"Maybe I don't understand as I ought, but there are things I need to do," I confess.

"Go and do what you must, but just know that you have many enemies, and that I am going nowhere."

"You will fight by my side during war?"

"I don't know," she disappointingly says, "but I advise you to see Bune, the all-knowing three-headed dragon."[3]

"It just doesn't stop," I say sarcastically.

Jahzara laughs.

"It doesn't stop because you need to control yourself and learn about what was taken away from you. With Bune, you can learn how to reign over your strengths with flawless skill, but he is difficult. All who have attempted to learn from him have failed."

"I don't think I'll have any problems with this Bune. When I return, I plan on solving all that is wrong."

"I will be waiting for you, I promise."

Our fate together is sealed with a kiss.

"I must go now, back to the Underuniverse," she says. Be safe and use all divisions of your wisdom."

I look at her confused because I have gone from being Azazel to being someone's "love."

"Why do you look afraid?" she asks.

---

3 See Note C

"A lot is happening. I am slowly piecing together the puzzle of my existence, but I'm still misled. I will see Bune and will not return until my lesson is complete; trust that I will gain more wisdom and strength."

"Good."

And with that, her beautiful figure vanishes. But the day's events are not yet finished. Upon dressing, I look up to see Anastasia in front of me.

It has been so long since I've seen her that I forgot what she looked like. I can't believe that the little annoying girl I grew up with turned out to be this beautiful looking woman. Time is a tricky thing.

"Azazel!" she screams as she runs at me with brute force, welcoming me with a kiss. "You're okay! Look at you now, just look at you!"

"Look at me?" I respond. "Look at you Anastasia; you look beautiful," I say, running my fingers through her delicately positioned blonde hair and lightly running my fingers over her face.

"Oh, come on now, I'm still the same old girl you grew up with, Azazel. No one has replaced you."

My face changes from happiness to confusion. I know Anastasia has always had something in her heart for me, but hearing it is another thing entirely. "Do you not remember?" she continues.

Here we go again, I think to myself.

"Remember what?" I ask.

"So it is true."

"What is?"

"Your memory is gone."

"I'm so tired of this."

"You got bad, Azazel."

"What?"

"You broke the Eternal's *laws*. He then decided to stop you, so he sat you down and took every memory away from you."

"How do you know this?"

"He told me to look after you since the night we shared our *bodies*; we were young. You had come from a talk with the Eternal and were telling me about it. I consoled you; you dropped to the floor in tears and then one thing led to another. He did not take your emotions away, just the memories he felt were leading you astray."

"Why am I now seeing you? You haven't appeared to me in the past, or have I forgotten?"

She laughs.

"Why would that be? This is the first time we're seeing each other. I've been in the Kingdom of the Council waiting to see you, but they would not allow me until I was ready."

"And what makes you ready now?" I ask.

"I know more about myself and my abilities, and I have controlled my emotions towards you. Or at least I think so," she says, trying to convince herself.

"So you have been living your life, but what about me? I mean, he is watching, I know he's watching; why isn't he helping me?" I question.

"I don't really know why, but whenever I would ask, he would just say it was not commanded."

I take Anastasia by the hand and we both walk back to Panthon.

"Where are we going?" she asks.

"To my other half," I explain.

"You have a woman?"

"I guess you can call him that, I love him dearly. He is the beast I made."

"You made a beast Azazel? It's really been too long. How did you ever construct such a thing, and out of nothing?" she wonders.

"You're not the only one who has hidden powers."

"You're still a show-off."

"I am not; I just made a friend in my *image*. I asked myself *if I could be a beast what would I be?* And so Panthon was born."

"There is no life down here Azazel."

"And that's why I took the carcasses of two dead animals and combined them."

"You are still amazing."

Upon making it to Panthon, Anastasia gasps in amazement.

"This is a big beast," she says, looking him up and down.

"Nine feet tall and with his own set of abilities," I say, slapping my palm on his side.

"Still a show-off."

"This is nothing Anastasia — listen to this. I was born way before everything else."

"What do you mean, how do you have this knowledge?"

"Jahzara," I reveal.

"Oh, her," she says in jealousy.

"You know Jahzara?"

"Yes, I know her, and so does the whole Universe of Heaven," she confirms.

"Really?" I ask in playful curiosity.

"You snuck her up to your quarters on many occasions," she says.

Laughing, I say, "I did that? And you still like me?"

"The Eternal knows best, Azazel, and if he says that you are confused then I believe it, plus I can see it. I love you for everything that you are and are not. You don't remember, but we grew close until you decided to leave."

"I had to go," I say, "he kept playing with my mind and I became more confused than ever. I needed to live in the danger of what I am. I have done nothing wrong."

"I understand. What did Jahzara say?"

"Not much, only that the Underuniverse is in an uproar over my past actions, but I can't remember anything."

"I'm sorry, I wish I could be of more help."

"It's fine, I need to work things out on my own anyways." We sat there in silence. Feeling what I felt for her, I could not stop caressing her face with my fingers.

"You are truly beautiful, Anastasia," I say.

"You didn't turn out so bad yourself," she says.

"I would have done so many things differently."

"Well, instead of thinking about what you could or would have done, why not start doing? Come back to Heaven with me, please."

"No," I say straightly.

"Please, Azazel."

"I don't want to see that foul place again."

"It is not foul, it is what I am. Am I foul then?" she asks.

"You are not foul, but what created you belittles my intelligence. I despise that Universe and its Eternal Sovereign."

"But I've been wishing for you Azazel. Do you remember all those adventures we would go on together? Remember the goddess of nature? Remember our first trip to Earth? I think about them all the time," she says, coming closer to me.

"Of course I remember those times, Anastasia. You were my life; you have my heart."

"Then let's create a life in Heaven. Follow me there now, please," she begs.

"I must not make any decisions in haste. I need to gather myself."

"Promise me this at least — once your mind is clear, that you will find me and love me in the same way that you have loved yourself."

I pause before I answer because Jahzara quickly appears in my mind, but I decide to listen to my heart.

"I promise," I say.

After I utter my response, I feel as though I do not deserve to be loved by either woman. But at the same time, I desire, I crave, and I lust for each of their love and I want it in abundance.

"Once I have situated my thoughts and arranged a set of plans, I promise to come to you," I recap.

She kisses me goodbye and flies back up to *Paradise*.

Before I can even gather my thoughts, another figure appears in front of me. Today refuses to be a silent one.

"You think you have them fooled, but you only fool yourself."

"Who are you?" I question.

"Who I am is not important. What you should know is I am one of the *beings* that obeyed your every command."

"For what reason are you here?"

"We need you to reunite us and to take charge against Heaven, but from what I have heard, you decline all motions."

"Go away," I say dismissively.

"I am Mephistopheles, the *being* who takes the rejected. I am here for you. You once gave the order of *beings* to take; now it is your turn to feel what they've felt."

"There's no way I'm letting you take my soul; I'm re-born. I'm searching for a new life, a new light. Something is being hidden from me and I need to find out what that is."

"I know how powerful you are. We need our leader back and he wants nothing to do with us; what is another motive? Your search has cost us our lord and you refuse to help unite the Amalgamate. Your actions require your death."

"Here's another motive: how about you find someone better?"

At my words, the *being* flies towards me but I dodge him by vanishing and then reappearing behind him. I turn my arm into a sword and, plunging it into his back, stab him several times. He falls to the ground but his back quickly heals. Seven souls fly out of his body while he lies on the ground healing himself. It seems impossible to defeat someone who has many *lives* to heal himself with.

When he rises from the ground, he looks back at me and breathes fire on the ground. The fire circles me and creates a wall that leaps into the sky. The *being* starts to chant *taaanak* over and over again until the fire engulfs me. When the fire dies down, I lie on the ground with sores, blisters, deep gashes, and destroyed limbs.

"Are you not the all-powerful Azazel?" he says.

He walks towards me but then pauses in shock; my body is healing itself.

"You need *lives* to live, but I don't," I say. "The one thing we don't share is immortality — your *lives* run out but mine doesn't."

He flew at me in rage, extending his long fingernails and digging them into my chest. I fall to the ground. We both punch and stab each other until finally, our fight ends with him shooting sticky saliva on my hands and feet to keep me tied to the ground.

"You have grown in strength, but your fate has come. Just as I have taken many who are cursed, I will now take your."

He stands above me with his palm towards my face. I can feel something being sucked out of me, but he had difficulty reaching it. Somehow, I manage to leave my body as it is in the present, lying on the floor, and I enter into his body.

Within his body, we fight once more. I attack his original *self*. Once I manage to figure out how to think my way out of his body, I cut his original *soul's* head off and explode from him. I then free my physical self that lies on the ground.

It was a different world once out of my body. I can see all the nefarious *beings* that would watch me and said or did nothing. It seems that so many depend on my actions, my existence, my power, but I just stand there looking at them before I tend to myself. I freeze this *being's* saliva and break it by setting it on fire. I re-enter my body and get up.

As I look around, I see none of the beings I saw when I was in this *other* realm. I need to be able to communicate with them in their world. They had looked at me, through eyes that desire peace, as if I was their savior. It may be through this realm that I find what I am looking for.

Although I know I cannot settle at the moment, I am growing tired and weaker from not knowing my strengths, from not knowing who I am. Is all of this set up? I don't know, but what I do know is that I need answers.

I must see Bune before I do anything else. I believe he will make clear what this *other* realm means to me. I have a trip to Heaven to complete.

The Trip To And From The Temple

I've been sitting in the same spot for the past thirty-five days; I don't want to go to Heaven. Panthon lies beside me and I can see his expression of disappointment in me. "You know how I feel," I say to the beast. A deep breath escapes his nose so hard that smoke comes out; he then lies on the ground behind me.

For thirty-five days, I have sat here meditating and feeling the energy of every *being* looking at me. Because of this, my senses are growing stronger. Through my meditations, I can't help but dwell on my memories of Olympus and Heaven. I do not dare step foot within either of those realms because of the history held there. Every time I think about arriving at either gate, my heart begins to race and my blood begins to boil. I only sacrifice it all for Anastasia. I keep telling myself I will go and that's it, that it will be fine. I have found out, thirty-five days into my meditation, that I am not the easiest person to convince.

Thinking back on Olympus makes me remember when Hercules and I would converse about our lives. He would be making a name for himself while I was stuck in Heaven, being a good little student. It disgusted me. How was I to know, at that time, what I was capable of? How was I to grow into what I am to be? I had to get away from that place to grow; I don't know how any other *being* was able to stay.

Besides Hercules, one memory I'll never forget is framed on the night I had both Athena and Persephone to myself. How did I get a goddess of Olympus and a former Queen of the Underworld together for an evening of passion? Of course, I was out of Heaven by this time and I lived in another realm. My age was of the twentieth millennium at the time and this experience was one I will never forget.

It is unforgettable because I enjoyed two of the most majestic women that ever existed. I grew up seeing Athena all of the time, and so I grew fond of her. When it came to Persephone, we became close quite easily. She was damaged, misused by Hades and taken as Queen of the Underworld. Once saved by her father, Demeter, she would come to my realm and wander. One day, I saw her and we spoke. From there, things took off in every aspect. But Athena and I had an honest relationship, even though her father hated me. Thinking back on it, his hatred towards me may have motivated my actions.

Back in the day, Olympus and Heaven held scholastic events, where we played games that were made up of teams. There were twelve teams, each consisting of twelve players. Only three players really mattered to me, and they were Hercules, Anastasia, and Athena. It was through these games I got to know Athena. We would sneak away to touch and kiss one another but would get caught by some lurking teacher.

I remember the games we played as teams; there were strength contests, fire talents, and events like who could freeze this or that the quickest or who could run the fastest. Silly little events, but they were all very fun and entertaining.

Athena and I were around the same age, so she would always be ready to do anything with me because of our playful relationship. After the games on this one particular time, I tried to talk Athena into sharing her self with me, but she declined. Later that night I snuck out of Heaven and flew to her window. We had our moment. Halfway into it she stopped and begged me to leave; I wouldn't see her again until I was of the twentieth millennium. It only took so long because I knew that her virtue would eat at her, causing conflict in Olympus. She would run back to me eventually.

"You must go Azazel," she had cried.

"Tell me why," I had demanded.

"This is not right."

"What makes this moment revolting?"

"You are my brother."

"Why should we let that stop us? I am not anyone's brother but Hercules' and even so, we are not blood."

"We share the same mother, Azazel, it is wrong."

"Nothing is wrong once the heart becomes involved. Do you really want me to leave?"

"Yes, we should never do this again."

"To prevent a strain in the atmosphere at dinner, I suppose," I said sarcastically.

"Don't be that way, Azazel."

"I am nowhere around Olympus because I am my own person, Athena. Who has told you these lies anyways?"

"My mother and father sat me down and explained it all to me some time ago. I have always felt an attraction to you but never acted upon it because of what I know."

"So I am truly the son of Lucifer and Metis?"

"Yes."

"Interesting," I reflect.

"I suppose."

"This is why your father hates me?"

"Yes."

"Fascinating," I say.

"If that is what it is to be called."

"We will meet again; I can foresee it. When you truly think about it, we are only half-bound by blood."

"Please leave at once, brother, so I may rest from what I feel."

"I swear I will break that royal chastity belt you wear with pride."

"Leave!" she demanded and, at once, I was gone.

Hereafter I would learn that Zeus would ask his daughter if she was alright.

"I don't know," she would reply, bringing her doubts about me into question.

I would not see Athena until sometime later, while I traveled through *Earth*.

Skipping ahead through time, I found Persephone mightily attractive, but what lured me to her was her pain. She just needed someone to understand, and I too desired a mind that could comprehend pain also.

"And who might you be?" I had questioned, as she stood by an ocean of blood.

"It's beautiful, isn't it? More beautiful than its natural clear blue water form."

"It's something else. It makes me wonder why such an all-forgiving *God* would kill what he created," I say.

"The human race never learned," she said. "They deserved it."

"I suppose, but where does that leave us?" I questioned.

"What do you mean?"

"Not everyone is satisfied with being a god," I said. "We have minds of our own, desires, wants, cravings. We are just as erroneous as any human being but are too enchanted to see it. I've seen how delusional I am and do now I pursue a recollection."

She eyed me up and down for a while and announced, "Persephone. I am Persephone."

"Beautiful name," I said, eying her.

"In Olympus, I am called Kore, which means Maiden. It befits me because I was raped and taken to the Underworld against my will," she explained.

"Who would do such a thing?" I ask.

"Hades."

"Zeus' brother? I swear neither of them are gods in any right."

"And your name?" she said, smiling from my comment.

"Azazel," I stated.

"That's a strong name, you wouldn't happen to be the Azazel of lore, would you?" she asked with a twinkle in her eye.

"Maybe," I say casually.

"You are quite the *angel*," she replies.

My skin cringed at the sound of the word *angel*, but I let it go because of her allure. She stood with long flowing red hair, pale skin and had the aura of a goddess. Her lips drew such attention that I mentally wished them upon *me*.

"And what leads you to say this?" I say.

"You defy the Eternal and show no fear; Aphrodite would allow this to be a moment of celebration for now and forever."

"Who can celebrate with such pain in their heart?" I asked.

"That is why pleasure is temporary, my lord," she said as she drew closer to me. "Through pleasure, one forgets about the woes burdening soul."

"And what would your king say?"

"I have no king; my father has saved me from his threshold. I must return once a year to the Underworld because of the struggle to free me from bondage, but that is all."

The moment her words ceased, her garments dropped to the ground. She so enticing that I could not help but touch her. I began to disrobe and laid her down on the sand. At that moment, Athena appeared, calling for my attention.

"Curse you, Athena," Persephone roared.

"I will return," I said to Persephone.

I did not worry about clothes. I immediately took Athena aside to speak with her.

"Brother, you are exposed," she says.

"You shouldn't care so it is no issue."

"You are insane Azazel. I have missed your personality."

"What brings you here, Athena?" I ask, looking nervously at Persephone.

"Father has yelled at me; I have told him what took place between us that night."

"Well, add that to the list of reasons to hate me, then. Why would you do that?"

"I felt guilty," she said, dropping her head and closing her eyes in disappointment.

"Nothing happened, remember? You told me to leave."

"Yes, but I cannot lie to my father."

"I am ashamed for you and your unnecessary honest ways," I say. "It is truly difficult to think of you as my sister."

"Then do not think of me as one."

"What?"

"I think about you constantly, Azazel. What you said that night, we are not fully related, but are half."

"This is too much," I said, roughly rubbing my face.

"I should have taken you when I had the chance. I do regret that now."

"I have something going on right now, Athena," I said, again looking nervously at Persephone. "I honestly believe you should just go back to Olympus and erase these absurd beliefs you have."

I told her this because I felt guilty, but then she looked behind me and then at Persephone.

After a couple of glances, she said, "I'll join you."

"What?" I said in disbelief.

"I will join you," she repeated.

"You will not," I sternly say.

"I want you."

"Wait," I say, but Athena began to strip. With her silky blonde hair flowing in the wind, and her perfect figure standing there, I was hesitant to return to my original temptation.

"Athena wishes to join us," I say to Persephone.

"I will have none of this," she replies.

"Why not?" I ask, my voice reaching a very high pitch.

"You are to be with me and only me."

"And you will, there will just be another who will receive my or your attention."

"I will not do this with you."

"For pleasure's sake Persephone, forget about the pain. This is a moment of celebration in the name of Aphrodite, in the name of all of love."

After a moment of silence, "Fine," she says.

Hearing these words, I look back at Athena and called her to us; we three uttered no words but spoke through action.

After our time together, we laid on the deserted land in peace and enjoyed a moment of taking comfort in each other's character. Our moment of passion had ended, but the memory would forever live.

"What is to happen now?" says Athena.

"I don't know," says Persephone.

"We live and continue as we were."

"Things will surely be different now," Athena says.

"They don't have to be," I say.

"That was amazing, my lord," Persephone says. "It was an honor to give myself to the legendary Azazel."

"Aphrodite would love you," Athena says to me.

"Aphrodite would break my soul with her sensuality," I reply.

"You are truly a love, Azazel," says Persephone.

"We all need love, do we not?" I say.

"I just became one with my brother," Athena cries.

"Do not be ashamed; if he was my brother I would have acted as soon as birth," says Persephone, as if I'm not here.

"I cannot return to Olympus," Athena then says.

"You must," I say.

"I will travel with you," says Athena to me.

"No, you will not," I respond.

"I cannot lie to my father or anyone else."

"I will fly you there myself should you decide not to return. It is not a lie if you never mention what just happened. Do not make any remarks to bring up the subject and it will forever stay hidden."

"He is right," says Persephone. "Things must be the way they were."

Just then, we heard the voice of Zeus calling for his daughter.

"I must go now," says Athena.

"Remember: stay silent. If it helps to lighten your conscience, we are not really blood, just half."

Athena placed her clothes back into order before she left for Olympus. She came over to me and delivered a kiss to my lips. She then faded right then and there in front of my face.

"So, you and your sister; is this the ultimate sin?"

"I don't know."

"Keep singing that song to yourself my lord, nothing will change what is or isn't a *sin*."

"I regret nothing," I say as we both get to our feet.

"And I'm sure you don't; neither do I. Is there anything to regret?"

"You keep calling me Lord, why?"

"Because you are a Sovereign God. We know of your *name* and status."

"So why are you here in this realm with me and not in your luxury?"

"Today happens to be the one day that I must go to where my heart saw the most pain. It is a struggle to force myself down here, so I wander about through this land until I am ready."

"Well, now you can see this day differently. You can enter into your hatred with a solemn memory."

"I will not forget you, Azazel. You are not what they make you out to be."

She came over to me and delivered a kiss to my cheek. She vanished down to the Underworld, where she would take a mental piece of me with her. I then picked up my belongings and began walking once again. Panthon soon appeared by my side once he heard the rustling and my journey soon continued.

Never again did I hear about Persephone until I had to travel to the Underuniverse for some supplies. As I entered a shop I heard two people speaking about her death.

"Didn't you hear?"

"Hear what?"

"She's gone and you know who did it?"

"Did Hades finally get his revenge?"

"I'm sure she wishes it were him, but it was Jahzara."

"Princess Jahzara?"

"Yes, and she did away with her in the worst fashion."

"How?" they inquired.

"She crucified her upside down and drank her drained blood."

"She shouldn't have lain with her king."

"Lord Azazel is trouble."

"Every male in all realms want her, yet he spends his time on *Earth* searching for something, defiling the name of his woman who fights for him. He has declined all of our traditions and yet still she lingers, even killing for his love."

"Azazel is a great man," chimes in one.

"I don't know about that. As beautiful as Jahzara is, I wouldn't want her watching my every move."

"Speak for yourself. I, along with many others, would do anything for the attention of that woman. Azazel is lucky, by the spirit of the Amalgamate, he is lucky."

Yes, nothing but fond memories when I think back on Olympus and on the Universe of Heaven. Honestly, I am afraid to set foot inside of this realm for fear of old enemies arising.

As angry and as powerful as I may be, I hate fighting. Nevertheless, I am growing tired of sitting here and avoiding what I must do. I look back at Panthon and wonder what I will do with him while I travel to Bune. Whatever awaits me I am ready. I desperately need knowledge of my self.[4]

I rise to my feet and open my wings; Panthon does the same. I pat him on the head and kiss him. He roars and moves away from me.

"Never been one for emotions, have you?" I say to him. "Do I look appropriate?" I next say to him.

He roars and takes off into the sky ahead of me. I smile and follow him into the Universe of Heaven.

---

4 See Note D

When we get there, I stand outside the gates and look inside the dimension in amazement. I never thought I would find myself here again. Upon my arrival, I notice some familiar faces guarding the main gate. From the distance, I match these figures to their faces and see that they are the archangels Michael, Gabriel, Raphael, and Uriel.

These were the archangels we were to look up to when we were little, but now I stand at their full height. They all look the same; nothing has really changed. Their wings shine with a bright white glare and their faces reproduce the same handsome nature. Their form ripples with the same aura of their Creator, but this was all something I could now match or even be greater than.

"The prodigal son has returned," says Michael.

"And he returns as a big man," Gabriel follows.

"What a pleasure it is to see all of you, those nice, bright, strong familiar faces. I have a query, though. It must get very tiring walking around here as the Eternal controls you with his hand up your back like a puppet. Is it not?"

"You carry the same filthy perception as your father. It is no surprise that you followed in his footsteps," says Gabriel.

"Maybe you are jealous that you and I do not share the same slavery." I reply.

"Pay no attention to him," Raphael says.

"You four await on my arrival with such anticipation; why?"

"Why not just repent, Azazel?" Uriel asks.

"Enough," says Michael. "What will redemption do for him? Has it changed him from how he was before?"

I then look at Michael with curiosity and think to myself, what does he mean *before*?

"Repent for what? If I am free to will then your *God* should have recognized his error by now, don't you think?" I say.

"Once again, Azazel, you are filth," says Gabriel. "You are a waste of time."

"If your *God* knew how depressing you really were, I'm sure you would be right there behind me on your journey for consciousness," I respond.

"We sit at the feet of the Eternal awaiting his orders. He knew of your arrival before you ever thought of it. We have met you here to escort you to him."

"Do I not know where I am?"

"We must go at once," Uriel declares.

"There you are mistaken my misguided fools. I am here to see Anastasia and not the Eternal."

They look at me confused. Michael gawks at me with hatred.

"That cannot be," Gabriel says.

"What is your business with her?" Michael asks. "We should not trust such an unworthy character due to his history of chaos. We will take you to our Lord."

"I will fight all of you before I allow you to take me anywhere."

With this, Anastasia appears, happiness etched on her face.

"Azazel!" she screams, pushing Michael aside to hug me. "You're finally here."

"This bastard belongs to you?" asks Michael.

"He is no bastard, and yes, he is with me," she replies.

The four angels part and Anastasia walks me through the gates. I walk with my head turned up at Michael and his fools as they watch with contempt. As she holds my hand, my mind falls into unwanted memory. So much has not changed and so much carries meaning for me. Soon enough, we are in her quarters. I am impressed.

"They are treating you like a princess now," I say to her once I get over her luxurious room.

"I've already told you I have grown as a woman and as an *angel*. I have earned these rights," she says.

Her room has gold plated floors with diamonds embedded within them, creating different designs with each plate. Her walls are also golden, but with designs made of many beautiful gems; her door is of a strong bronze material. Her room is so graceful that I immediately begin to feel content within my self. She then walks to her bed, which appears to be one of royalty and lies down.

"I cannot believe I am here again," I say, taking a breath and looking around.

"Neither can I. This is a truly a memorable day," she says.

"They were going to take me to *God*, and for who knows what to happen."

"I know; that is why I came for you."

"Repaying the favor I see, after all those times I saved you."

"Don't be smart," she retorts.

"And now you can make it storm upon my head without disturbing your neighbor below."

"Shush up," she says playfully. "Come by me," she demands.

"I'm fine right here. I am still in awe of this room of yours."

"Azazel shows fear and respect; this is new?"

"You believe in your comical ways don't you?"

"I will not bite," she says.

I make my way over to her bed. The moment I sit down she begins to disrobe. I immediately cover her body by hugging you.

"What are you doing?" I frantically say.

"What is wrong?" she asks.

"You should not do this, Anastasia."

"But I love you."

"You are highly ranked among *angels*; think about that."

"You are worth it, Azazel, *we* are worth it. Your hands already hold me, now caress me," she says seductively.

Many thoughts run through my mind, but I do as she asks. For some reason, I cannot turn away from her affection. I take her within my arms; her body innocently shakes. After our moment together, we gather our breath and lie in bed, holding one another.

"You are truly sweet, Azazel."

"Am I?"

"Yes."

"And your *God* may now look upon you as he sees me."

"Does that matter to me?" she murmurs.

"I would think not."

"You are correct. So you have sorted your mind?"

"Yes."

"You will leave me?"

"I will leave everything; I don't even know what to do with Panthon."

In hearing his name I hear a great roar from the other side of the bedroom door.

"I will care for him," she offers. "It would be like caring for you and it would fill the void of your absence."

"I don't know, I will let you know what I will do with him when the time comes. But I will be leaving to see Bune very soon."

"I wish you the best."

"I wish I could know how long I will be gone."

"That doesn't matter, you must attain the necessary knowledge you need to become one with yourself." I look at her as if I do not know her. Why have I forgotten how much she understands me? "Just come back in one piece," she pleads.

"You are truly something else."

"What makes you say this?" she says with playful curiosity.

"You still have a heart for me, even though you know all I've done and still do."

"You aren't okay; I cannot blame you for what you do."

"Then why not blame the Eternal?"

"He is not to blame; he does what is right, even when we do not see it."

"A bit extreme to think, isn't it?"

"You should not speak of him in this way."

"Forgive me," I say.

Anastasia leans towards my face and kisses my cheek.

"You are forever forgiven with me," she says.

Thinking to myself, I wonder how I will deal with Jahzara and Anastasia when I return. I believe that I will be the source of much pain.

"I should get going," I say, ashamed about thinking of Jahzara at this moment.

"I wish you will come back to me upon your enlightenment."

"I will," I say, knowing that I am lying to her.

"My body and mind await you," she sweetly says.

I then dress in silence because I cannot bear to speak or look at her.

"Anastasia," I say, breaking from silence.

"Yes," she replies from the comfort of her sheets.

"I love you," I say truthfully.

"And I do love you, more than my *God*."

I leave her room and go to Panthon. As I look in his eyes I debate whether or not I should see the *God* of the Universe. I take a deep breath, suck in my pride, and make my way to the temple within his Palace.

Outside of the Palace, I tell Panthon to sit tight. I do not intend for this visit to be long, but hopefully I can get some answers. As I say my goodbyes to Panthon, the Palace gates open and his voice commands me to enter. His voice shakes the very ground that I am standing on and even made me stagger. Eventually, I get my footing and enter through the gates and into the temple area. Behind me, the gates shut and I can see in Panthons eyes that he is not happy. We were a great distance from one another at this point, so I cast my thoughts into his mind to calm him.

"Everything will be fine," I say, as he stands ready for attack.

The long walk to *God* brings back memories and feelings from when I was just a little boy. All those times I had gotten into trouble landed me here on this same walk of shame, but I was never scared or demanded forgiveness. Walking to *God* now, I still feel the same fearless attitude flowing through my body, but now I am weary of what might take place. I'm hoping he will answer some things for me.

Once inside the Palace, the door shuts behind me so hard that it alarms me into drawing out my wings.

"Walk up to my throne Azazel," *God* commands.

As I make my way towards him, I see that he is just as I remembered. He is but an infinite wall of ice immersed in an infinite wall of fire the color of amethyst.

"You will draw no answers out of me," he says.

"Right," I sarcastically say, "you are all-knowing."

"You forget many things, Azazel; most importantly, you forget that I see."

"I am not perfect."

"No, but you are of perfection. You lie with woman after woman feeling nothing, feeling no shame. You are the chosen one, yet does this give you a reason to corrupt those around you?"

"I corrupt no one."

"I see different."

"Perhaps you must have received praises so loud and lovely that you did not notice the two thousand essences of little children I've freed," I boastfully say.

"It was seen and acknowledged, Azazel, do not doubt that."

"Souls you knew were trapped but did not free yourself," I continue.

"And why do you think this injustice was done?"

"You know all; tell me."

"I will tell you this, Azazel, that all you go through is a test. It is a mental, spiritual, emotional, and physical test you must go through to find what you are looking for."

"Why?"

"Why do you seek knowledge of your true identity?"

"It matters to me."

"Does it?"

"I would think so; I have been doing everything possible to understand myself thus far."

"Why?" *God* asks.

"I don't know why."

"Why can't you remember?"

"I don't know, but from what I've heard and do believe, you've taken my memory."

"Only certain parts."

"Why have you done this to me?"

"You will find out."

"No!" I scream and propel fire from my mouth as I yell. "I demand you tell me why at once!"

"So, you demand from me?"

"Yes."

"Who do you think you are?"

"Justify your actions to me now!"

"Do you realize and understand who and what I am?"

"I spit upon you and what you are. I have created my own beast with my own hands and it is more beautiful than anything you could have ever conjured. I spit upon your hypocritical tyranny and the injustice you thoughtlessly commit, and not only to me, but also to your own *beings*. You are nothing; just like me."

"And from whose image of a beast did you use to create your own?"

"That is irrelevant," I quickly say.

"You think an expression of anger will solve your problems?"

"Who are you?" I mock. "You have no idea what it feels like to be ignorant, angry for no reason but sad because of that anger. You do not care to help those that know nothing."

"And this is because of the free will determined for you?"

"And then you insult me when I live in my ignorance; why?"

"I do not insult but rather try to tame reasoning into a calm ocean of predictability. Why is it that I disagree with you? It is not because I hate you, but it is because I know you know it is wrong, and I know you have the mind to think otherwise, and yet you still act."

"You are heartless," I say. "You do not know. You are ready to forgive when the action can benefit you. Why is the manner in which I was born no issue to you? Why have you not yet asked me to forgive you?"

"That is for you to find out."

"Why am I torn between two worlds, two women, between life and death?"

"All of your answers will come to you in time." Through all my anger and frustration, I begin to cry, placing my hand onto the wall before me. "You must remember, my son."

"I am not your son," I interrupt.

"You must never forget that I first experienced everything you now feel. Your father did tempt me many times, but I kept my mind, because I cannot be disturbed. I know what it is to have pain, which is why your will to do as you please is justified."

"Why do you hate me?" I say.

"Why do you hate me?" he replies.

"I don't know," I respond.

"I do not hate you. You are crude, and so am I. But you are love, and so am I. To hate you would be to hate myself, and because I cannot find a reason to sufficiently hate myself, I refuse to look for a reason to sufficiently hate you."

As I stand there in silence looking down and contemplating my next words, a tear runs down my face. A hand, followed by a bodily form then comes through the wall and gently holds me.

"I love you," I say as I plant my face into his chest, but I cannot be you," I add.

"I know, Azazel, I know."

Just then, the Seraphs surrounding his throne join us and we all came together as one. Never have I seen the four six-winged and four-headed guards leave their position. This is the first time I feel as though I exist.

Walking out of the Palace, I feel as though something has been accomplished. I still have hatred towards *God*, but now that hatred has understanding.

Once I make it back to Panthon, I notice that he isn't alone; Anastasia is with him. It appears she is protecting him. A large crowd has gathered around them at the Palace entrance. From the distance, I can hear clearly what is happening.

"Whose creature is this?" a voice says. "You defend who? Isn't this the same *angel* who believes he is *God*?"

Anastasia was protecting Panthon from the crowd. She must have heard the ruckus and then came to help.

"Why don't you all just let this animal be? Who is he disturbing?" says Anastasia as she stands in front of Panthon.

"And why should we?" a voice says.

"This beast was foully created," says another.

"She protects this disgrace of an animal because she loves the one that created it," said Michael the archangel.

"Don't you start," Anastasia warns, looking at Michael.

"That's right," I say, as I make my way onto the scene and into Michael's face. The crowd immediately backs away, but the three other archangels stand behind their leader. "Do not say another word, Michael."

"How dare you utter my name from that filthy mouth," says Michael.

"Peace, Michael," soothes Gabriel.

"Peace means nothing to a half-blooded pest like this!" spat Michael.

I then raise my fire-covered fist, but Anastasia caught my hand and brought it down to rest at the side of her thigh.

"You better do as she says," Michael continues. "Who are you to come into our kingdom, our home, after all this time, and demand respect?"

Once again, we met with our noses touching, and this time, I wrap my wings around his body.

"I do not want nor need respect from this place or its inhabitants," I say to him. "I left in search of peace; let it be nothing to you."

"That's what you think, Azazel? You think you left of your own will?"

"Speak!" I yell.

"You have not only offset the Underuniverse but the Heavens also."

"I can care less about either," I say, releasing him.

"We will escort you out," he says, gathering his breath.

"I need no help — I know exactly where I am going."

I turn and grab Anastasia's hand. I then summoned Panthon. As we walk by, Panthon jumps up at Michael, scaring him. Once we make it to the gates of Heaven, Anastasia and I say our final goodbyes.

"Thank you for watching over him," I say.

"For a big animal, he has a soft heart."

"As I said, he is in my *image*."

"Take care of yourself, Azazel. I meant what I said earlier — in mind and in body, I wait for you."

"And I await the moment where I can again smell the sweet scent of your hair from within your sheets."

"You are special," she says, stroking my cheek. "You too, Panthon," she says, stroking his head. "Come back to me in one piece."

"Will do," I say.

With these final words, she kissed my cheek. I climbed onto Panthon, and we flew back to *Earth*. As we descend, I watch her standing there, holding her gown as she wipes fast-flowing tears from her face. With a powerful wind, I blow ten single different types of flowers up to her.

As children, we would learn of *God's* creation, and there were ten flowers Anastasia would always remark on. My abilities were becoming stronger as I saw through this action. The strong gust contained a red rose, daisy, carnation, iris, orchid, lilac, lily, wildflower, sunflower, and one tulip. Each flower would change its color upon her sight, except the rose, which would remain red. The flowers would represent the emotion she would be feeling at the moment she gazes upon her gift; the rose would not change color because it was the one representing how I once felt in her presence.

Once I return to *Earth*, I sit in thought about when I would see Bune. I desperately need to learn more about my self, but now I am afraid of what will be revealed. Anastasia is also on my mind. I truly love her, but I cannot forget Jahzara, who carries my heart, and I hers until our rightful deaths.

In the middle of my meditation, the violent shaking of the ground disturbs me. The earth beneath me showed no sign of cracking, and yet it vibrates with such anger. Immediately, nine extraordinary looking *beings* surround me. They are not here for war, but for peace. The one who speaks first announces himself as a Duke of the Underuniverse; the other eight just stand silently, analyzing me.

"I am Astaroth, Duke of the Underuniverse, and we have come to speak with you, my lord."

Astaroth stood as a strong and unsettling figure. In his right hand, he carried a large and sharp sword engulfed in blue flames.

"You remember us, no?" he continues.

"I have no recollection of who any of you are," I say as I stand at the center of what appeared to be my doom. "Why are you here?"

"My lord, I am Ipos, and it is unfortunate to see you in this way." Ipos stood with a strong and muscular body, and with the head of a lion. "We have served under you before, while you did serve under and with the Amalgamate. We come to you for guidance."

"What is wrong?"

"We need the mighty Amalgamate to come back as they were, and you are the only one who is strong enough to complete the task. You have fueled us in the past, and we need you once more."

"Who am I speaking with?" I ask.

"I am Amon, I reign over forty legions within the Underuniverse and yet fall to your superiority. Is it true that you remember nothing?"

"Who are you, with the three heads?" I ask, ignoring Amon's question.

"I am Asmoday, and I am a king and a great warrior."

"You have the head of a bull, a ram, and a man."

"I know this, my lord. Before the Universe of Heaven divided into two, the other half becoming the Underuniverse, we were all once members of the Universe of Heaven. Our appearance is due to being created by the same mind."

"You live on this *Earth*?" I ask.

"Correct," says Asmoday. "It is true that some of us reside beneath the surface, but some don't. We have lived in the Underuniverse since before the commencement of time, just as you have."

"Nonsense," I say,

"We are here to find you, my lord. We desire you to sit upon the throne and to triumphantly lead us into war."

I stood, confused.

"I need none of this — I already have a lot on my mind as it is."

"And we understand."

"Announce yourself," I say to the individual that spoke.

"I am Ose, one of many presidents of the Underuniverse."

"You are in the form of a leopard?"

"Yes, and I am also a great warrior. We have all been in war with you on countless occasions; you commanded all of us at some point."

"All we need is for our lord to remember his rightful place and take his woman by his side and reign as he used to," said Astaroth.

"You said since before time, Asmoday?"

"Yes."

"I have been alive since before the commencement of time?" I ask.

"Yes," said the sizeable flaming bird behind me.

"Who are you?" I ask.

"I am Phoenix."

"I don't understand — I am only twenty-five millenniums."

"Someone has lied to you, my lord. I am Allocen — a duke of the Underuniverse."

"What was I?"

"You were *God*," Astaroth said. "One day, you just vanished and became one with this realm. You roamed it in search of nothing, and after many confrontations with you, you still fail to remember anything."

"*God* has erased my memory..." I realized.

"And this does not give you further motivation to destroy his Palace?" asked the leopard, Ose.

"I reign over forty legions, my lord," said Amon, "but my true strength came from you and from your words of wisdom. It was you who bestowed the gift of immortality upon me."

"Were you my disciple?"

"Yes, my lord!" he cried in amazement.

Things were starting to come back to me, or maybe I just made a sound and obvious guess.

"Your woman waits for you," says the phoenix. "She is held by her father, Apep, from ever seeing you again. He wishes death upon you because you are the rightful heir to the throne. Your father has been captured, and it is written that you must take over the kingdom and have your woman give birth your heir."

"And where is this nonsense that you speak of written? I will have Jahzara, but I must return by my own will."

"She had to produce crafty acts behind her father's back to get to you, but in the end, she would be punished," the Phoenix replied.

"He hurts her?" I snarled.

"No, but you need to kill him."

"Who are you?" I ask.

"I am Apollyon, the prince of darkness and king of the bottomless pit. You, too, gave me the strength of immortality, my lord, and I, along with all that you see here, will fight and die for you. We are here to help you regain your lost identity and to seat you back on the throne."

"Never have I adopted the titles that have been thrown at me, but I do believe you. I must see Jahzara."

"You must go disguised, my lord."

"And who are you that speaks in concern of my safety?" I asked, turning to the speaker.

"I am Barbatos, duke and earl of the Underuniverse."

"Do you all give out titles down there? You all have one or carry the same."

"No my lord, you issued these titles to us since before the beginning of time."

"Not I?" I said incredulously.

"You grew to have so many powerful and favorite disciples at your side that you had more dukes, earls, and kings than you desired."

"I must have been as confused then as I am now," I dismissed. "This is nonsense. I do not know any of you, and if you have come to fight, then fight!"

"We are not here to fight," said Amon. "You are far too great to battle with, as we have seen you destroy some of our more powerful companions."

"Did you receive the *being* of marble?" I ask.

"Yes," confirmed Amon. "The Underuniverse was very angry at this gesture, but those of us close to you were amused."

"Your loss of memory has aroused a lot of hatred towards you in the Underuniverse, and so they come to see if it is true. You are cowardly to the rest, but to the intelligent, you are very bold and should be commended," said Ipos. "As saddening as it is to see you in this way, my lord, we pray to Amalgamate that you receive your *eyes* and lead us into the anticipated dimension."

"We do not come for war, but have come in peace," said Astaroth.

"You are all very loyal to me. But I must make sense of all this. Barbatos!" I yell.

"Yes, my lord."

"I will take your advice to disguise myself, and then journey to the Underuniverse to see Jahzara."

"She would greatly appreciate that," says Barbatos.

"Go — I will now tend to my love."

"You sound like my master of old," says Allocen.

"Allocen," I call. "How powerful was I?"

"As powerful as any Sovereign Creator," he replies.

"Was I as powerful as the Amalgamate?"

"Why, of course, your blood came from Lucifer, my lord — you are infinitely powerful," he continued.

Interesting, I thought.

"Leave," I command. I would then journey to the Underuniverse — hopefully, a shorter trip than to the Heavens.

I have discovered my age, and yet I looked so fresh, strong, and youthful. My heart races at the thought of seeing Jahzara again; I believe that she is my rib.

The Trip To The Underuniverse

After the nine *beings* vanish, I begin to prepare for my next journey. This expedition was not really necessary, but I did not mind going out of my way to see Jahzara. I keep putting Bune on hold, but now I can actually get Jahzara to tell me how to get to him — upon her announcement of this all-knowing dragon, I had failed to inquire about his whereabouts.

Just as with my trip to Heaven, I plan on bringing Panthon with me. He is alert during my brief meeting with my past disciples, and I believe that he too was ready for this trip.

Before we move, I conjure up a hooded trench coat and a bag, and then fit my bag over my shoulder. I sling the hood over my head, so all that is seen is an open patch of darkness about my face. Once ready to go, I begin running in a straight line, taking off with my wings. Panthon and I fly into the sky, circling *Earth's* entire surface, and then dive into the Underuniverse, vanishing through the ground.

While descending, I can't help but question why I am going down there; I want to see neither Heaven nor the Underuniverse again. Before I know it, the overwhelming stmosphere produced by this land interrupts my thoughts. Once we arrived at an entrance into town, I tell Panthon to sit tight and, should anything bad happen, wait for my call. Panthon lies down by a burning bush and goes to sleep. Sometimes, I am slightly jealous of him. When will *I* ever get the chance to rest? I then make my way into the Underuniverse's center, but am detained by a nearby conversation.

I saw and heard two *beings* speaking of the Lord Azazel coming back for war.

"So, he has come back?"

"That's what I've heard."

"Who does he think he is?"

"He's more powerful than any *being* or Sovereign in any of our realms, I'll tell you that."

"And that is why every *being* here will attack him at once; does he not understand what he has done?" I heard one say.

"He has indeed abandoned us, but we must not despise our Lord."

"He is just a *figure*; Amalgamate is our true Lord that deserves all praise. And while he quests, may I add, through the *earth* for some *thing*, we sit here in angst because of him. Cut his head off, I say."

"You can be killed for those words."

"Then it should be me, along with everyone else, who should be put to death."

"I commend your passion, but it should also be noted as stupidity," one of the *beings* said harshly.

"And then he comes for war; what's wrong with him?"

"It is only what I've heard; he comes for war and for his woman."

"Well then, now that makes sense. If I had a *woman* that compared to Jahzara and did not have a family with her, I too would wage war."

The two then share a laugh.

"I do not know what to make of this, but Jahzara will hold a ceremony about it all."

"That should be somewhat enlightening."

"You speak as if her beauty is all that she carries."

"You are wrong — I have not heard about this ceremony and anticipate what she will say."

"It is always a pleasure to see pure beauty," the *being* revered.

"Yes, but she is not like us — she is like him."

"What do you mean?"

"Azazel is Lord of death, disease, pain, anguish, and destruction, this is true — but he is also good, a judge of regeneration, wisdom, reason, life, and love. I've seen the good in him. He has the Eternal's compassion."

"Do not dare taint the Eternal's image in my eyes," says one with disdain in his voice.

"Believe me or not, but why would the Lord of all, the king of death and the mediator of beauty, wish to vanish?"

"No one knows."

"Well, I know what I know, and I know better. He left because of something disturbing his heart."

"You idiot!" one of the *beings* chided. "Do not let anyone else hear you. You are lucky that I know you. Anyone else would turn you to ash right now."

"Gamble or not, I stand by what I believe."

"Let us go to the ceremony then. I refuse to hear another one of your rants."

"Yes, let us go and hear the blasphemy that comes from the Universe's most seductive lips."

As the two men break apart for the ceremony, I follow cautiously behind them. I want so badly to kill them, or to make sense of my self to them, but I hold back and let them lead me to Jahzara. I must not create any more problems here; I am here for Jahzara, and that is it.

The path we took led me by the forest where I first met Jahzara, and it looked no different. The three- and four-headed animals still flew among the burnt, leafless trees and fire filled streams. At that point, I paused and failed to notice that my guides had left me. I walked into the forest, and lo and behold, Jahzara was running her fingers through a liquid river of fire and wearing what appeared to be the same dress of the past. Did my eyes deceive me?

"Jahzara?!" I cried.

"My love!" she says aloud. "I can hear you, but cannot see you."

"Is it really you sitting there?" I ask. She looks around until her eyes land on me.

"Azazel!" she screams.

"Quiet," I whisper.

"I cannot see you," she says. I then remove my hood.

"You are beautiful," she says, making her way to my lips.

"What are you doing here?" I ask.

"I am nervous about today's ceremony, so I came here to get away."

"And that gown..." I began, teasingly.

"Do you like it?" she asks.

"I love it — it is as I remember it."

"It is a newer version," she says. "I wore it hoping I would see you before the ceremony."

"How did you know I would be here? Suppose I didn't show?"

"Well, I heard you were coming, and so I figured that, mysteriously, you would be here. Whenever you would visit in the past, you would end up here, so I always made sure to be here."

"Oh," I reply.

"It is great to see you; I still have the feeling of when we last made love."

"I am here for you," I exclaim.

"I heard of your return through word of mouth, but was not sure of its truth."

"I have come to see you, but I do not want bring war. I want no more conflict."

"You have come to take me away with you!" she said excitedly.

"I have yet to see Bune — until then, I will make no other decisions."

"And why are you wasting time?"

"I am not, but distractions keep arising."

"You must see Bune."

"I have come to ask you where he is."

"We will get to that later; for now, we must be short with one another." I stood with my head down in deep thought until she raised my chin with her hand. "What's wrong?"

"How many times have we met here?" I ask.

"Oh, countless. Seeing you and having you not remember me on every occasion grew to be annoying, but I cherished every moment. After all, you would remember more and more with each visit."

"You were right."

"About what?"

"*God* has erased my memory."

"I said some things about him, but I wouldn't mind seeing the Universe of Heaven one day."

"Do you mean that?"

"I keep telling you, we don't belong here. We should be living in peace."

Hearing those words only drew more confusion, but also joy, to me.

"Then why do you sit and do nothing about this tyranny around you? You can leave."

"Not everyone is as bold as you," she states.

"No, but you are like me in sharing what no other seems to possess."

"Which is?"

"We have minds of our own."

Jahzara then drew out a sorrowful sigh.

"I must consent because my father rules this Universe. Should I oppose him, surely I would die."

"Nothing will happen to you, and no one will hurt you."

"Good," she said, placing her hand on the side of my face. In the distance, someone shouts her name, and immediately I throw my hood back on.

"Princess, what are you doing here, and who is this?" they call out.

"He is..." she paused. "He is but a friendly passerby."

"Are you sure?"

"Maybe you alarmed him," said Jahzara.

"What a strong and bold *being* you've picked up," I whisper to her, laughing.

After she hits me in my side with her pointy elbow, she says, "Don't be stupid."

"Are you alright?" asks the *being*. "I see a struggle."

"I am fine, and there is no struggle — you can go. You have done enough."

"We await your presence. King Apep has sent me to find you; he is growing tiresome," he advised.

"You will not be waiting much longer," she says. The dark figure then disappeared.

"And what is this about a *being* I've picked up?" she says, repeatedly hitting me.

"I'm just having fun, Jahzara."

"Your jealousy is stupid."

"What do you mean?"

"You have killed many *beings* over me — it is why I kill for you."

"I don't remember."

"In time," she says.

"You must go, but I want to see you after."

"Will you come to me after?" she asks.

"I would love to, but I cannot be exposed."

"You are right, but I will miss your touch," she purred.

"I will touch you however you like once I return," I flirted.

"You will be changed."

"Yes, but before I am, you must go to this ceremony of yours." Jahzara then leans up and gives me a sweet, warm kiss.

"I will see you after?" she again tenderly asks.

"Sure," I say.

"Follow me halfway, and then I will let you go," she says, as she took my hand.

She did as she said, and halfway to her ceremony, she let me go; I then walked on. I took a different route, and somehow I ended up encased within the multitudinous crowd. As I look around, I see all of the faces I had let down and betrayed, but because I couldn't remember them, I felt nothing.

Soon after my arrival, Jahzara begins to speak. She stood on the mountain in front of Apep's Palace. I have to admit that I was anxious to hear what she would say.

"*Beings* of the Underuniverse," she began, "welcome."

The crowd let out a tremendous roar that she allowed for a while, and then began again.

"We are gathered here at this moment because of the long-time comer, Azazel. My love, your Prince, he is here and among us. He does not present a threat to you but rather desires to make right of what went wrong. Disregard the ignorant image of belligerence that was painted to you through rumor because they are false. You all have questions to which you would like answers, but Azazel will not give you what you want. He would like to, but he cannot.

Many have physically tried to extricate the truth from his mouth, but they just fall victim to death. Let us not forget the marble figure that he delivered to us in the past. I consider him luckier than the others who have tried."

I don't know why, but that statement made me smile.

"I bring you all here today," Jahzara continued, "not to discourage the hatred toward Azazel, but to celebrate the fact that our Lord has graced us with his presence, and we should be grateful.

"Now, about war, I must touch on this subject. Do you not want to rule the entire Universe of Heaven?"

At these words, the crowd made so much noise that the ground began to shake.

"*Beings*," she started again, "who are you, and who do you serve? When the time comes for war, I can tell you who I will be fighting for. *Armageddon* was only the first war; we will not be defeated again."

"Bring Azazel to us!" A voice yells from within the crowd.

"I do not need to bring Azazel to you," Jahzara replies, "because he will come and do as he pleases. His history is indeed flawless, and he is the greatest *God* to grace this Universe, but do you not believe in your own strengths?

"Who are you to believe what another says? Do you not serve the Amalgamate, or do you now bow to the weak spirit guiding the Universe of Heaven? It is said — it is written — that one superior union shall come together and wage war for freedom. He has created us, and yet he does not want us to be thinkers. I want you to answer — is that just?

"Who here remembers our famed *beings* of reason? These *beings* examined the spirit that created them, and they learned that the other Universe can be defeated. We will cast a victory so triumphant and magnificent over Heaven that it will instantly catch fire. We will take back what is ours, reign with supreme power, and enslave the rule that has enslaved us.

To all sects of the Underuniverse, I thank you."

Throughout her speech, I stood in awe because this was a different woman from what I was used to. As she walked off her stage, the crowd cheered and chanted her name endlessly. I became unsure of whether or not I wanted to see her again.

I had no idea how I would do just that, so I simply waited in the forest where we last spoke. She eventually showed up and with open arms to hug and kiss me, but I halted her greeting.

"What was all that about?" I instantly questioned.

"All what?"

"That speech, it was so backward. Why would you even agree to do a speech like that?"

"I told you already; my father would cut my throat if I spoke any different."

"What I heard sounded believable."

"Well, that's the point, isn't it?" she says.

"Don't be that way to me Jahzara; I thought we both had the same mentality."

"Do we not?"

"Clearly we don't!" I yell.

"Lower your voice," she said, pointing a finger in my face.

"I believe that you are good, but I also see that you are naturally perverse."

"Does it not remind you of someone?"

"Should it?"

"You have just described yourself," she says, "except you look upon the female image of what you are. Do you not see why we must be together? We are one and the same, Azazel."

After hearing her words, I stood in silence because they were beginning to make sense to me. The woman that stood in front of me was not as perfect as any other, and yet she was. Just like me, she was truly ignorant, and I now saw that she might not be what I wanted, but what I needed.

I need a woman that can understand and cry with me when needed, or go to war with me by my side. I need a woman who can bear the cursed seeds that should be my children and still naturally love, teach, cherish, and tend to them. She is what I need and fulfills my will in all aspects; maybe she is also what I want.

Becoming lost in my thoughts, my silence has become so insulting that she caresses my cheek and says, "Have I done something wrong?"

"No," I say.

"I am just trying to help you make sense of it all," she says.

"Is it true that I have taken you as my queen, in the past or at any other time?"

"You have never taken me, but I am called your queen because of the foretold prophecy."

Her words instantly catch my attention.

"What prophecy?" I ask.

"That Azazel will save his love's heart from the torment of time. Every *being* knows that I fulfill the vision; it means you will take me, and so I am known as your queen."

"Is this prophecy true?"

"I don't..."

"Who told you this?" I ask before she finishes her sentence.

"The three witches up north."

"And have they ever been accurate with their predictions?"

"Oh yes, of course — they have predicted all your visits to the Underuniverse. Their last prediction of your arrival came some years ago. We all have anticipated this day."

"You must take me to them."

"They live so far and secluded from everyone."

"And why does that matter?" I ask.

"It doesn't, my Lord, I just care to have you see Bune."

"I will, and we will talk about that after I see these witches."

"As you wish," she submitted.

Jahzara then took me by the hand and we flew to the witches. As we soared above everyone, I watched below and observed the Underuniverse in awe. Could I have really ruled down here? Did I truly have the strength, knowledge, courage, and patience to command these millions? Clearly I did because I had met nine of my closest disciples, but I just did not see myself doing this.

"Here we are," says Jahzara, interrupting my thoughts.

The area looked so decrepit, the witches living in an old tilted box-sized home surrounded by branches.

"Are you ready?" I ask.

"Of course," she responded.

Before we knocked on the door, the door opened, and three females appeared in front of us.

"May we help you?" said the first woman, who sat at what appeared to be her reading table.

She sat with candles in front of her as she read a book. This woman, along with the other two, had long black hair, but they each had their own appearance. The woman reading her book had slimy, rubbery skin that fell from her bones. Her face was so dry it looked as though her soul had been sucked right through her face. Everything on her looked feeble, and while she talked, every now and then, her jaw would dislocate, and she would have to place it back into position.

"We come in peace," says Jahzara.

"I come for answers," I say.

"Who is it that comes looking for answers?" says the second woman.

This woman stood behind the one who read at the table and carried her own eyes in both hands. She had no slots for her eyes in her head, so she held her eyes up to see. She too looked the same as the first woman, except her skin was very dry and rough, as opposed to being slimy and rubbery.

"Yes, who is this hooded *being*?" said the third, and this woman looked different, standing slender yet curvy.

Her skin was a beautiful tan, and her hair flowed with her body as she swayed left to right from mixing something in a big pot in the kitchen. She had a beautifully sculpted face and a wonderful voice that threw me into a deep trance.

"Don't you look at our niece in that way!" says the first witch.

"Who are you?" asks the second.

"What do I say?" I whisper to Jahzara.

"Show them," she advised.

I removed my hood and said, "I am Azazel."

Each woman halted in the action they were doing and stood in front of me. Next to me, Jahzara smiled.

"Stupid women," she uttered.

"My Lords, please forgive us; we did not know," said the third witch.

"It's fine," I say.

"Our attitude to you was sour."

"It is fine," I repeat.

"I am Ethel," said the first witch. She touched the second and said, "This is Gretchen, and the youth is our niece, Isabella."

"It is a pleasure to meet you all," I say.

"Oh, but it is an honor to have you grace us," said Gretchen. "Please, have a seat; we will tell you all that you wish to know."

"Bring our Lord a refreshment," says Ethel to her niece.

"Do the same for Jahzara, also," I say.

"No, it's fine," says Jahzara humbly, "never have I failed to exist in a room before — I'm growing used to it."

"Forgive us, my princess," said Gretchen. "We are overjoyed by his presence."

"I will have your coat," says Isabella.

"No, you will not," says Jahzara with fury as I opened my mouth to give my thanks. "Remove your hands from him."

Jahzara's sharp response made me smile, and then I ask that a chair is brought for her to sit. "Be calm," I whisper.

"If she looks at you like that again, I will take her youth from her," she whispers back.

"May we begin?" Ethel inquired.

"What is this disgusting liquid I am placing into my body?" asks Jahzara.

"Next time, don't just take anything then," mouthed the niece.

"It is hawk feather, vintage goat milk, blood of a whore, the tongue of an Ox, the meat of worms, dirt, and the sweat from each one of our foreheads," says one.

Jahzara and I caught eyes for a moment, and she slowly placed the drink down onto the table.

"This is the worst visit..." began Jahzara.

As she spoke, I cut her off by saying, "Thank you for your hospitality and kindness."

"Are these two befitting of one another?" whispered Gretchen into Ethel's ear.

"And why would we not be?" asks Jahzara.

"I will take your coat," said Isabella as she grabbed at my arm.

"I told you to stop!" Jahzara says in almost a hiss.

"Isabella, please — he is fine," says Ethel.

"Is she hard of hearing?" Jahzara asks.

"I am here because of a prophecy of yours that I have come across," I say.

"And what does this prophecy tell?" asks Gretchen.

"That I will take my love, and we will live...but I need to know more."

"We can help you," said Isabella.

"Why does her voice now haunt me?" says Jahzara.

"Calm," I whisper.

"I will fetch the cards," says Gretchen.

"Please do at once: give me your hand," says Ethel to me. "Your palms are empty," she says, looking at me in surprise.

"He is truly immortal," said Isabella in awe.

"Is there a problem?"

"I've never dealt with an Eternal," says Ethel. "I see that you will be most difficult to read. Because you have no lines running through your palms, you have no timeline for anything; it is quite impressive."

"He is *God*," Gretchen said, walking back to the table with the cards.

"Okay, here we go," says Ethel as she shuffles the cards and lay eight down onto the table. "This cannot be done," she said.

"And why not?" I respond.

"Once the cards have been placed, they go from image to image. I have never seen anything like this. Each card is to have only one image — a king is a king, or an angel is an angel, but each individual card scrolls through many. This is miraculous."

"Miraculous is not the word," says Jahzara. "This is a waste of time."

Soon after Jahzara spoke, the cards ceased switching through images and finally land on their rightful destination.

"This is most impressive, yet tragic," says Isabella.

"What do they say?" I ask.

"The top four display two kings and two *Gods*, while the bottom shows a deviant character, a queen, triumph, and death."

Jahzara asks, "He is immortal, so how can this be?"

"Sometimes, death does not speak to who is having their prophecy read, but rather to those around them," said Ethel while I sat there in silence.

"What nonsense do you speak of," says Jahzara.

"I say only what I see," Ethel coolly respondes.

"And I will have my love?" I ask, looking down with a frustrated gaze.

"That is clear to see, my Lord."

"You will also be most powerful, my Lord," says Gretchen.

Immediately, I rise from my seat and head for the door.

"Thank you for your time," I say hurriedly.

"It was a blessing and an honor to see you in person," says Isabella.

I then rushed out of the door and took to the sky. I flew to the Underuniverse entrance, where Panthon lay. Jahzara came behind me.

"Why the rush?" she asks.

"I must leave at once — how do I get to Bune?"

"I did not want you to see them."

"You knew of this fate?" I say.

"The last time we made love; I took a hair from your head and brought it to the witches. They predicted your next visit to the Underuniverse and told me of your fate. I did not believe them then, and I do not believe them now. You will protect all that you love, won't you?" she asks.

"Of course I will, why wouldn't I? I couldn't be in there anymore, Jahzara; I should have never gone to see them," I admit.

"Maybe this is good; it does not hurt to know what is hidden, right?" As her long red hair blew in the wind, I look at her face with a passionate smile. "Why do you look at me as if I am prey?" she asks.

"Because I want you," I reply.

"You do not have to wish," she says, sliding onto me and wrapping her arms around my back. "I am yours already." We then kiss. "I'm already yours," she repeats.

"I must go, but I must know how to get to Bune."

"He will take you on his own. I have informed him of you. He resides where his student was born; it is his method."

"So then I must return to *Earth*."

Just then, Panthon looked up at me, and I down at him.

"What is to happen with your beast?" asks Jahzara. "I will care for him."

"I don't know."

"It will be like taking care of you."

"I think I will hold on to him."

"You will give him to another, then?"

"I haven't made up my mind."

"Leave him with me, Azazel, let him protect me," implores Jahzara.

"You do not understand — he is all that I have."

She looked at me kindly.

"I know, and that is why you must let your love handle him."

"Where would you keep him?" I ask.

"With me in my chambers until you return."

"He is no pet, Jahzara," I warn.

"I understand."

"Keeping him imprisoned in a room is like keeping me held in a room."

"Do you not trust me?" she asks.

I hesitated. "It's not that."

"Do you trust another?"

"Why say this?"

"I will kill whoever else wants you."

I look into her eyes and say, "And do I not do the same?"

"Yes, but never have I been with anyone else," she says.

"You are correct, and I am with no one but you."

"Is that so?" she says.

"If you wish, I too can question your loyalty."

She stood in silence.

"You may watch Panthon — I trust you," I say.

Her face flashed a half-smile that wished to be full, but her pride would not allow it.

"Thank you," she says, planting her face into my chest. I could then feel and hear the happiness in her voice.

"I am sorry," she says. "Maybe I am childish."

"And I do the same over you. I suppose it is normal. The moment I heard that Apep was holding you against your will, I had to see you and let you know that I would return for you. Also, I wanted to give you something."

"What is it?" she questioned.

I took her hands into mine and shared the beauty and feeling of everlasting life with her.

"Now we are one," she said.

She watched her palms as the lines within them began to fade, and then said, "The feeling is different."

"I will return for you, the both of you, as soon as I am freed," I say.

Panthon stood and stretched his well-rested body. He began to purr heavily and walked over to Jahzara as she welcomed him. "It's a good life, isn't it Panthon?" I say. "You leave your owner for a beautiful woman, as if I never existed."

"He comes to me as you do," says Jahzara.

"And now you place yourself on high because of this?"

"Once again, Azazel's ugly head of jealousy rears itself and is caused by his own beast. I will watch over him; he will be in good hands."

"Never have I been alone," I admit. "I will miss him."

"Go — wait for your calling," she advises.

After I watch her for a while, I take off and fly back to *Earth*.

"Take my coat!" I yell from the atmosphere, flinging it down to her.

She stood there, awaiting it while she watched me leave with tears in her eyes. Why did I toy with these two women — or was I? Each has won a side of me, but I want Jahzara the most.

Once on *Earth*, I wait for my *call*. The moment I arrive, I hear a voice saying, "Are you ready?" Immediately after, I respond, "Yes." I then drop to the ground in an unconscious state and awake in an empty Olympus. Jahzara said I would be taken to my place of birth; she was right. Looking around, I notice that I am naked and begin to panic.

I see nothing but hear an echoing voice around me.

"It is amazing how the mind distinguishes necessary and appropriate *clothes* to hide what is most thought of as private."

"I suppose it is interesting," I say back to the voice.

"Stop hiding," says the voice.

I immediately take my hands away from my body and bring them to my side. After I doing this, Bune, the figure producing the voice, appears.

"The Creators of the Creators sought my counsel on the frame and stature of thinking and feeling creatures; it was decided that they should only retain so much of their experience before it would be forgotten. Their manufactured damaged *being* forced their memories to be taken from them once they became new souls for a new life. Yet one would think they could or should at least feel their loss to pursue a new, different, or better outcome, but they spat on their existence by revering emotional and prideful curiosity. Just think, the equation for their recovery was given to them, but they could not get over themselves to see it. Interesting, no?"[5]

"I suppose it is."

"Why are you afraid?" asks Bune as he curled his body around mine.

"What makes you think that I am afraid?"

"I can see, hear, and smell it all over you."

Bune was a gigantic red and blue dragon. His eyes were terrible to look in to because they were all white, and his breath was so hot that it felt as though he would accidentally melt me.

"You have nothing to worry about, do you?" he implored.

"I do not."

"You have come seeking knowledge of self; am I wrong? And you wish to attain wisdom that has been erased from your memory."

"Much has been removed from me."

"Jahzara loves you dearly, Azazel."

"This is true," I said.

---

5 See Note E

"So, why do you toy with her emotions?"

"I do not," I say defensively.

"She is not alone; you do the same to Anastasia."

"Once again, I do none of what you say."

"Their love for you can be fatal to them; enemies do not need to be aware of a threat in order to become an enemy."

"Enough," I finally say. "I am ready."

"You will not avoid any thing while in my presence."

"I will not," I confidently say.

"Then let's begin."

In The Beginning

The Council created every *thing*. They were five *Sovereigns* that traveled out of the Infinite realm to create a realm of their own.

When leaving the Infinite realm, they each took elements of it with them. Standing on a crystal floor disconnected from the empty universe around them, they each dispensed with their elements into the atmosphere, giving the broken environment ingredients to not only produce life but to consistently sustain it. Their words were written into the core of every component for life.

When one element broke apart to form another, the code of their particular character would be translated into that element, causing it to become the physical manifestation of their mind. The elements then, while they watched what would occur, continued to act without their guidance, creating every *thing* and every one.

Doubtless, the most critical part of their world's conception was the language system used to honor their philosophy of "being." While the Universe and their elements for life labored to create a Heaven and Earth, they developed a certain spirit of Wisdom for their thinking and feeling creatures. This Wisdom was an ethic adding awareness to their conscience, making them mindful of right or wrong judgments.

Together, they, using the knowledge they retained from the Infinite realm, created a law of life. This law would contain the principles of the Infinite, yet it would be a revelation of how their five minds interpret them. With this law's point being the complete mindfulness of their thinking and feeling creatures, when sincerely pledging faithfulness to the spirit of their Wisdom, those creatures may learn the secret of government to transcend the very *nature* in which they are born.

Certain *God*s were sent from the Infinite realm to create another devoted to the mind of the Infinite. The hope was that every created realm would learn of the Infinite wisdom to perfectly reflect that character of the original realm, but these five *Gods* had their own intention — they cared to act without the Infinite will. They cared for a realm to function according to its own spirit, and this was allowed by the *Infinite*, who gave every *God* the right to do as they will.

The Infinite had committed the creation of a realm to five *Gods* who, being knowledgeable in the science of the Infinite wisdom, create — through the imagination of their perception — whatever should be created. Sent into every developing element was a fundamental principle of their Wisdom. By their Wisdom, every *thing* either lived or died. Their Wisdom was within every bit of the atmosphere's matter, creating their vision's intention and destroying whatever was not a sure fulfillment of it.

The first structure the elements made, which was their Temple, was formed above the atmosphere. Within this temple was a Hall of Judgment with five thrones. Each *God* sat on their throne. It is from here that they examine their creation and perfect the Wisdom their thinking and feeling creatures should obtain. The elements then formed the *Earth* of their Temple, making that sphere livable.

Before man, but after the *Earth* and the *Heavens* were formed, *beings* were created. They were born in a different light than *humans* because they were created as many organisms in one pool, whereas humans were made independently. Among the many *beings* created, Lucifer was chosen as one of the highest-ranking. This would be a decision that, although satisfying the Council, would evidently break the *Gods'* hearts, but would also allow them to see who was loyal to their rule.

Nevertheless, as livable as that realm should be, when on it, no creature should live in ease. An equal, lesser, or greater force challenged everything on *Earth*, and their thinking and feeling creature should experience the same. The Council, knowing for their male and female to reach their highest potential, and that a contrary mind of "being" must examine their character, decided to create a figure born for deceiving. They would call this figure *Lucifer*, according to the leader of that realm indifferent to the Infinite.

The Council put their Lucifer in charge of the invisible welfare of *Earth*. The *Earth's* balance should depend on how his counsel would be given and received. The Council created him with a most brilliant and illuminating understanding for honoring the Temple within the Infinite realm and the Temple of the Council. The *Gods* decided that *Earth's* primary governor was their deceiving messenger because if able to perceive his wisdom and the subtleness of its spirit, *Earth's* members may uncover the wisdom of the Infinite to better their person.

Therefore, when the Council created Lucifer, they encoded his mind with a form of understanding that mirrored their collective definition of the Infinite realm's character. Because he must fulfill a crucial task, they made his mind with great care, sealing his thoughts with a code of "being" that was sensually alluring to lesser minds. The operation of this minister's mind must, therefore, be a little less perfect than theirs, and should keep the attention of lesser minds while still having power to rule over them.

"He is perfect," said one, as the five watched him lying on the floor of their throne room, mass and energy slowly forming his body.

"He is our most intricate *son*," said another.

"He will either be the *Earth's* fall or its regeneration," said another.

"And you honestly think he is prepared for this?" another asked.

"He has all five of our minds within him, yet in an imperfect way. He will mislead *Earth*, and he will succeed, but if we have made him as well as we think we have, he will be the reason *Earth* never knows the Infinite."

"And must *Earth* know the Infinite?" questioned one.

"We are here only because of the Infinite. We are members of the Infinite assembly. If *Earth* fails to know her Temple, and if she fails to know the dimension strengthening their bond to one another, then we have failed, and the Infinite is disrespected.

"If we have made him as well as we think we have," he continues, "then he, being *Earth's* test, will destroy it, and will cause the *Earth's* principle to mysteriously pass away. I see nothing wrong with this because we have created the *Earth* to be very sensitive, and when it senses wrong, it will let its members know."

"He will be the means magnifying our legacy forever," says another. "We have seen our brothers and sisters fail to complete their project in and under the Universe because they couldn't perfectly create a Deceiver. Here lies our Deceiver, and he is above them all."

"Wake up," said one, kneeling and placing their right hand on his forehead.

Soon enough, this *God* brought her left hand from her side and faced her palm upwards, conjuring a glass bottle with water inside. The water soon took on the form of a gas, filling up the glass until it broke the bottle's cap, slowly rising and traveling into the nose of their deceiving messenger. The glass, now empty, and still in the center of her palm, shatters into a liquid and transforms into another gas, rising from her palm and traveling into his ears and mouth.

"The sorrow and knowledge of many worlds will be the air in his lungs," she says, her right hand still on his forehead. "Wake up," she continues, "wake up."

Upon his stirring, the Council clothed him and updated him of his task. As with every *Deceiver* before him, he gladly accepted, having no intention to do anything but the program encoded within his character. The *Gods* then brought him out of the throne room to show him the *Earth* forming on its own.

"Put your imprint on creation," says one to him.

They then flew a little closer to *Earth*, yet a great way off, as the distance of the sun is from the earth. Lucifer held out both arms, his palms facing up. A ball of energy, the color of Amethyst, formed above his palms. Within the ball were sentences written in a specific code of dialect and arranged in an order that only he and the *Gods* knew. When this ball's energy reached its height, it lifted from his palms and thundered loudly over the realm, causing a rain of ash to fall from dark, wool-like structures. These structures soon began to blend with the whiteness of the forming clouds and the falling ashes, the language of "being" seeping into the atmosphere.

"Now, create your own *kind*," said one to him.

"Create ones similar to you, to help you," says another.

They then turned their back to the earth, flew into the galaxy and, in the open cosmos, allowed him to create his congregation. Lucifer held out his arms, and with one palm facing up and the other palm over it and facing down, a ball of energy formed between them. Within the ball was another code of sentences. When the ball's energy reached its height, it shot out from between his palms, entered into the open realm, and caused a thunderous combustion to occur, revealing nine hundred and thirty bodies floating in the air.

"How do I wake them up?" Lucifer asks.

"They are already awake," said one. "Just perceive it."

Lucifer then breathed out of his mouth, his lips taking on the shape of a weak kiss. A blue-like substance emitted from his lips, pouring over the floating host and encircling them, as if in a womb. The substance dissolved into the host, and Lucifer, with his eyes closed, began to imagine them fully conscious. When he opened his eyes, all nine hundred and thirty were on their knees with their faces pointed down. Lucifer, amazed and feeling both fear and awe simultaneously, looked at the *Gods*, and with a smile, they looked back at him.

"Now build the place of your temple, your Labyrinth," said a *God* to him.

Lucifer again held out his arms and placed both palms facing up. Another ball of energy filled with more code began to form. This ball floated up and out of his palms, divided into two, and hovered over the earth, causing a loud clap. A realm had now opened at the center of the earth. The nine hundred and thirty creatures of Lucifer lifted themselves and flew into the two created realms.

"Create humans now," said the one whose right hand labored on his forehead. "Create this kind of creature as you think it should be."

Lucifer and the *Gods* flew closer to *Earth*, hovering in the clouds' mist. At this point, the earth and everything above and below it was formed and fully functional; animals, plants, and the sun, moon, and stars included. Lucifer held out his arms, and once more conjured another ball of energy filled with the code language. At the height of its energy, the ball separated from him, floated over the earth, and divided into four million little balls of energy, falling onto the earth and pervading it. Soon enough, thinking and feeling creatures, according to his imagination, began to surface, finding usefulness in their environment to bless and be blessed by the environment.

"Leave them alone for now," said one of the Gods to him. "Only when you feel them inquiring of you, should you respond."

"Only when you feel them directing their thoughts and feelings to you, should you act," said another. "You cannot force attraction, and you cannot force love, but if you want their respect, you have to read their energy."

"We have made you special," another remarked, "and your rank is one that only neglect can diminish. Do not be negligent."

"Yes," Lucifer said.

"We have an assignment for you that is dear to our heart," said another. "We need you to lead this lesser creation."

"I don't understand," he replied.

"Through you, they are peculiar. They are not as you are, and they are not as your nine hundred and thirty, but are a kind of creature of their own, and must have their minds cared for. They will rule *Earth* with a kind of force to become one with it. They and their realm will become one as they recognize their secret *Deliverer* as returning their energy to us."

"I don't understand," Lucifer repeated. "I am to serve a lower kind?"

"You serve us," they said.

"Go on," he encouraged, lowering his head and closing his eyes.

"To be whole creatures, they need the pressure of examination. You must be the one who causes them to make their choices according to our character. You must direct them into living a certain kind of life, so that when they *die*, and when their minds open, they may return to us. Those who do die and commit unlawful acts will have the chance to live again and make the right choices before returning to us. We need you to guide them to this destiny; it is through you that they reach their highest potential. Do you see?"

"I do, and will do as you say," Lucifer says, being bound by other thoughts and feelings.

The Council dismissed Lucifer. Descending into his temple, Lucifer discusses his new role with his created assembly.

"It's an injustice," he said to the crowd. "Can you believe that I am chosen for this?"

"It appears to be an honor," says one.

"It is not," he replies.

"What are you to do again?" asks another. "I don't understand."

"I am the one who must guide the Council's new kind of creature," he answered.

"What is this kind going to be?" asks one.

"Why should you have to suffer with the ignorant?" asks another.

"Why can't we have *Earth*?" another questioned.

"I do not know," Lucifer says, attempting to calm them.

"You should do as you will with them," says one.

Feeling as though he must get a closer look at his creation, Lucifer says, "I will go to *Earth* and see what I have created. I will return after."

Lucifer travels to Earth and finds the Council hovering in the clouds.

"They are beautiful, aren't they?" says one to him.

Lucifer says nothing.

"Lucifer, this is to be your domain, and these are to be your subjects."

"If these are to be my subjects, should they not desire me as I desire you? Should they not pray to me as we pray to you?"

"You are to act before guidance is needed," said one. "There is nothing to be jealous of."

"I am not jealous!" said Lucifer defensively.

"Is that so?" says one, knowing about his conversation with his assembly.

"I will do as you say," he conceded. "This is my kingdom, and I am to treat it as you would."

The *Gods* smiled.

"This is no kingdom of yours, Lucifer — this realm is your domain. You are to be here and guide the people to know *right*."

Feeling a little indifferent, Lucifer returns to his domain. Once again, his crowd gathers around him, their curiosity fueling his thoughts and emotions.

"Are you sure we have to serve them?" says one.

"I think I would rather submit to death than help what I've created reach a level of mindfulness equal to our own," added another.

"Is it fair?" Lucifer asks. "I am to serve them in their realm. I am their slave." Looking up and out toward his audience, he adds, "Help me and I will share their realm with you, and when it is ours, we will take the Council's realm."

"Why should we wait until later to take the Council's Palace?" asks one. "I would rather you start to strategize now."

"Patience," says Lucifer. "Everything will happen in time."

Although saying this, in his heart, Lucifer began to rethink his position; no longer would he talk — he wanted war.

"Enough!" he barked, as others began to speak up. "They have given them the key to life and have not once thought about me; even to every male on earth is a female given. Should I have no wife?"

"The *Gods* have shown that they don't care for us anymore!" one yells.

"If they truly cared, they would not have issued ranks or positions," says another. "They would not have made us look at one another in ways that cause jealousy."

"I will to lead a war against the Almighty Council," Lucifer decrees. "I will to overthrow them and take my rightful position as God of the Gods. And as I take that position, I will be an even greater God than them; all will worship me for my thoughts." Then, looking out into the audience, he says, "I trust you will not fail me in this war."

"Hail Lucifer!" says one, beginning a chant.

Lucifer, plus his nine hundred and thirty, travelled from under the *Earth* and up to the Council's temple. Overhearing the noise of a crowd, the Council's chief Captain, who had his commander in chief by his side, asks about the commotion.

Entering the building, Lucifer says, "You will see," making his way to the Council's Hall with his followers behind him. He stands in front of the Council.

"Why have you come to break our heart?" they ask.

"What is this heart you speak of," Lucifer replies.

"You have said you will to overthrow our reign and become the king of what is on and above *Earth*. Are we wrong?"

With a smile, Lucifer says, "You are right."

"Why would you break our trust?"

"Why have you made me serve what is lower than me in beauty and in intelligence?" Lucifer counters.

"There is nothing to be jealous of."

"I am not jealous!" shouts Lucifer. "I want justice; I want a true position. Why else would you have me with so much power? You were to be overthrown eventually."

"What made you think this?"

After a long pause, Lucifer says, "I am done."

"We are disappointed," the *Gods* say.

Immediately, Lucifer charged the Council's throne and threw himself toward them, but they put out their hands and sent him to the ground. Behind him, while all *beings* continue to fight, using their minds, the *Gods* held Lucifer to the ground, watching him. Somehow, Lucifer makes it to his feet and attacks three of the *Gods*; this enrages them.

The *Gods* then expel Lucifer and his assembly to *Earth*, barring their entrance into their sphere. Lucifer then decides to embark on his first act against his subjects — he would confuse the *divine* language. He knew there was a particular weakness within the male for the female and the female for the male, and that with the two carrying different characters, one would be more liable to bring the other to his coarse manner of thought.

Knowing that this new kind frequently spent time with the Council's messengers to learn of their culture, Lucifer changed his *beings'* appearance to raise no alarm when they approached the newly created kind. These ministers subtly introduced into the new kind's culture a certain spiritual knowledge and language, causing their mind to refrain from the Council's manner of "being" to mirror the *image* of his realm's natural and religious character.

This is how it all started. Over time, and until *Heaven* and *Earth's* last battle, Lucifer would manipulate *Earth's* philosophy to re-invent the spirit of the Council's assembly.

Along the way, because he knew that the Gods held him in eternal contempt, Lucifer did have a child of his own. With a son, Lucifer would endure all the pain brought forth upon him because he knew someone would avenge him one day. He knew his son would also free him from *torture*, which is why he took the form of Zeus and seduced Metis into intercourse. It was a plan that would land him a child most powerful and intelligent.

Throughout the beginning of *Earth's* existence, Lucifer traveled to Mount Olympus. At one particular time, Zeus had been called to Heaven, so Lucifer found his time to strike. Upon arriving at the gates of Olympus, Lucifer transformed into Zeus' image and stumbled through the area to find his kingdom. Once he found Zeus' throne, he found Metis looking out and onto the people. He came up from behind her and took her by her waist, hugging her softly from behind. The two then engaged in conversation.

"You are in a good mood," said Metis.

"To have a queen as exquisite as you, why wouldn't I be?"

"After our argument last night, I thought you would hate me for years to come."

"Argument?" Lucifer questioned.

"Do you not remember?"

"Of course I do. I just care to forget it because I love you so much. Time is so precious to waste fighting when I can marvel at the beautiful work the *Gods* have done with you."

"What has gotten into you, Zeus?" Metis questioned.

"Not a thing," Lucifer said, bringing her to his chest.

"You are different," she says.

"What do you mean?" Lucifer asked, throwing her from him.

"This is not the Zeus I have seen of late. It is as if you forget that we argue about how you fail to desire me but lust after others."

"I do none of what you speak of!"

"And the argument begins again," she says.

"No, it does not," says Lucifer calmly as he takes her hand. "This will be forever silenced as we lay in bed together, your figure upon mine."

"You are truly a wonder, Zeus."

"*We* are truly a wonder," he corrected, leading Metis to their bed.

Hereafter the deed was done, and when they finished, Lucifer took his original form. Metis jumped up in fear at the sight of Lucifer in her bed.

"I have just allowed the light of darkness to infiltrate my womb!" she cried out.

"You have done this world a great justice," he says.

"Get out!" Metis yelled.

"I will leave, but my child stays within you to grow most powerful," he says over her yelling.

The commotion alarmed Olympus, and the kingdom's guards enter at once. They stopped, frozen in their tracks as they saw Lucifer. Rushing to attack, Lucifer creates a wall of fire separating him and Metis from the guards.

"My child will rule by my side," he says, violently holding her face.

"You are pure evil!" she screams.

"And you are most gullible. You are indeed beautiful, but Zeus carries on with many. Now, am I really that evil? You may have a child to love now; isn't love what you want most?"

With those last words, Lucifer vanishes along with his wall of fire, descending back in to the Underuniverse.

Metis tried her hardest to keep her child's existence a secret, but she couldn't. She wanted to say it was Zeus' child, but the guilt of lying was something she couldn't do. After the baby was born, Metis did love him for many months, but then she eventually confessed all to Zeus. This confession would lead the child to face a path on his own; he would have to carry the cross that his father placed upon his shoulders.

"Azazel, you are divine. I do not know how something so precious could have been created from hate," said Metis as she cradled him in her arms.

"What is this that you speak of?" asked Zeus, overhearing. "No child of mine would ever be conceived in hate."

"It has been some time now, and I think the truth needs to come to out," Metis began nervously.

"Truth on what?" Zeus asks, confused.

"This child is not yours," she says with her head down.

"You can mother this child all you want, but do not keep it from me."

"No, Zeus, it was not you who I laid with on the day when this child came about."

"What do you mean?" asks Zeus.

"Lucifer took your image on the day you left for Heaven and seduced me into believing it was you."

"Can you not tell me from a fake?" he incredulously asks.

"I'm sorry," Metis says, looking at her child.

Zeus did not look worried but rather neutral; his overwhelming anger sounded through the sky as lightning and thunder hurled through a newly gray atmosphere. Zeus then pried the child from Metis's hands and went outside.

"Let him go, Zeus!" Metis begged as she tried to stop him from walking through those large golden doors of the kingdom, thunder and lightning echoing in the background.

"Out of my way!" he yells, shoving her aside.

Zeus went to the most glorious mountain in Olympus and held the baby in the air. He brought him behind his back, and with one arm, launched Azazel into the Cosmos. Azazel lingered among the emptiness of the galaxy until a Sovereign of Heaven picked him up and brought him to his realm, washing him in the waters of his love.

Azazel did have a life in Heaven, and he did get into all sorts of trouble, but he was never alone. He always had Anastasia by his side, and she too shared something with Azazel — she was a *being* of similar yet lesser fashion. Apep's wife, Tamanna, had an affair with one of Heaven's Sovereigns. After he found out what had been done, he took the child into his kingdom and banished the Sovereign to the Underuniverse. This Sovereign had taken in two children that were conceived with cruel intentions and let them grow up with one another, or so they thought.

Azazel grew up in this Sovereign's realm alone for many years and would travel back and forth from Heaven, *Earth*, and the Underuniverse. He was rebellious, but this Sovereign always tried to help him make sense of his experience.

While the people of *Earth* suffered cruel and harsh judgments leading up to *Armageddon*, it was Azazel and his father who led *Earth's* people to adopt devious practices. Azazel would leave his Sovereign caretaker, and each time he returned, he would ask for forgiveness. He had a good heart, but being born from two different worlds had horrible effects on his mentality. Eventually, this Sovereign grew tired of Azazel and put him out of the Universe — on earth, his mind would cause the realm's conclusion.

In the Underuniverse, in the not so distant past, the Amalgamate sat on their throne as Lucifer spoke to his son.

"My son, you have served me well."

"Father, I have done all that you command."

"You do not know how long I have waited to have my son by my side so that we may conquer together," Lucifer said proudly.

"As I stand in front of the four who form the Amalgamate, I look at you, father, and a fire burns inside of me for Heaven's annhilation."

"There will be a battle, my son, and as long as you mislead *Earth*, its character will suffer, and its heart, along with its patience, will grow weaker. You must join me in battle on that day so that I know I have someone I can trust by my side."

"Yes, father."

"These people are ignorant, with their political, economical, and religious worries. For billions of years, I have deceived the *chosen* while you developed as a thinking creature. We have ruled the Underuniverse, Hades, and *Earth* since before the beginning of time, my son, and now the time is coming where we must rule Heaven. I lost the first battle because I was weak — my intelligence and strength weren't what they are now. But with you, I will surely have an edge to victory."

"How much longer must I deceive the people?" asks Azazel.

"Why should you question this and not play with the pawns until you are bored? When you are bored, then you may do as you like."

"I am growing tired of this mission, father — I feel like I can be more useful."

"Are you not happy? Do you not enjoy your human experience?"

"I do enjoy, but I need more."

"You must not understand," Lucifer says in disappointment. "Did you not see as I took the form of Leopold the Second? Do you not remember the elegant cries of mercy, the silence of the night, or the smell of the Congo? It was uplifting."

"Yes, I do remember, and it was remarkable."

"Some people don't even want to believe or remember that it happened — that's how good I am. With you, people will never say that it didn't happen because they won't get a chance to. What you are doing will lead to the *Earth's* end; we will have the *chosen* with us. We will win. All I need, what you must do — as if you have a choice — is to fight successfully with me. You, along with my three other halves, will take back what should be rightfully ours."

"I will," said Azazel.

"Leave me, for when you are through, you too shall join me on the throne. You are born to immortality, my son, and that will be evident as we head into war."

Azazel then flew back to *Earth* for several years to finish what he started. His human figure was strong and brave, and established a very great lie on the human mind, performing a species of thought he attributed to *God*. He held power on earth for some time, and then, when he finally grew tired of the experience, he led the world into a devastating *war*. Many *bodies*, and those who protected them, were killed for their beliefs. It was during this time when the *scroll* of the dimension unrolled, taking revenge on minds that should have better understood. As the sentence was given, Azazel fled to the Underuniverse, where he would report to his father once again.

"It has been years since I've seen you," Lucifer welcomed.

"Yes, it has, and I have returned to say that it has begun."

"No longer bored, are we? Everything is going according to plan."

"It was horrible, father. I couldn't watch it any longer; the people began to question why I didn't suffer as they did."

"I know, I saw. And doesn't it make you look at things differently now? The spirit of Heaven is weak."

"Or maybe we are the pawns," Azazel reasoned.

"Have you switched sides?" Lucifer questioned.

"I apologize."

"All of this is because of you. Enjoy your legacy. Wasn't it *God* who banished you because of your curiosity?"

"Yes," he admitted.

"You are just like me. You have a brain and your own disciples. Did they not show loyalty to you by being right there as you carried out your career on earth?"

"You are right."

"Son, bask in the moment because we are not wrong. We are none of what has been depicted of us by the ignorant. Simply put, we are thinkers."

"Thinkers," Azazel voiced, as if trying to gain confidence in the word.

"Go and see your work and take pride in your rationality."

Azazel soared from the Underuniverse, but he did not go to *Earth*; he flew by it with disgust and sorrow, and then entered into Heaven. He made his way through the gates and into *God's* royal throne.

"Why are you killing those you say you love?" he asks.

"Why have you chosen to deceive them so that they receive the return of their attitude?" God countered.

"Because I am ignorant; what is your excuse?"

God was silent.

"I want for forgiveness once again," Azazel submitted.

"Why?" God questioned, pitying him.

"It isn't my choice — I am unhappy. Why did I have to be born? Why was my birth one of hate instead of love? Why me?"

"I will forgive you for as many times until the end of time, but each time you break my heart by erring again."

"I know."

"You were forgiven from the moment you were born, Azazel."

"Why is it so hard for me to live, to do right?"

"There is no such thing as good or bad, my son — there is only what is right and what is wrong."

"Then, do I have no such ability to distinguish the one from the other?"

"That is something only you can answer."

Azazael thought on this, and then asked, "What separated my father from any other?"

"Lucifer was cunning, intelligent, and powerful. He had intelligence far superior to any other creation of mine, and so he overthought about what should be, rather than what is. With you, you can be content with whom and what you are. With him, there was no such chance."

"I am afraid of letting him down."

"And I have never drawn fear to your heart?"

"I don't mean it that way. I have a life with him, and I have my own army, but I would give it up for you. I need to."

"You certainly carry his same sweet-talking mouth. Go from me and prove your action is stronger than your word. And I am your Father; I have made all — including Lucifer — so as you bow, worship, and hurt him, you disappoint me, and not him."

"Yes, Father."

"Prove your loyalty."

Azazel left Heaven and flew back to the Underuniverse. He came to the throne of the Amalgamate and entered as Leviathon held a conference with his *beings*. "Welcome back, my Lord," said Amon to Azazel. Azazel walked past Amon silently and stood on the throne next to his father, who sat on his throne.

"I conclude," said Leviathon. "We are to strike and strike hard. We lost the first battle but have had many victories since. The biggest victory came at the beginning of time, and our latest victory came from Azazel. We are now stronger and wiser than we were before, and we must execute. We must deliver the blow to stop the Universe of Heaven from existing. Lucifer was banished because he was too great of a presence for *God*. His heart was too passionate, and so he had to be put away. Instead of ending the catastrophe that took place, Heaven chose to let his man suffer at the hands of brilliance. We must not feel pity for Heaven. And to finish, I must add that we will have the immortal Azazel in battle with us, so we are truly as strong, if not stronger, than that wisdom which created all *things*. Let us triumph!"

After Leviathon's speech, Lucifer pulled Azazel aside.

"Where were you?" he questioned.

"I did as you said."

"You watched the humans suffer for this long?"

"Yes," said Azazel shortly.

"You are my son, indeed," said Lucifer, sensing his deception. "Why did you venture to Heaven? You reek of its disgusting and trifling fragrance."

"I only went for more understanding," Azazel pleaded.

Lucifer lifted his hand, flipping Azazel and sending him into the wall so that he formed an upside-down cross. Lucifer then knelt beside his head and said, "I am not too proud to kill my own son. Unlike God, I will kill you right where you stand. Immortal or not, you will be dealt with."

"I understand," Azazel said.

Lucifer dropped him.

"You are to join me in battle, do you understand?" he barked. "You are my pride, my joy, my son, and my strength — let's go into battle with the same mind."

"Yes, father."

"No!" shouted Lucifer. "You are to have the heart of a beast and the mind of a thinker, what is wrong with you? Have you turned incompetent as well as foolish? Speak with more pride," Lucifer said, watching as Azazel rose to his feet.

"What is the matter?" said Belial upon hearing the noise.

Lucifer looked at Azazel with hatred and said, "There is no issue."

"We will prepare for war," said Azazel.

"Listen," Lucifer said, putting his hands on Azazel's face. "Be a good son, and we will win. I will bless you with the crown that you deserve."

"Yes, father," replied Azazel.

Lucifer walked away and left Azazel standing alone, his head down.

"What's a handsome *being* like you doing with his head hanging low?" said a tempting female voice. Azazel looked up to see Tamanna standing by the entrance.

"And what concern is it of yours?" Azazel harshly responded.

"Do you miss your woman?" she asks.

"What?"

"It's fine — she has told me everything between you two. You love her, yes?"

"I do."

"Then you must fight, Azazel. Take her now because she desires nothing more than to have your child."

"I will."

"You are such a shy young man," she said tenderly. "You are good. Lucifer should have had you with another."

"What are you doing here, Tamanna?"

"I have come to check on my Lord's son — on the future prince of the Underuniverse. I will be there in battle, and I wish to see you there, too."

"And you will," Azazel promised.

"Bye," she said in a way that struck fear.

Azazel sat in that room for hours, even days, thinking about everything. He would ultimately break his promise with God once again, and then what would happen? He would surely be severely punished if he went against his father in war, so would he risk it?

As the days passed by, *Armageddon* approached, and the dominions prepared to clash. With Azazel on the wrong side of the controversy, surely the misled would win — but he had other plans.

Forethought

Every *judgment* released upon the human race had stopped; *Armageddon* began. All sides prepared for war, but Azazel lingered in his chambers with Jahzara. Sensing his stress, she came to comfort him before he made any decision.

"I don't know what to do," he says in frustration.

"Think of it like this — you go and fight, conquer Heaven, and then we will be together. We will be Supreme Royalty, and our Empire will be indestructible."

"My problems are bigger than that and cannot be put to rest that easily. I am torn between two worlds."

"And I am not?" she quickly rebuts. "You have no idea what its like to live as the daughter of machination and to know that I you are not like your father. You are not the only one torn between two worlds Azazel; never forget that. I suffer just as much as you do."

"I wish you did," says Azazel.

"So I can be like you? Nobody wants to live in confusion and anger throughout their life. Your immortality only adds to your pain," she reasoned.

"Motivation is a virtue of yours, I see," Azazel says sarcastically.

"I'm full of sorrow just like you, Azazel, which is why I continue to believe in us. Since birth, you were meant to be mine — I know it."

"I was born to be trouble," he says miserably.

"You will be fine; if you chose not to fight, then I will be by your side. Whatever you do, Azazel, I will do. I respect all that ruins you and support all that runs through that crazy head of yours."

"Why are you not my wife yet?" Azazel says as he lay on his bed beside her.

"You have me nightly; it is just an improper having of me."

They both share a smile at her comment.

"Tell me that I will be fine and that my father's blood will surge through my veins when we charge Heaven," says Azazel springing from the bed and pacing.

"No," she responds.

"Tell me I am stupid in my thoughts."

"No."

"Tell me that I am *God*."

"I will never."

"Tell me something!" says Azazel in desperation.

"I will not say anything to suffice your ego or to change your mind. You are good, Azazel — evil just comes naturally to you because your father is Lucifer. And it is harder to do that evil because you desire to be your own — you want freedom."

"Yes, you're right, that is it," Azazel realizes in astonishment. "Freedom is what I feel like. I want to be free, and I want to be held to nothing; I just want control."

"You can have that freedom if you like, but only you can know what is right for you. Until then, you have the strength, power, intelligence, bravery, and wit of *God*, and you must make the right choices."

"You are right."

"Why, of course — when has there been a moment where I was wrong?"

"How did I land such a strong, wise, and stunning woman as you?"

"You fell into my life, and I had to take care of you ever since."

"I'd be lost without you, Jahzara."

"You are a hopeless case," says Jahzara with a smile.

"Am I now," says Azazel as he jumps on top of her in bed, kissing her neck playfully.

"A lost cause!" she says out loud, and laughing.

"True, but I've found my cause in you," he says in a moment of seriousness.

"No pleasure before war," says Lucifer as he quietly enters the room. "We need you at your full strength."

"Father," Azazel says in fright.

Lucifer makes his way from the entrance of the room and over to the bed where, now frozen in shock, Azazel and Jahzara sit.

"A fine one you have here, son," Lucifer says as he plays with her hair. "Be gone now," he adds, waving his hand in the air and causing her to disappear.

"You are ready, aren't you?" he says to Azazel.

"I am ready to fight by your side."

"That's good to hear because you wouldn't want to look weak in the eyes of your woman, would you?"

"She's not like that," Azazel says with pride.

"Do you think so?"

"I know so," he says confidently.

"I was the one who introduced the idea of a woman for a man. I know exactly what they are capable of and how their different thought processes are from yours, not mine. You may think you have a diamond of a woman, but if you look closer, you will see that she is nothing more than an ordinary rock."

"So you have come to speak about the war," Azazel says, hoping to change the subject.

"I have come to ensure your loyalty once more and to warn you of Heaven's trickery. If I am to be captured, it will be you who rules this throne until you retrieve me. I have faith in what we have, but one must always be prepared."

"A thinker," Azazel says.

"Yes, a thinker — that's more like it. You must think, and that is all there is to it. With the Amalgamate by your side, there is no way we can be stopped."

"I'm ready, father."

"I hear our army forming; General Apep and his men prepare for war. We must also."

"I will meet you there, father."

Lucifer and Azazel separate, the two headed in different directions. Lucifer goes to the Underuniverse's entrance to complete the Amalgamate, while Azazel leaves to find Jahzara. Now together, they join the Amalgamate, along with Apep and his wife, Tamanna, to form the front line of attack.

As one, they charge toward Heaven. As they reach *Earth's* atmosphere, *one* on a white horse meets them; behind him is an army. The two forces meet above the *Earth*. Many of *Earth's* inhabitants die from the debris the *war*; the landscape's physical structure also dies with them.

As the opponents battle, Azazel takes Jahzara back down to the Underuniverse. Lucifer sees Azazel's actions and becomes enraged. It is at this moment that Lucifer becomes weak and susceptible to capture. A bright beam from one *being's* palm hits him hard. The *king* of *darkness* is then thrown into a cage and sentenced to an empty realm for one thousand years.

In the Underuniverse, Azazel and Jahzara arrive in an empty world.

"Are you alright?" she asks.

"I think so."

"I believe you made the right decision; you now have no part in the battle's outcome, and that is good."

"I'm stupid — I have to go back," he quickly says.

"No," Jahzara says. "This is your decision, and you must live with it. You're here for a reason — you want a new start."

"He saw me."

"Who did?"

"My father — he saw me leave."

"I'm sure you are mistaken," she says, hoping to comfort him.

"No, if he could have reversed my existence right then and there, he would have. I have betrayed my father."

"Have you really? What is that saying he is always preaching to you, that you are neither good nor bad, but are rather a thinker? Should you be persecuted for a belief that you two share?" she reasoned.

"I don't think he cares about that," Azazel says pitifully. "All it looks like is that his own son left him in war. He needed me, and I let him down."

"Come with me," Jahzara says, taking his hand. The two soar to the Underuniverse's atmosphere. "Look down."

"What is the point of this?"

"Do you love the *beings* of the Underuniverse?" she asks.

"You know I do. My *men* that I love are up there now and fighting a war they believe I am a part of. I would die for them."

"Then maybe this will be yours, and you can rule it how you see fit. This will be your kingdom, Azazel, and you can make it right; you can lead us."

"You are hopeful, but I see things differently. I see nothing but doom in my future."

They pause at the sound of the devastating warfare raging on both above and below them.

"Who do you suppose is winning?" Jahzara wondered.

"Heaven," says Azazel. "The Underuniverse is no match for Heaven. The Amalgamate is nothing compared to Heaven's Royal Mind, and that's why I was needed."

"You need to stop. Soon it will be over."

"I need a way to escape," he says.

"And I will be there with you." Jahzara squeezes his hand reassuringly.

"You're fine here. You need to stay where you are because I will find you from wherever I am."

"Do you not realize how hurtful it is not to have you?"

"I'm sorry," he says, dropping her hand. "But I need to do something to set myself free from this invisible burden I carry."

"It will all be over soon. I promise you will find your way. You have been destroying the *Earth* by Lucifer's side, and yet you have a good heart. You will find a way."

"I hope so, because I don't know why I do what I do."

As the two embrace in the warmth of a hug, *beings* began to rain down into the Underuniverse and burn as they hit the ground. Azazel and Jahzara watch from the atmosphere as their kind suffers their justified fates. Although most perished, some did not; Azazel's nine disciples and their armies who honored him, and Jahzara's parents, along with their army, survived.

Azazel tells Jahzara that he will go to his chambers to think; she wants to come, but he advises her to go to her family. In his room, Azazel paces at the thought of ruling an entire empire until one of his advisors enters, bestowing knowledge upon him and encouraging him to lead his people to an even stronger attack on Heaven during the next battle.

"My lord, stop this at once — we need you as levelheaded as can be."

"And what are we to do now?"

"We must collect ourselves and free him."

"What am I to do now? I must run this universe on my own — this universe of weak-hearted souls defeated by Heaven?"

"This is true, but you must not cast harsh ideals upon your people. You have run the Underuniverse before; what is the problem now?"

"The problem is that I served under the Amalgamate — I took orders from my father, and so I never truly commanded on my own."

"Do not doubt yourself," encourages the advisor.

Right then, Leviathan, Belial, and Satan were attempting to regain their own thrones and regroup for another attack to free their fourth self. Damage was undoubtedly done to the Underuniverse, leaving Azazel to run his father's empire, something he was ultimately not happy about.

Azazel did as his advisor requested and ruled for some time. He did not take Jahzara as his queen but instead handed all power over to Apep, who was Lucifer's chief general. One night, Azazel clothed himself in a long dark coat that covered his entire body and vanished from the Underuniverse and fled to Heaven. Before he left, he would see Jahzara.

"You have made such radical decisions, and now you leave us in a state of chaos? What are you thinking?" she asks.

"I know, but I must do as you said; I must find a way for me to escape, and I think that I have."

"And what is this brilliant idea?" she sarcastically asks.

"I will go to Heaven once more and make a peace treaty that will change *things*."

"Then I will come," she demanded.

Azazel stops her.

"I will not forget you, Jahzara, I will return for you," he says.

"Everything you do is unfair to me," Jahzara says, childishly.

Azazel couldn't help but smile.

"You will wait for me, will you not?"

"You are an idiot to believe I wouldn't," she grinned. "I understand that you have to do this; just come back in one piece."

With those last words, Azazel made his way through to the Underuniverse's entrance. He looked back and thought about the many memories of this place, for his idea of an escape would not allow him to stay. With a deep breath, he made his finger into the form of a knife and held it at the top of his forehead, running it down through his left eyebrow and past his eye. He took the blood that came from the wound and marked the ground with it. The cut would leave a scar; only damage by others allows him to heal correctly. If he committed the act upon himself, the wound would heal, but not in the same fashion.

"Goodbye, but not forever," he said out loud, and then he shot up to Heaven.

His random disappearance would cause suspicion and accusations of treachery, which led to an angering of *beings*. Chaos ensued in the Underuniverse, and Azazel's head was something most desired. And yet, all the while, Jahzara would continue to fight in his absence to protect his name, staying mindful of her king and protecting his legacy.

The Final Baptism

The flight from the Underuniverse to Heaven felt as though it would never end because memories accompanied him on his trip. As Azazel flew, he thought about his first trip to *Earth* and then to the Underuniverse. He thought about the *beings* that tried to kill him. Then he thought about Jahzara until he remembered Anastasia and how they partially grew up together. Lost in thought, he began to wonder why he ever left Heaven. It was Anastasia's curiosity that kept him away from her, but he was always drawn back to her. In a way, he saw a connection between her and Jahzara.

"Why must you keep bringing that foul girl up to Heaven?" Anastasia had said to Azazel one day after class.

"I did not know there was a problem," Azazel said with a smile.

"Why do you even want her attention? There are more suitable women, you know."

"If that is true, then tell me — who is most suitable for me?" he said as he put his arm around her neck.

With her head down, she says, "I don't know; it is for you to decide."

"And why has my decision upset you?" he asked, though he knew the answer.

"Because she is pure evil," Anastasia responded.

"If you got to know her, I think you two would be the best of friends. She's really a nice girl, but I think I know what it is — it's her hair, isn't it?"

"What?"

"Just because she has that red hair, she's evil, right?"

"Oh shut up, you idiot."

"Say what you must, but I can see it in your eyes," said Azazel, teasingly.

"Can you also see that I want to turn you into a tree, and then have you turned into a shelter?" Anastasia said stubbornly.

"All of this violence in Heaven...you must stop this at once," Azazel said mockingly.

"All I am saying," Anastasia said, knocking his hand from around her, "is that you are in Heaven, and there are consequences or having affairs with those who disobey *God*. My father had an affair with a woman from outside of the realm and he was dealt with."

"And how has Jahzara disobeyed *God*? I am the one bringing her here; I am the one who sleeps with her in my bed. Should I not be the one to face the consequences? And where are they?"

"You have yet to suffer because you are being taught a lesson."

"I don't know what I'm doing, Anastasia; I'm searching for something that I don't know. I want neither Heaven nor the Underuniverse because they do not have my mind," Azazel said anxiously. "If I stay here, then I must abide by *laws* and be what I am not. If I go to the Underuniverse, I must be a prince and cause harm through more *laws*. I want nothing that this life can offer me."

"Stop," Anastasia interrupted. "I see and understand your worries, but I am here for you. I have always been here for you, but you fail to see that," Anastasia said, walking away in frustration.

Azazel stood and just watched as her figure moved with the motion of a weak heart.

He then left that memory and moved to all the times he would spend hours and days with Jahzara at his mountain in the *Desert*; thinking back on Jahzara always made him smile because he enjoyed the fact that there was a female out there who shared the same pain that he did. He also depended on her; she loved him in the way that he expected to be loved. He recalled the many times they had *engaged* on Mount Azazel, but then he also remembered her voice of reason.

"You cannot do this forever, Azazel," she had said to him once as they rested on a cliff.

"I know."

"You must choose what is right for you because I can feel the energy from Heaven when you hold my hand. I'm not welcomed there."

"Neither am I, but what am I to do about it?" he asked.

"You need to start taking it seriously because I do want to have a life with you; you need to find out what you are missing."

"This is delightful scenery, isn't it?"

"Azazel," Jahzara said sternly. "All these mountains are mine."

"Hey!" she yelled, trying to regain his attention.

"A beautiful creation devoted to my name by humans; just look at it."

"Control yourself," Jahzara said to silence him. "Whatever it is that calls to you, you need to discover it. Maybe you just need to live on the earth for a while, or in the Underuniverse next to your father. You need to experience in order to determine what is right for you, and I will be there."

"You keep saying the same thing over and over every time we're together; is there nothing else that you can say?"

"You mean is there anything else that can distract my love for you, Azazel? No. I will keep saying the same thing until you do as I say and until you're at peace with life."

"I wish you would stop," Azazel said.

"I wish you would think," she responded.

"What is all this constant pressure anyway? What evil intentions do you have?" he teased.

"You idiot, there are no cruel intentions, just concern. Is there truly no love between us that you should doubt my actions?"

"I do not believe in love."

After a brief moment of silence and disappointment, Jahzara says, "Well, I will love you until you understand its overwhelming feeling."

"I don't believe in it, but with you, I try to."

"Do you promise?"

"I hate liars, so you have no worries with me breaking a promise."

"I have sworn myself to you only, Azazel; be careful with my heart."

"I know."

"You have to think of ways of finding peace within yourself."

"I will."

"It is not fair that I must leave my own problems and take on yours constantly, no matter how much I care for you."

"I know."

"I need you to do this for us," she implored.

"I will make a decision by tomorrow," he promised.

Jahzara flashed a wide smile.

"My confused *God* is so cute when he's serious," she said as she laid her head down, resting it on his chest.

"Yes, I am," he replied, and then the two fell asleep.

That was the last memory he would relive before getting to Heaven. As he walked to Heaven's throne, he remembered that after he and Jahzara had met on the mountain, that next day, he would come to *God* and ask for release from Heaven. That was the day he left to live in the Underuniverse — a day about which he would forever be indecisive.

Upon his arrival to the throne, he stood outside the main gates and lingered a little. Before he could even take a breath, Michael and Gabriel welcome him.

"Look who has come home," says Michael.

"A delightful surprise," Azazel snapped back sarcastically.

"We are here to escort you to the throne," says Gabriel.

"Do I not know where I'm going? Has the layout changed?"

"Be quiet, and let us walk you," Michael fires at Azazel.

"How about this — I walk your spirit into mine, so you can be no more?" replies Azazel.

"I'll be sure you are defeated worse than your father, you son of a liar," says Michael.

"Your words are tough, and you do look strong, but we both know I can set this whole place on fire faster than you can report it to your God. And once you are on fire, Michael," Azazel threatened, "I will personally control your flame so that you burn for ever. And I am immortal, so it will be no problem for me."

Michael touches his nose to Azazel's and the two look one another dead in the eyes.

"I will be on my way," says Azazel.

"Nothing you can do will ever redeem your actions, you illegitimate child," says Michael.

Returning to Michael, "If I did act on my emotion, I and not you would get blamed, so you are lucky," says Azazel.

"It is not I who am lucky but you who keeps receiving the blessings of the Eternal and wasting them."

Azazel looks at Michael and turns around, walking towards his destination. He said nothing to Michael in response because he knew that what he had heard was true. Azazel had a plan to revive his reputation; he would make it right.

As he walks, he feels just as he did as a child when he would get into trouble.

"It was only a matter of time," God says.

"It always is, isn't it," Azazel replies.

"You have come for redemption, to reconcile my love for you."

"Shouldn't your love for me be never-ending?" questioned Azazel.

"Of course, and just as it has been many times before, you are forgiven before our meeting."

"You have very charming greeters."

"They only act against individuals that ruin my *name*."

"Have I truly ruined your name?" Azazel asks smugly.

"We both know of your history and struggle as a *being*; it is not for others to judge, and why should one care?"

"I can care less; I know where my heart rests."

"And where might that be?" queries God.

"Somewhere I am not," he states.

God laughs.

"Tell me the reason why you are here."

"I have come to you for the ultimate cleansing — my final baptism."

"Is this due to the pressure of Jahzara or Anastasia?"

"Neither," Azazel says firmly.

"Your inclination is natural, then?"

"I am and have always been of my own mind. I need to find peace; Jahzara has just wanted this for me more than I do for myself."

"What have your own thoughts led you to?"

"I want you to erase my memory. I want you to make me whole, make me honest in thought and in action so that I may know what is right. Should I do as I did before, feel as I felt before, then it is final. I will be for what is *wrong*, but should I prevail, my mind will be as is your mind. I wish to forget all that I know, love, and hate, so that I may start over. Not as a child, but as a new *being*."

"This is truly noble and yet can be tragic."

"It will be what it will be," says Azazel.

"Should I proceed with this request, you will not know of your abilities, of your mind, emotions, weaknesses, strengths, or loyalties. This can be devastating because although these things may be gone, you will remain the same. And in doing so, you can regain certain memories upon the situation and then act accordingly. Knowing you, Azazel, you will be prone to mischief."

"If that is so, then let me be. Take me in and hear my plea. Forgive me and then let me learn not to do it again."

"Did you not think about your relationships, Azazel? You have a whole Universe of unsatisfied *beings* depending on your wisdom and leadership. Should you go through with this, they will put you to the test."

"And since when have I become afraid of tests? Let me prove to you that I am more than an experiment gone wrong."

"I must ask again — is this what you wish, now that you know even more chaos will arise with your disappearance and newly erased mind?"

"Yes," Azazel says firmly.

"Then it will be done, but first, I must remove your section from my *Book* to ensure new pages for you possible recovery from death to life."

"I am immortal — how can there be a death for me?" he questioned.

God took out his *Book* and flew through the pages until he landed upon Azazel's record. He ripped the pages from the book and handed them to him.

"Everything I have allowed to come into existence must live, learn, make the right decisions, love, and then die. All that comes into existence serves a purpose, maybe not to for a universal affect, but to ensure their own personal wellbeing. I will let you see your past, present, and present future. I show you your life and death not to tease or to provoke emotion, but to let you see for the sake of seeing. With your current wish, it will do you no good, but relive what you have and have not lived."

Azazel read his record. He saw memories he remembered and forgot, future events that disgusted him, and then some that made him proud. As he finished reading his life, he approached his death and saw his final days, or what his final days would have been if he had not made this new request to the throne.

He stood in tears, and through his crying, managed to say, "I will feel the pain of death that I have caused others."

He put his death down and ran back to his memories of Jahzara and Anastasia. He read of the many people he could have spoken to and that could have impacted his life, realizing how much love other *beings* — good and bad — had for him.

He reviewed his life over and over again because he had second thoughts about his request. He saw how he would wander through *Earth* after losing his memory, and it wearied him. He saw the disappointing acts of violence he would perform, and it made him wish he had never existed.

He read the table of contents and opened to his desired section. He stood read about himself as the earth's enemy mind, about Jahzara and what part she would play in his life; he even read about Bune. He saw the torment he would go through in trying to understand who he was and how deciding between two worlds would destroy him. As he read through his life and death, he felt bad about living, but he knew he could make it right with one decision. He held his life in the center of his palms, and in an instant, the pages caught fire. He was ready for a new existence.

"I will do as you wish, but I will not erase all your memory," said God to Azazel.

"It must be done in the way that I ask."

"If I were to erase all of your memory, your future would not be intended. I will leave certain memories and the ability for you to regain or create those memories you desire. You may think a complete absence of thought is the key, but you are mistaken."

"Do what you will, but take away from me the character that has caused my downfall," Azazel conceded.

At that moment, *God* places his hand upon Azazel's heart and takes his lingering essence; he then touches his forehead and clears his mind. Azazel stands in a zombie-like state until a new *lifeline* is breathed into him.

"Speak to me," God commands.

"Have I done something wrong?" responds Azazel.

A New Past Age

Azazel would live as he wished. His memories of love, hate, good, and evil *deeds* were all gone; he carried on naturally. He had his memories of Anastasia, but they were only memories he held dear to heart. He did not remember her as a woman, but rather as a girl when he was a boy. He would not remember anyone unless he came across and embraced him or her — certain smells, for example, would force his memory. He had flashbacks of Jahzara and of his past life, but he never put any further thought into them. He lived as though he had not lived before, and, although random flashbacks haunted him, he was content.

~ ~ ~

In the Underuniverse, the three forms of Lucifer and Apep plot for another war to set Lucifer free and to take back Azazel.

"They have brainwashed the prince," Leviathan says to Apep.

"My Lord, I promise that both father and son will be retrieved."

"Your daughter kept close to Azazel, do you think she knows something?" says Belial.

"I doubt it, but she will be questioned."

"It has been five hundred years since Lucifer has been captured, and in the next five hundred years, we must grow stronger and wiser.

This is no longer about destroying Heaven, even though we have another chance after Lucifer's release from," says Leviathan.

"It will all come together in the next years, but do you truly want to have the prince back?" says Apep.

"What are you saying?" asks Satan.

"It is rumored that Lucifer saw his own son betray him in war," Apep says.

"Blasphemy!" Leviathan yells.

"I apologize, but it is only rumored. It is said that Lucifer caught the eyes of his child and became weakened at the sight of his actions."

"I will believe none of this unless it should come from Lucifer's lips," says Beliel.

"Yes," Apep agreed, bowing his head.

"Be gone — there is much on which to strategize," advises Satan.

"As you wish," Apep says before leaving them alone.

~ ~ ~

During the next five hundred years, Azazel would continue to lead *humankind* toward what, according to *God*, was right, but he would have Anastasia by his side. She knew what he had requested, and so her happiness and love for him would only grow at the thought of a new start. Her obsession with him would equally grow — so much so that she would seduce him by lying about their past. She made sure to take advantage of his memory loss and the stipulations and possibilities around it.

Azazel and Anastasia watched over the earth, being worshipped as *God*. Heaven's throne had to eventually silence these notions of them because such a deviation on *Earth* would not happen again, like as it happened in the past.

"You are not to blame," said God to Azazel and Anastasia. "But you must leave him, Anastasia."

The two were separated, and it hurt them badly. They had expressed a new bond and love similar to that when children. The only difference now was Azazel's memory loss, which Anastasia was not altogether unhappy about because she wanted to be the new Jahzara.

One day, Azazel and Anastasia stood on a large mountain above the sky, watching over the earth and enjoying their time together. Their interaction was peaceful and much needed. Anastasia was finally becoming something more than a "friend" in Azazel's eyes.

"It is truly something to see, isn't it?" says Azazel.

"It is; these creatures are interesting. They accept the reform their thoughts and feelings must go through. They have, despite the influence of their companions, chosen to care for their heart.

"This next age will be special. I already know that I will have my hands full."

"You'll be fine; you have strong hands," says Anastasia, smiling.

"It's been nice having you here with me," he says to her. "Tell me something, Anastasia," he continues.

"Anything," she says.

"Why is my memory so hazy? I mean, what's wrong with me?"

"There is nothing wrong with you or with your memory," she says, wanting to tell him the truth.

"I feel different."

"That's because you are different."

"I know, but I feel like there's more I have to know. I'm unsure about something, and I need to know what."

"Everything will reveal itself," she says, flying down to speak with the *people*.

Azazel sits and watches her roam around. He wants to harm the *people*, but he doesn't. He fights his inclination by getting up, breathing out fire, and flying down to join Anastasia.

Flying to the *Earth's* surface, he thinks about how his angry release of fire must mean how unhappy he is. Of course, there is nothing to be unhappy about, and yet lying within him was an emotion he couldn't understand. A mental claw ripped at his brain as new and intense feelings surged throughout his body.

While walking through the towns of the *Earth*, he stops and admires the work created by the *beings*. The buildings had been made of nice, strong, sturdy fixtures; the ground was also well paved. The beautiful glow from the *sun* illuminated the land to its true beauty and exposed the spirit within the *people*. Azazel truly admired their beauty, and he especially admired Aurelia's.

Whenever they would pass one another, Azazel would get that weird cringe in his body, drawing his breath away. Aurelia was the most beautiful creature he had seen, and although he remembered Jahzara and saw Anastasia on the regular, his mind was not the same as before. Moments would rise so that when he glanced at Aurelia, he would actually think about Jahzara, but only to a certain extent. Aurelia was tempting, but he knew he must stay away from her.

Aurelia stood with nice, light brown hair and a body that made Azazel want to risk everything. Her complexion worked well with the sun, exposing her aura. Her walk really caught his attention, so he made sure to always watch whenever she passed by.

Although her physical nature was more than enough for him, Azazel also loved how honest she was as a person. By nature, she had a good heart; Azazel saw her goodness in how she waited for a husband. "*God* will bless me with one," she said in a conversation Azazel had tuned into one time.

To get into her thoughts, Azazel tried to impress her by doing little things; he was *God*, but the then *beings* didn't understand the range of his powers. He couldn't use supernatural strength to impress her, so he had to show the softer side of himself and display sincere emotion, or at least make it appear that it was sincere.

Upon arriving on *Earth*, in the center of a town, a group of children approached Azazel. This frequently happened because he looked different from any other *being*. For one, he wore a scar — rare for *beings* — plus his wings and body displayed a certain originality about him. He was a natural amusement, and he enjoyed the attention; he honestly loved his role serving these *beings*.

"Azazel, can we go for a ride?" asks one brave skinny child.

"I wish I had wings so that I could do anything I wanted," says another.

"If you could do anything you wanted, then we'd all be in trouble," says a little girl in the back of the pack.

"Don't say that; nothing can destroy this *place*," says Azazel to the children's laughter.

The boy looks around and then says, "I will destroy nothing; I just wish that I could fly and sit on a cloud."

"Clouds are not that comfortable — they only look comfortable. You can fall asleep, but then in the next moment, you fall to the ground because you're too heavy," Azazel says.

The children laugh amongst themselves and look up at Azazel.

"Why should a cloud drop me if I fall asleep on it when it was stable before I fell asleep?" asks the first skinny boy.

"That is a very good question," says Azazel. "Just because you are thinner than the hair on your head and lighter than the wind, it doesn't mean that you should fall."

"Then what is the cloud's problem?" says another little girl.

"Maybe the clouds are trying to tell you something; do they not move into images when you look at them sometimes?"

As he says this, Azazel looks over his shoulder to find Aurelia coming out of a shop and watching his interaction with intrigue.

"Maybe you are not meant to sit on clouds. Maybe you are to create an image with your life, just as the clouds do."

"Well, that's no fun," moans a child.

"Still want to sit on a cloud?" asks Azazel.

"No," the whole group says in disappointment.

"I'm never on clouds; you never see me relaxing on one because I know that they will kick me off to give me a lesson," Azazel says to the disappointed faces.

"They are like parents then," says the girl in the back.

"Since when did parents become bad?" Azazel questions.

"Since the beginning of time," says a little boy.

Immediately, Azazel thought of his father, and this conjured up more memories. He tried to imagine how life would be if his father had not let pride interfere with his position.

Snapping out of his thoughts, Azazel says, "You know what else parents are good for?" The children look around at one another. "Protection," Azazel says, turning the ground they are standing on into a surface of snakes.

All the children ran away, screaming but with smiles on their faces, and as they ran, the ground turned back to normal. Azazel stood, watching and smiling at how silly they looked running away.

"That wasn't nice," says a voice behind him. "Although it was quite entertaining; you do have a way with children."

"They are just like us," he says, turning to the speaker and freezing in his speech.

Aurelia was in front of him. The moment they caught each other's eyes, his breath began to subside again. Through mumbles, he finally utters, "Their later development begins now."

"I don't think the clouds are parental figures as much as you are, in your own way; you enforce your own law. Why would you tell children clouds are lessons? That makes no sense. You will shatter how they see you."

"I may be who I am to everyone else, but I'm no different. I would give it all up if I had to," Azazel says confidently.

"And why would you do that? Who or what would you give it up for?"

"I would give it up for a different experience, for a different life. I would give it up because I've already lived this life and know what it is and what it is not."

"So, you would be more than happy to live in the ground as a worm?"

"If it's interesting to me, why not?"

After a moment of silence, Aurelia finally says, "So you are unhappy?"

"I..." Azazel begins, but then pauses. "I don't know," he finally says. "Lately, I've been feeling different, and I don't know why."

"I'm sorry that you've been feeling this way, but don't use it as motivation to frighten the little ones," she smiles.

"I apologize," Azazel says, flashing his teeth. "I should know better than to pervert the minds of the little ones through lies about clouds."

"You are something else," she says admirably. "Your wings are beautiful — may I touch them?"

"You...," he says.

Before he could finish his sentence, her fingertips massaged his feathers.

"They're amazing; how do you live with them? They must get in the way."

"You get used to it. You're carrying food," he says, sensing a need to shift the conversation's direction. "A celebration? I also see wine."

"Yes, a dinner," she says, answering his question. "It is my mother's birthday, and we are celebrating."

"Excellent," he says.

"It's difficult to stop her from walking out that door and doing the shopping herself. She is a strong woman when you try to stop her from doing something she already has her mind set on."

"Thank goodness you lived through your near-death experience to do this for her," teases Azazel.

"You laugh now, but if you had to see her, you would know."

"Then why not invite me?" he quickly says.

"Look at you, inviting yourself," she says, smirking.

"Well, I am a strong woman, so to stop my intentions once my mind is set on something would be devastating."

"You are quite a manly woman," she says, laughing.

"I would love to prove how manly," Azazel says.

The two stand silent for a moment.

"You are something," she says, breaking the silence. "Then I formally invite you to my home tonight."

"Your mother will love you for your fine choice of invitation."

"You are interesting, but it's what is beneath the surface that I would like to crawl in to. And," she says seductively, "if you like the way I walk, then let me know so that I can walk for you." Azazel then watched as she turned around and walked away.

Azazel immediately throws on a devilish grin, but then it begins to fade as he remembers his office. He is to lead the *people* to what was right in deed, in thought, in behavior, and in act, refraining from improperly handling them.

Leaving the area and walking around various streets, he meditates on two choices: he could go to the party and show Aurelia who he truly is, or he could fight his urges and fulfill his responsibility. Of course, it was just a party, but with celebration comes the feeling to simply let go.

A Return To Form

Azazel battled many thoughts, but he finally decided to attend Aurelia's mother's birthday party. He appeared at the doorstep of temptation dressed as well as he knew how to. Before he could even knock, Aurelia opened the door. The love and laughter of the room was so loud that knocking didn't really seem to make much sense when he later thought about it.

"An *angel* who is late; imagine if all *angels* were this way."

"I'm no *angel*; that's my excuse," he says.

"Some excuse," she responds. " Come in, but as a warning, I told my mother about you coming."

"Yes, the woman of the night. Let me see who almost killed you for wanting to surprise her."

"This will be something to see," she says, taking a deep breath.

"Where is my daughter?" a voice yells from inside the house.

"Enter at your own risk," says Aurelia to Azazel. "I am here, Mother, and with your surprise guest."

Immediately, everyone turns around and looks toward the door. They smile once seeing Azazel, and then through the crowd appears her mother. She shoves people left and right, grabs many necks and throws many heads, just to see Azazel up close. She flies past her daughter to give him a very large and welcoming hug.

"It is a blessing to see one of God's dearest."

"Thank you," Azazel says as he tries to catch his breath from the hug. "You are a strong woman," he says.

"Strong," she says. "I am stronger than I was a year ago."

"Scary," Azazel says.

He looked at this woman of six hundred and seventeen years and saw no difference from that of a thirty-five-year-old. In this age of *life*, these *people* mature in ways where their true age doesn't show. In this realm, the aging process is slowed, making the *beings* look and feel younger than they actually are.

"What a nice, handsome thing he is, isn't he, Aurelia? I think you two should get together; get me some grandchildren."

"We'll see about that, mother," says Aurelia hesitantly.

"My daughter would rip you apart, Mr. Azazel, if you give her a chance."

"Mother!" Aurelia says out of embarrassment.

"I have no angelic grandchildren."

"That's a shame," Azazel says.

"You two should never meet again," Aurelia says, exasperated.

"Hush up, child; this young thing has needs too. So what if he is whatever he is. Is not the image of a *man* standing here?"

"Is it not?" Azazel echoes, looking in her daughter direction.

"Maybe something more devious," says Aurelia.

"This smart-mouthed girl has never seen what's been in front of her face. Men falling at her feet, so what does she do? Nothing. And why?"

"Mother!" Aurelia cautions.

"Why?" asks Azazel.

"Because she's stupid is why," replies her mother.

"No more wine for you tonight," says Aurelia.

"Will someone bring wine for me and make it quick!" yells Azazel.

"I am going to enjoy myself because this is a glorious day, and my God has allowed me to celebrate it on many occasions. This bottle of wine is his life-saving gift."

"You have a tremendous spirit," says Azazel to her mother.

"I will go now," says Aurelia's mother. "If I pass out from the celebration, please, drink for me."

"Will do," says Azazel.

"Go on now," implores Aurelia.

"I now see what you mean," Azazel says once her mother leaves the two of them alone.

"Let's go outside and speak; it's too loud in here," she says.

As the two walk outside, Aurelia takes Azazel's hand.

"I can't believe you yelled for more wine," she says.

"Your mother is entertaining."

"It's nice seeing you here; I thought you weren't going to show because you were so late."

"I just figured that if your mother is who you say she is, then a celebration is never over. Even when it's over, it's still happening."

"You are right with that one," she says, sighing.

"And your mother likes me; any earlier and I would not have seen the real her. The way she came at me was frightening, but it was honest."

"That is my mother — honest, even when sober. You look good, by the way," she added.

"Well, I have to."

"And why is that?"

"Because I made a promise to you; this is who I am."

"I like it because it looks like you, and so I must re-introduce myself."

"Comedy does not run in the family, I see."

"You want to talk comedy, what's comical is how you got dressed up and never even spoke to more than two people or even enjoyed the party. You show up looking nice when you could have just come as you. You did all this to impress me; I see how your eyes move up and down when you see me."

Azazel looks at the ground in silence as she speaks. He flashes a grin every time she hits on something right.

"It's a beautiful night, isn't it?" Azazel says, breaking his silence and shame.

"Don't change the subject — I know the thoughts you have about me, because I have them too about you."

Azazel instantly moves his eyes from the sky to her face.

"I don't care that you are *God*," she continues, "because I know that there is more to you. You put on a show, but when no one is around, your actions are natural and endearing."

"You are something else, Aurelia."

"You are too, which is why I want to take care of you. And I didn't just decide this; I've been going back and forth on this until I've drawn myself to tears. You've tried for my attention when all you had to do was be yourself. Naturally, you are good at heart, Azazel — I just wish you would see it."

Azazel, looking into her eyes, sees her passion displayed. In his heart, he knows that he only wants her for unjust pleasures and cares nothing about her. He then runs through his duty to the *people* once more, and once again thinks about how this situation unfolded. He immediately feels upset with himself for even wanting to betray Heaven and ultimately committing a great injustice against himself. Through his frustration, he wills to now think before he acts.

"I appreciate all that you have said, and I love your demeanor, but I cannot do with you as I please. I want you, but in a selfish way, and I must let you know."

Aurelia smiles.

"It's fine, Azazel; I understand. I don't want you to get into any trouble or get more lost with your thoughts than you already are."

"Thank you."

"It will be fun to imagine what could have been, don't you think?" she mused.

"I disagree; I think its torture to think about it. Get back to your mother; I bet she needs you."

"Will do, Azazel."

Azazel then flew to Heaven. Before he could lie down on his bed and rest on his pillow, Anastasia enters into his room.

"What you did just now was very commendable."

"Do I not have a private moment to myself around here?"

"We all know, Azazel; it's Heaven."

"Yes, that's right, how could I forget?" he sighs.

"You're really helping yourself."

"I did nothing," he says disappointingly.

"You did more than you think; you wrestled with your self."

"Please," he says, turning away from her, "don't remind me."

"Why are you acting like this?" she questions.

"Nothing that I thought or felt was wrong, you know, when you think about it. I had true feelings for another, but this person just happened to be one of the *Select*. And to make matters worse, I found out, from her own mouth, that she was willing to completely give me her self."

Anastasia's demeanor began to fill with a jealousy that she quickly struggled to tame. Calmly, she says, "You too are part of a member of the *Chosen* and *Select*; you're the Chosen One, Azazel. You don't seem to understand the giant leap you just took."

"Giant leap?" he sits up and looks at her. "What giant leap? You speak as though the world would crumble if I had done any *thing* with this woman. You speak as though my life belongs to a threshold of pain that can only be released through acts of injustice. You speak as if a victory has been won, but there is no victory; it's just me, Anastasia."

"And little by little, you are discovering you."

"Why are you acting so strange? This could have happened to any *one*."

"And yet, it didn't. You're coming into yourself, and we are all proud. You have this position and power for a reason, Azazel."

After staring long and confused into her eyes, Azazel finally rambles, "I need to be alone."

"Thank you," Anastasia says before leaving him.

~ ~ ~

In Heaven, the Council discusses Azazel's progression over the past six hundred years.

"He shows improvement."

"He is, and yet, I wonder if it is all an act."

"If it is an act, then deceiving himself only forces negativity upon his destiny."

"I commend him. He proves that he deserves every blessing given to him."

"Yes, he is worthy, but does he truly deserve our blessing? Will his past resurface and drag him into the depths from which it came?"

"He will fight and struggle because of his mind."

"Poor soul."

"Poor soul indeed," mourns one.

"The courage it takes for one to admit cowardice is one that deserves a new beginning for recognition."

"He will show his true colors eventually."

"His heart is stronger than the wings of a butterfly, and yet, his mind deceives his soul into believing the imagery it depicts."

"He will be fine."

"He will rise from his past ashes to carry a new form."

"He's still weak."

"Although minuscule, the essence of this victory is one that does not destroy his effort to cure himself. He does, in fact, desire purity."

"He has been battling rightness since birth, yet he manages to ignore his true being. Yes, he is finding the success that he sought, but there is more to come."

"There are three hundred more years until those from the Underuniverse are released," warns one.

"And also to be released at that time is Lucifer," states another.

"His true test of success is bound to clash with him during this time."

"He did not fall victim to the female; he is learning."

"He did fall victim."

"He was a victim in the sense of thought, but not in the sense of action. He resisted his heart to listen with his mind. Although a triumphant victory, he must battle himself still."

"Preparations must be made, and accordingly."

~ ~ ~

During the next four hundred years, Azazel would successfully lead this *people*. He would lead this host through the Gates of Heaven and right to its throne.

Once Azazel standing in front of the throne with this *people*, he was given the memory and knowledge of his "being." It was through this act that Azazel could now understand that he could use *life's* elements to do as he wished. His other strengths were still hidden, and because of this, his development was designed to blossom. Once the ceremony for the new *beings* had commenced, Azazel was given another command: to go back down to *Earth* and watch over the *beings* that once lived within the Underuniverse. This would be his greatest test yet.

"You are to be the one who leads this next host to my intention," *God* said to Azazel. "These are the worst *creatures*; you must not succumb to their habits and fail to let them the *Just* character."

"Yes, Father."

"There is hope within every being that I have given breath to. They may not see it, so it is you who must show them. They will roam *Earth* and reproduce just as the first host did. Through you, they should know decency."

"I have not failed you yet, my Lord; I will do this."

"You will be greatly rewarded upon your success; bring them home to me."

"They are already yours, Father; I will show them that."

Azazel left Heaven immediately and flew back down to *Earth*. He was the only one down there, but not for long. Upon the release of imprisoned *beings*, they all surfaced to one side and watched Azazel from the other.

The Amalgamate were finally reunited and Lucifer stood before his son once again. Now, it was those *beings* of the Underuniverse on one side and Azazel looking on from the other; obvious tension arose. After a long pause, Lucifer finally breaks the awkward silence.

"It feels good to be free!" he yells. "It is now the way it should be. My people, look before you and see the true appearance of a coward, but do not hate at him. I have anticipated this moment because I knew it would happen and because I did, there are no hard feelings. Maybe there is anger, a lust to kill the weak seed I have delivered, and yet, I think of how powerful and intelligent he is. Come to me, my son," he says, with arms wide open. "Welcome home."

Through Lucifer's speech, Azazel stood confused. He walks toward his real father, and as soon as he reaches Lucifer, he says, "What are you talking about?"

"Does he not remember?" Lucifer boasts.

"I am no coward, and what you see before you, Lucifer, is a Sovereign."

"A Sovereign? I see no Sovereign; all I see is a *being* deceived by God."

"Deceived?" Azazel questioned.

"Wait a minute," Lucifer mumbles. "Look into my eyes," he says as he draws closer to Azazel's face. "You have no memory — disgraceful!"

"What do you mean? I remember everything. There is nothing that has slipped my mind."

"How did you do it?" Lucifer says, gritting his teeth. "Where did you go after you left me?"

"My home is with *God*."

"Your home is with me!" yells Lucifer. "And your whore, you left with her?"

At that moment, Leviathan looks at Apep, and while Apep looks at Jahzara, who has her head down.

"I should kill both of you right now," Lucifer says.

"Leave him," Jahzara calls from within the crowd.

"You stand where you are," Apep whispered to her, but she sprang past her father and out into the open.

"He has done nothing wrong!" she continues.

"Yes, please, join your prince," says Lucifer.

"Prince?" says Azazel.

"You have a lot to catch up on, son; I suggest you do so before we attack Heaven once again."

"I will kill you all before you step foot in front of those gates," Azazel barks.

"Jahzara, your *man* appears to need you. You can't and will not stop us. Regain what has been lost from you, and quickly," advises Lucifer. "We will go and live in this land, but only to destroy it; be wise, Azazel."

Every *being* then flew into the area and began to settle, leaving Azazel and Jahzara time to talk.

"It has been a long time, Jahzara," began Azazel.

"We were forbidden to reach this land until one thousand years had passed. If there were no barriers, I would have seen you sooner."

Jahzara then sunk her head into his chest as they stood silently. In a rush, a flood of memories came back to Azazel. He pushed her off and began to look at her as if she were a familiar stranger.

"My woman..." he says.

"Yes," she replies, as their bodies meet again.

"I have to lead all of you to an *understanding*."

"That's not going to be easy," she says.

"I remember our past, but I don't remember anything my father said."

"Maybe through touch you will remember?" Jahzara offered.

"Maybe I wanted to remember you so bad that it actually happened."

"Whatever it was, you need to remember because there will be another war."

"Another war?"

"There was a battle — *Armageddon*; you were there. Things turned out the way they were supposed to, and here we are."

"I feel worthless because I can't remember."

"It's not your fault. I told you to do what was best for you, whatever that may be, and you did it."

"I remember you saying that," Azazel says. "What was best for me?"

"I don't know."

"I feel lied to; I need to feel complete. I'm too content; there has to be a reason why I keep having these dreams and visions of things that I know nothing about. My memory goes beyond what I can imagine, and I need to know what lies beneath this *world*."

"So, you remember nothing about your past with your father, or anything else?"

"Nothing," Azazel confirmed.

"And you remember me and the life we had?"

"I always remembered you; there was just something stopping me from feeling any emotion. Seeing you, hearing you, touching you, it has all helped in bringing everything back to me."

"Do you know about your abilities?"

"My otherworldly strengths?"

"That's not all there is; you're stronger than that, Azazel."

"What do you mean?" he questions.

Just as he finished asking the question, his memory returned to him in full.

"What did they do to you?" asks Jahzara.

"Nothing," he quickly says.

"They have lied to you; you need to be with me. You need to be with us, with people who understand you."

"I can't just go with you; every *one* of you needs to reach an *understanding*. If no one does, at least I hope that you accept my God so that we can be at peace together."

"It will not be that easy for me; I can't," she explained.

"You know, I wanted to hurt and kill all of the *Select*, including *beings*, but I didn't. I should have seen this side of mine. The fire I breathe out in frustration was a sign of who I am. I was just too brainwashed to believe it."

"You have done what was best for you, Azazel, but I am chained to the *law* of my father. If I ever spoke a phrase other than, 'Praise the Amalgamate,' my father would kill me."

"I will free you, somehow," he promises.

"First, you need to realize the conspiracy. Your *God* is no good; he's unfair and unreal, and you need to know where your heart lies. And even more importantly, you have to remember beyond what you know so that you can stop this war."

"I figured you would want me fighting alongside my father."

"Lucifer is your father, but you control your own fate. Fighting is inevitable, but if you do fight, I want you fighting for no *one* but for yourself."

"You are still a wonder to me; how could I ever forget what we had?"

"You cannot forget what was stolen."

After a brief moment of silence, Azazel suggests, "Go to your father; you are in enough trouble for standing up for me."

The two separate. Jahzara goes out in search of her father, and Azazel takes off in Heaven's direction, but he has other plans.

Azazel goes to the Amalgamate and asks for privacy with his father. He figured that maybe if he were close enough to Lucifer, somehow, energy would release to rejuvenate his memory. Although he didn't want to be next to or even see his father, he had to suck it up and hope something would spark his memory.

"It is a surprise to see you," Lucifer greeted.

"I've come to learn about my history."

"It is a shame you have given up your memory."

"Given up?" Azazel questioned.

"You may fool everyone here, but I know what really happened. I do not know why you would want to erase your memory, but the only way it would happen is through your consent."

"I don't know why I would want something like that, either," he said.

Lucifer looked his son up and down.

"You have grown in strength; I can feel it."

"I can't tell."

"Well, I can, and you will be an even greater force alongside the Amalgamate," said Lucifer.

"What do you mean?"

"You were to fight next to the Amalgamate in *Armageddon* because your power, strength, and intellect were far greater than any. Now you are even stronger, and we will get our victory."

After hearing about the battle once again, this time from Lucifer's lips, Azazel's vision went blurry, and he dropped to one knee.

"Pick up yourself and stop acting *human*," barks Lucifer.

Azazel's heart began to race as the battle of Armageddon came back to him. He remembered how he felt when going into war; he remembered going into war and then falling back and seeing his comrades perish as they fell through to the Underuniverse. Every emotion fell back into place, and that dysfunctional puzzle met its final piece. His anger boiled within him.

"I remember now," he said.

"Get up and talk," said his father.

"I remember it all now, father," Azazel said, as if asking for forgiveness.

Along with this discovery came the treasure of his loyalty. Once again, Azazel felt as though he would have to choose between two worlds, and so, once again, he was at a crossroads. The feeling of betraying his father came back to him, and he wanted to make up for it.

"Light dawns on Marblehead," Lucifer said, laughing. "Where do you stand?"

"With you," Azazel said firmly. "I will not fail you again."

The smile Lucifer gave Azazel shook the grounds of Heaven and brought tears to *God's* eyes. Azazel had not remembered everything, but through his actions, he proved that he was not fit for the newness he sought.

From Whence He Came

For the next five hundred years, Azazel would try to help the *beings* of the Underuniverse understand their error against Heaven, but he would fail. It was also during this time that he and Jahzara would re-discover discover their relationship. She wanted to have a child with Azazel, but he wanted no part of it. He didn't want any one else passing through a living experience.

Azazel spent his time on *Earth*, wasting it away with members of the Underuniverse. He believed that Heaven was his natural home, but he was starting to see differently. He spent five hundred years violating his divine office. Azazel made up his mind that he would fight side by side with his father and bring justice to his people. Although Jahzara disagreed with him, she couldn't say anything because she too was just as confused as he was. Once again losing himself to his thoughts, he brought sadness to those who had faith in him.

By the six hundredth year, plots to invade Heaven were beginning to be taken seriously. The leadership of the Underuniverse five hundred years strategizing in *Earth's* newly developing realm, and then it became time for war.

"It is the sixth hundred year, and I believe we are ready," says Lucifer to his army. "We have been living here for too long, and have grown comfortable, when we should have been claiming the realm."

"My nation," added Leviathon, "now is the moment we take all and keep it, and standing at the right of the Amalgamate, Azazel."

"Hail to the prince of all!" says Belial, the crowd repeating his ballad.

Azazel makes his way through the crowd, holding Jahzara's hand. Those in Heaven that watched observe the scene in awe.

"I have been blind," says Azazel. "I do not know what happened to me, but I will make this right. It is I, the Amalgamate, and my wife to be," he says, bringing Jahzara close to his chest, "who will do what the prophecy has spoken of. My brothers and sisters, this is why I was born."

With these final words, and a kiss from Jahzara to seal it, the crowd goes wild; a charge towards the heavenly Estate ensues.

"My God, why do we not make a move of defense?" says Michael.

"At ease," says *God*. "Although they are strong, their hearts weaken as they near."

Upon entering the *Kingdom*, the large gates open to a surge of light, which sent all but a few of them back to *Earth* and to their deaths. Azazel and Jahzara remain, along with Lucifer, Leviathon, and a few members of their army. They destroy a good amount of *beings* and cause havoc to the kingdom before they reach their intended destination.

"That's right," says Lucifer to Azazel. "This is how it should be."

Azazel fought his own set of *beings* and then caught Anastasia's eyes, who stood cornered and awaiting his wrath. The two stare at one another so long that Azazel's defense weakens.

"What are you doing?!" yells Jahzara, who sees what is happening from a distance. But Azazel became weak. His heart bled tears of confusion within his veins that sent him to his knees.

Anastasia runs over to him, and he pulls her in. With his head on her stomach and his arms wrapped around her, he senses something within her body that sent electricity through his. Jahzara then burns the twenty angels around her and then flies over to Azazel, slamming Anastasia to the floor.

"I'm almost there!" yells Lucifer. "He is not far!"

"What are you doing to him?" says Jahzara to Anastasia.

"You wish that he loved you as he loves me," Anastasia barks back.

The two exchange powerful attacks, but neither fall. Anastasia, stomping as hard as she can with one foot, causes four stone walls to appear around Jahzara, but Jahzara breaks them down and hails a hard rain of fire on Anastasia. Anastasia merely catches the fire and sends it back to Jahzara. No matter how hard they try, they can't seem to annihilate one another. Azazel, watching these two women fight over him, rests on the ground; remorse wasn't the word to describe how he felt.

"Finally!" Lucifer yells as he rushes towards the bright light containing Heaven's chief Sovereign.

Everything froze when Lucifer said this. *God* stepped out from the wall containing his essence and walked down his throne with his right palm facing out. He walks up to Lucifer and touches his forehead; Lucifer is immediately engulfed in flames. Lucifer's remain are taken and stored.

Heaven's chief Sovereign then travels to Azazel, touching his heart to erase his memory, and then throws him down to *Earth*.

"I love you," he says as Azazel's body floats down and through Heaven's surface.

He did the same to Jahzara, but once she reached *Earth*, she continued down through *Earth* and into the Underuniverse. Every other contrary force within the Estate is then destroyed. Once again, he fades into the wall of his brilliance and takes his throne. Now seated, time revives.

Once everything unfroze and the present began to move again, the host stands in confusion about what had happened. They look around and see not one *enemy* in sight. After a time of observation, Heaven's Council enters into the room of the divine wall to discuss Azazel; Anastasia was within listening distance.

"Anastasia, are you going to speak or just listen?" says one.

"I mean no harm," she replies.

"We know you don't, but we know what you will do."

"I must see him," she says.

"Why does your love for him run so deep?"

"Because my hate for his sorrow runs deeper than anything else."

"He is not who you think he is."

"I know this, but I have faith in him."

"Faith is it?"

"Yes," she says confidently.

"Faith in what?"

"I don't know."

"Think on my question until we speak again," suggests another member of the Council.

"Thank you."

"Go down to your love and try to talk sense into him."

"I will try," she says.

~ ~ ~

On *Earth*, Azazel wakes from his unconscious state and begins to search for answers about where he is and how he got there. With no recollection of the battle that took place, he sees his environment and thinks about a reason for him being there. *God* had taken his memory once again but had also given him knowledge of his powers. He walks and studies this world to balance his thoughts, but he can't piece anything together without the help of forced action.

"The days are long, and the nights even longer. The sun has darkened, while the moon has turned blood-red. There are no stars, for they fell centuries ago. This search feels like forever. The air is both hot and cold, but it is not warm. The air feels like all heat is trapped behind the darkness of the sun, but then the heat escapes and brushes over my skin like a tease," he says, thinking to himself.

"I do not know how long I have been here in this empty realm. I have no memory whatsoever, but what memories do remain are flashbacks of what must have meant something to me. Looking around, I see nothing but a flat, dry, and rough looking land. The sky looks angry and the weather feels aggravated; something makes me feel like I am the cause of it all," he continues.

"*Armageddon* took place not too long ago. Its memory is so fresh that time seems to be no issue. I remember is leaving both Heaven and the Underuniverse, but I can't quite remember what I was doing in Heaven in the first place; I despise that place, along with its chief Sovereign. And although I question my belonging in Heaven, I cannot remember why I fled to the Underuniverse. I have vague memories of both worlds, but I can't seem to piece it all together."

The sight of Anastasia in the distance interrupts his thoughts. The two walk toward one another as if they had been separated for millennia.

"You're alive," says Anastasia, touching his face.

"Of course I am, why wouldn't I be? I haven't been gone for that long — or maybe I have."

"Don't you remember?"

"Of course I do; *Armageddon*? I was there; it's a bit unclear, but I know I took on a false *form*."

"No," she retorts. "There was another battle after *Armageddon*. You don't remember?"

"I don't know. Why was there another war?"

"He must have taken your memory again."

"Who did what?" says Azazel.

"Come back, Anastasia," says a voice from above.

"Why do you bother with that tiresome *Being*?" asks Azazel.

"I deal with him for you."

Just then, Azazel's eyes became white as Anastasia's slowly filled with tears.

"Let him be," says the voice.

"Stop hurting him!" she yells.

"He does not need to know anything. I will not ask for your presence again; remember, this is what he wanted."

Anastasia knew what was happening: *God* was erasing her presence from Azazel's memory.

"I do it all for you," she mumbls to Azazel's frozen face. "I do it for you, and for our family."

Anastasia's figure then fades, causing Azazel to return to the present. "Come back!" he yells, curious about the diminishing female figure before him, but it was too late. He wasn't sure if what he saw was real, but something told him that it was.

Azazel continued to walk and to attempt to piece together what had just happened. Was he having a vision, a dream, or was he just making things up? But his thoughts were interrupted by new thoughts that he could not understand. A rush of memories from the Underuniverse came to him, and so he gave it his undivided attention to them.

"When I do think back on the Underuniverse," he says to himself, "all I have are scenes that skip, but the more I think about them, the more things start to become clearer. I have these flashbacks of me as someone in command, of someone in high rank; this must mean something.

"Could I be *King*? It doesn't make sense. One scene replaying constantly is one of my disappearance or my last night in the Underuniverse; I keep trying to make sense of it. It always starts with me in a room and pacing nervously. Then, out of nowhere, one of my soldiers or commanders — someone who is to be an advisor to me — interrupts me. His presence does not stop my pacing, but we do have a conversation."

~ ~ ~

"My lord," he says, stop this at once; we need you as levelheaded as can be."

"Tell me what I should do," I respond.

"We must collect ourselves and free him."

"What am I to do now? I must run this universe on my own, this universe of weak-hearted *beings* that were defeated by Heaven?"

Sight

The session with Azazel now takes place in a setting most fitting. A wise dragon intends on taking his past and present and using both to hopefully shape his future. Although conscious at their first meeting, Azazel has been kept in an unconscious state for some time.

"Let your body feed on itself," says Bune before enclosing Azazel within an amniotic sac. "Relax, breathe, and rehabilitate," he continues.

Bune then carries Azazel, now balled up in amniotic fluid, from Olympus to the center of the cosmos, where the two are to be situated for a period of time. Bune, watching over him, regularly releases dirty fluid rising within the sac. Doing this allows the sac to refill itself with a clean liquid; hereafter fresh fluid consumes the body and helps to nourish all of its cells.

Azazel's sac lay in the cosmos, but it was connected to *Earth*, Olympus, the *realm* dearest to him, the Underuniverse, and Heaven. Azazel took what he needed from his sources of life; the dirty fluid meant his mind underwent and accepted its stage of purification. That fluid needed to be released so that the stage of purification could continue uninterrupted.

To speak first with Azazel, Bune recruited the lovely Guanyin — the goddess of mercy. She was the one who heard the cries of those afflicted with all sorts of pain and vowed to never rest until they were alleviated. This was a no-brainer for Bune because there were none more currently afflicted than Azazel. Guanyin, after the amniotic sac's time of use elapsed, would speak with Azazel and finally hear him. Never had she been able to make contact with him, so she too anticipated what this meeting would bring.

"So, he rests in a sack of his own fluid?" asks Guanyin upon her arrival.

"Yes, of course," Bune says quickly. "How else is one to purge the character of infection? But I do drain the unclean liquid. I allow the body to marinate in filth for only a short time before I release the negative water and allow the process to quickly begin again."

Through a grunt of disgusted curiosity, she says, "His body is connected to different Universes; how can one purify ones self if one is still connected? Isn't this experience to be one of solitude, of disconnection for connection?"

"And solitude it is," agrees Bune, "but is there such a thing as pure purity? It appears that all other *beings* have adapted to the perfection of impurity. Speaking of impurity, it is necessary to take a center position on what can connect one to levels of solitude. To rid himself of what he struggles with, of what haunts him, he must be in sync with every *home* he acknowledges, and in every way. I believe this to be true, and with more filthy fluid I have to release, it only means that he is helping himself."

She moved her eyes from Azazel's naked floating body up to Bune. Squinting and thinking about what she had just heard, she says, "Interesting."

"Why, of course," says Bune.

"When will he break through to consciousness?" she asks.

"I anticipate it will be soon," he says, inspecting the sac. "Some cracks lay on the surface, so he should fall out of the sac at any moment."

As Azazel lay lifelessly in his sac, his mind is all too alive, taking him through a dream-like journey that felt too real. He is stationed in an open land and focused on the moon, and although he sees no one, he is not alone.

The light from the blood-red moon shone on the river in front of him, portraying his reflection. The water turned to blood as he cut his palm and let it sit in the river. As he took his hand out of the river, the deep wound in his palm began to heal, but the river remained stained with his regret.

The waves his middle finger made as he dragged it through the water only distorted his reflection into what he wished it were. He would disturb the water until his reflection disappeared, but when it would return, it would aggravate his sorrow.

Behind him appears a female figure that makes him smile, causing him to forget all that troubles him. The wind worked perfectly with her hair, as did his passion for her. Still kneeling by the river, he watches her reflection behind him through the water. The trees then blow in the distance and then come to a sudden stop, as though nature cares to speak with him. Looking at his palm, he wonders why there are no lines in it, and why he feels a loss when noticing the female has disappeared.

As the trees again begin to move with the wind, he feels a breeze brushing through his hair, moving his thoughts. As he watches the river, he puts his hand over the water to slow the current. The beauty in watching the water move at a slow pace was not that it moved slowly, but that every shine, curve, and drop appealed to the eye, and so much so that it was hypnotizing. It was as though the wind told him to slow down and watch what was never seen, and so he did.

The female figure returns and touches his shoulder, causing the river to flow normally. Because she knew him, she knew he would be here, , and because she did, she felt his remorse.

His response to her touch wasn't immediate; he just sat and watched the river. As the winds picked up, so did the current, which drew concern. Further down, he saw that the blood-filled river split into three directions. He didn't know where those directions went, but he prayed that all the water flowed into a center path. Looking closer, he sees bright *beings*, each guarding a path, but they appear to be in conflict with one another.

Each *being* wants all the water to flow into their path, and because they fight, the river moves down all three paths. Suddenly, the moon comes down from the sky and floats in front of Azazel's face. It drops into the water, turning the river into solid crystal and breaking it apart into pieces. The shattered pieces ascended into the sky and take position as stars. Once this is complete, the water refills and once again begins to flow.

The female figure behind him still lingers, and her touch still did not draw his attention. He is captivated by the river and continues to run his hand through it. The stars of shattered crystal then begin to fall from the sky and impale his body. He screams out in pain, but after the event is over, his body heals itself.

He notices the *beings* quarreling so badly that they leave their positions. As the river flows freely, he looks to the sky in happiness and sees two male *beings* with golden wings and strong demeanors looking down at him. They speak to him, but he cannot understand them, and so he merely watches with a smile. When he turns around, he sees the beautiful face of the female figure, and the two begin speaking.

While no sound came from their mouths, she spoke highly of his good looks and admired his bravery. She is a wonderful sight to see, and she too knows that his beauty is one that deserves no words. The two take hold of one another and share a passionate kiss. Soon enough, they connect on the riverside and share an experience they believed they'd been missing. Their long-lost voids were now filled, and whether he knew it or not, it was real.

The two sat by the river and observed their reflections. No longer did they have an image, but as they looked deeper into the river, they saw the two male *beings* behind them. They were gone through no physical disturbances of the water, and this made them smile because their disappearance had been natural, but what worried them was that their immortality had no chance against their reflection's fate. And once again, he was given the impression that whether he knew it or not, it was real.

Outside of his mind, Bune and Guanyin continue to discuss Azazel and the strangeness of his mind.

"I've never been able to hear or feel his anxiety," says Guanyin.

"You wouldn't," says Bune looking at Azazel. "He doesn't think, nor does he feel. Well, he does, but he does not do it sincerely. For one to feel, one must go through appropriate motions or stages; this is to comprehend how to trigger to desired emotion. Azazel has continuously played with his mind, resulting in him not being able to piece together any answers. But with me, he will get those answers."

"Are you sure?" she asks.

"I have faith," Bune says with a touch of suspicion.

"The wise Bune doubts?" teases Guanyin.

"It's not doubt, but he has a mind; a certain demeanor has not allowed me to reach him. Usually, I am in-tune with my subjects; I know them. I know him too, but he's different."

"And?"

"And I believe he will do just fine," he says confidently.

Floating over and touching the sac, Guanyin says, "It's so cold; I would have expected it to be at least warm."

Removing her hand and looking even closer, the cracks in the sac release a chilled steam that made Guanyin look on in wonder.

"Like I said; he's different," says Bune.

Soon after Guanyin released her hand, Azazel was released from the sac. While Bune and Guanyin watch intensely, he floats in the fetal position. Through the silence of the Cosmos, coughs and gasps for air are heard as Azazel tries to collect himself. In a panic, he stands up straight, covering himself.

"What is going on?!" he yells.

"Hello, Azazel. I am Guanyin."

"Get this woman away from me!" he shouts, looking around and further panicking. "Where are we?" he asks. "Wait, why are we in the Cosmos?"

"Calm down," says Bune. "I apologize."

"Apologize for this invasion of privacy? Watching me as I am naked?" he says, noticing the slime and throwing it off of his body. "What did you do to me?"

"I've come to speak with you," announces Guanyin. "I'm here to see how you are doing."

"How did I get here?"

"Be easy," Bune suggests.

"I don't remember anything at all," says Azazel.

"Clearly, you're confused," Guanyin reasons.

Azazel freezes, looking at Guanyin.

"Who is this woman, and what happened to me back at Olympus?" he says.

"If it helps, I am of neither sex," said Guanyin. "I can take the form of a female or a male; I do as I see fit."

Bune and Azazel look at one another and then focused their attention back on Guanyin.

Looking her up and down, Azazel says, "I've run into something like you before, but backwards," he pondered, scratching his head.

"I didn't quite know that," Bune says in a low tone.

"What's going on?!" Azazel yells once more.

"It would be best if we spoke privately," advises Guanyin.

"Or I can leave," says Azazel.

Bune then breathes out fire from each of his three heads and constructs a flame-barred cage around Azazel.

"Are you serious?" says Azazel sarcastically.

"Yes," says Bune. "While under my supervision, you do not have any of your powers. You are far too powerful and dangerous to be walking around freely. You will be given your strengths back once we are through. You are here to learn, not to leave."

"How is trapping me going to help?" he asks.

"I'm done with him," sighs Bune.

"Oh no, you get me out of here," says Azazel.

"Take him; do what you must with him, then bring him back to me."

"Of course," says Guanyin.

"You know this isn't right, right?" pleads Azazel. "You can't force someone to see something that isn't there."

Guanyin touches his cage, and then the two quickly travel to Olympus. The moment they arrive, the cage around Azazel is lifted, allowing him to roam free in curiosity. He and Guanyin have landed in Metis' and Zeus' room on the night Azazel is to be conceived.

A cloth appearing around his waist, "That's not Zeus," Azazel says, walking towards the portrayed image before him. "What is this?" he asks.

"How do you know that this isn't Zeus?" Guanyin asks.

Walking even closer to the hologram and waving his hand through their imaginary bodies and disrupting their frequencies, he says, "It isn't hard to forget the face of someone who hates you. This, this is an imposter. Just look at him — I've never seen Zeus display this much emotion."

"That doesn't mean he isn't a different person around his wife."

"He has many women; he would never have to use seduction like this."

"Do you know the story of your birth, Azazel?" asks Guanyin.

"What's wrong with her, why can't she see?" he questions upon seeing Metis' holographic form.

"Do you know anything about your birth, Azazel?" Guanyin repeats.

"No!" he fires back. "There's no story; there's nothing to know."

Azazel then froze, giving way to thought.

"What's wrong?" asks Guanyin. "This is your history; this is the night you were born. These two *beings*, Lucifer and Metis, this is who your parents are."

Watching Metis with intensity," I've never seen her before. I mean, I have, but not like this," he says, rubbing his chin. "It's hard to explain."

"This is what happened that night, and disregarding all you have heard and remember, you were not conceived in full hate. Your mother loved you dearly, even before you were born; you have a lot to be thankful for."

Guanyin and Azazel watch the interaction between his father and Metis. Azazel looks on with rage as he saw how his mother was taken advantage of. The scene of his parents making love replays, and then Lucifer reveals himself. Azazel sees and hears the words from his father's mouth, and finally, things begin to clear within his mind.

With his head down, he hears the cries of his mother after the night became silent. He thinks about how he pledged allegiance to Lucifer, how he opened his heart to his father, and the whole time he was being used. Azazel lifts his head and walks to his mother, who is lying in bed. He stands over her as she lay crying and tries to touch her, but his hand easily cuts through her image. Minutes later, Zeus would come in and demand answers as to why she cries.

"I just miss you, is all," she says.

"They said there was a commotion in here," Zeus says curiously.

"If my tears woke others, then I apologize; I must have let my thoughts get the best of me," she says frantically.

"Calm down," says Zeus. "It is you I come home to, not any other."

"I don't know if I should be as content with that as you would want me to be," she replies.

Azazel stands in the background and sees the life he is brought into. He wants to desperately make himself known and to do something, but he can't.

"Why would you show me this?" says Azazel.

"Because you need to know. You need to know the truth and I know this because I can feel you now."

"He knew he would be dealt with by God," says Azazel, returning to the hologram. "I shouldn't even be here. He only wanted me so that he could live free, so that he could take something that ultimately isn't even close to being his," he says, puzzling events together.

"But remember, your mother loved you dearly," says Guanyin.

"Not only did he rape my mother, but he also raped me."

"How do you feel?" asks Guanyin.

"I don't know," he says with a confused look on his face. With his head in his hands, he adds, "I shouldn't be here. Why would he think to do that? Is there no other way? Did the thinker finally stop thinking?"

"Do you feel any sense of forgiveness for your father?" she asks after a moment of silence.

"No, there is no forgiveness," he says. "There's really nothing going on inside of me. It makes no sense to ask why and how. The act is done. I don't want to be alive; I never did."

"What do you mean?" she asks.

Walking closer to her, he replies, "You saw the same thing I did; I wasn't even conceived. I was...I was forced into existence. Nothing should be forced to live."

"Then nothing would exist."

"Exactly," he strongly says. "There is no point. The point of life, or the supposed meaning of it, is to praise a Sovereign who refuses to act for the good of what should live."

"To understand, you would have to have his mind, Azazel. His mind is not like ours."

"Aren't we his creation?" he says. "Understand this," he continues, "when I was twelve millenniums, my father told me that, to hear *God* say that it made him sorry to know he made *man*, was a triumph. My father no longer cared about his life at that moment because it now became a duty to bring every mind into his way of thinking. And he had me, even at that age, ready to die for his philosophy. Both *God* and my father fall to the same weakness that created error: pride."

Guanyin felt Azazel's heart. He truly believed that he shouldn't be alive. And that saddened her.

Time had gone by before she spoke. Because she felt that Azazel needed that moment, she allowed him to have it. Looking into his eyes, she asks, "Where do you feel you belong?"

"Not here," he says.

"Be more specific," she probed.

"Not alive," he responded.

"Take my question seriously, Azazel," she says. "Now answer honestly."

"If I had to say, I belong to myself."

"You'd be happier alone?"

"Yes, I'd be at my best if I was alone and if death were not an option."

"I know," she says. "I have shown you all that I have desired to, and I hope you have taken something away from this. You are one of a kind, Azazel, and I believe great things will come to and from you. Don't forget this; you are blessed. You are blessed."

Guanyin then touches Azazel's cheek with her fingertips, returning him to Bune and once again floating in the Cosmos. When she touched him, she continued showing him his life through a sharp and fast-moving highlight reel. Azazel saw everything, including how to fully cause his powers to release energy beyond any Sovereign. He saw his life and began to feel shame, shame that he took the many roads he did to get to where he should be. Now standing in front of Bune, he realized why he was there.

"Back so soon?" says Bune.

"I've learned so much," says Azazel.

"I asked her to take you away from me, hoping you would find what you need without returning back to me."

"I would like to proceed," says Azazel.

"I was being polite when I said to bring you back to me," says Bune. "Welcome back."

"That was good, but I want to see more."

"Have you discovered what you must do with your life?" asks Bune.

"Not quite, but I know I'm onto something."

"Well, if you have not one idea, I'm sure that what I show you will spark something."

Bune then turns and points to the sky.

"Do you see that?" he asks.

A small ball quickly flew past them. Bune brings Azazel closer to the image. They see Azazel being thrown into the Cosmos as a baby and watch him linger in the air.

"This is you," announces Bune.

"I get that," Azazel replies.

Azazel then looks down, and from a distance, he recognizes Zeus.

"This, for a time, was where you hailed," says Bune.

Azazel watches himself float in the atmosphere, but what didn't surprise him was that he heard no crying.

"He's a little strong one, isn't he?" says Azazel.

"You're that strong one," says Bune, "and you still are."

Moments later, Azazel's small figure is swallowed up by six shadows.

"What's happening?" he asks.

"Come by me," advises Bune. "This is where it gets interesting."

The six shadowy figures soon revealed themselves to be Lucifer, Leviathan, Belial, Beelzebub, Belphegor, and Asmodeus.

"What are they doing to me?" asks Azazel.

"You will see," says Bune.

The six figures circle the baby, and then each figure takes a portion of the child's character so that he would forever remain a servant to them. His body would remain, along with his mind, but he would not have a mind on which to reflect on in a time of need. It was this lack of essence that kept Azazel drifting into all worlds; this is what kept him from *living*.

"So, wait — I don't have a *soul*?"

"Correct," says Bune.

"But I was in the *eternal* realm once."

"That might be true, but it didn't last very long, did it? And you couldn't really do much in it, could you?"

"Well, no," Azazel says.

"You have the mind to get there, but without a conscience for it, you don't belong there."

"While I was there," Azazel reflects, "something made me feel like I belonged. Ever since then, I've been trying to get back."

"But you can't," says Bune.

"But I can't," agreed Azazel. "I'm tired of this life," he says, looking down. "It's not real. I'm just a pawn, and I know I'm better than that."

"One is only as good as the environment from which they come," says Bune, trying to aggravate something within Azazel. "And that is said of the weak."

"Then I need to be better than the realms," says Azazel. "Life becomes special and a necessity when you realize you need to die to preserve it."

"Something has sparked, I'm guessing," says Bune.

"Nothing has sparked, more like everything is engulfed in flames. If I need my *soul* to let fate share its bittersweet taste with me, then all who took it from me will suffer. I'm coming for it."

"Very good," says Bune. "It appears that my time with you is through, so once I bring you back to where I found you, your powers shall be returned."

"Thank you," Azazel says. "My *eyes* are open."

"Do not thank me; it takes a woman. It always has, and it always will. It was Jahzara who came to me on your behalf. This woman pleaded your case and believed that you did not know what you were doing; she gave the impression that you were some sort of lunatic. And now that you know your life, one can only imagine how I saw you. I knew you were troubled, but one is never so troubled that there is no path to follow. You needed to see everything you saw because it was time, Azazel; you needed to grow up. You stand before me as a different *being,* as someone who knows where his *conscience* belongs. Once acquired, I know you will find peace."

"I have a lot to do and think about once I return."

"Indeed," says Bune.

"Hopefully, I won't have to see you again."

"And if you do, I'm not helping you," says Bune through a heavy chuckle. "Go; I have more fools to deal with."

"One last thing," says Azazel. "What makes you so wise?"

"Nothing makes one wise; it is our decisions that force change, experience, and knowledge. One day, they will call you wise too."

Bune then breathed out a fire that completely covered Azazel. The fumes act as an anesthesia, making him pass out immediately. When he waking, he is on *Earth* and in the same way he was before he left. It felt like a dream, but his mind felt more alive than ever.

He got to his feet, and it felt like he hadn't moved in years. He now had a mission. He had something to look forward to. Since he couldn't find a good enough reason to live, he had found one to die.

Vengeance

"His movements are getting sharper," says one.

"He will succumb," says another. "He is alive, but not for long."

"He will embrace the slumber," says a third.

"We have yet to have a Sovereign of his caliber," says the first. "His movements are getting sharper."

"I refuse to believe that he will quit the realm's design to awake," says the second. "We only need him asleep for a few more moments, and then the slumber will become permanent."

"He may be close to breaking the design," says the third, "but should he remain in this condition for even a few more moments longer, he will be our greatest prize yet."

"Let them all mindlessly wander in the lost realm," says the first. "It doesn't matter how close they are to breaking free. Once they pass the allotted period of time, they belong to us."

The Council of the Eternals watches Azazel. He is showing signs that he is close to waking up. His randomly flinching body and his changing facial expressions reveal that he not only wants to revive, but also that his regeneration is inevitable.

The Council will not relinquish their rule over the dimensions. Being granted power over dimensions, and over their character and construction, they have devised a means to protect their position from prophesied challengers. Individuals born to overthrow their rule must prove their worth: they must demonstrate and manifest tact in government.

But the endeavor is rigged. None are to escape the matrix they create. Being creators of dimensions, these Sovereigns have constructed a realm for minds. They have become the Judge and the Jury of prophesied Eternals, inventing a realm of provocation as a trial of fitness.

Every mind entered into their experiment is sent into a fixed realm. Creating a matrix familiar to their projected thoughts and feelings, the challenger is encouraged to believe that their experience is real, opening them up to care to remain in the realm. Should they fail to break the realm's design, they will forever remain in the slumber of their experience, but should they awake, they will replace this Council, becoming the sole Eternal of the dimension.

The Estate of the Eternals is filled with many Sovereigns. Being given their office at the beginning of time, they conceitedly defend their place and position. Champions, since the beginning of time, have been prophesied to overthrow the Council of the Eternals, but have, due to the Council's persuasive machinations, repeatedly fail.

But in the midst of the Council is a Sovereign that has other plans. The *other* realm is to serve as a remedy for gaining awareness of time and space, and where others have fallen, Azazel excels, using that realm as a means to consciously understand what he must do in reality.

"Something is wrong," says one of the members of the Council who, seeing Azazel's movements increase, begins to greatly worry.

His movement is increasing because the frequency between he and the Empress is growing stronger. The host watching Azazel is unaware of the Empress and his wives in their vicinity.

After realizing their failure to correctly interpret the writer's advice, they left the Estate of the Eternals to once again find the Eternal's writer. Understanding that their initial conversation was with the wrong writer for the wrong Eternal, they took note, and in hopes of its usefulness to Azazel, of what they saw in the Estate of the Eternals. Exiting that Estate and returning to the Palace of the Eternal, they find the right writer that had assisted in Azazel's judgment.

"Each member of the Council of the Eternals is an Eternal Sovereign, and for every Eternal, there is a writer," says the writer to the Empress and her companions.

"The last writer sent us to where we should not have gone," says one of Azazel's wives, "but I believe the trip was for a reason."

"That is correct," says the writer. "Each of us, as writers, have only one responsibility, and that is to make sure the spirit of the Eternal's words easily translates, for the sake of creation, to the elements of creation. We cannot override the work of one another, but can labor together, for better or for worse, with the spirit of what is written."

"Why are there so many writers? Why not have one writer for the Council?" asks another one of Azazel's wives.

"Each Eternal has a disposition," explains the writer." "It is written that every Eternal should have a *Conveyor*, or an *Assistant* fulfilling the law of their thoughts. This Conveyor and Assistant is what my colleagues and I are. We are writers for our particular Eternal, and because they each have a law inscribed into their character, only one writer is assigned to properly manage their imagination."

"And you are the writer responsible Azazel's judgment?" says the Empress.

"I am responsible for no judgment," says the writer. "I am responsible for the coming together of desired elements and for assisting in the outcome of what is wanted."

"So Azazel taken away from us, and from his own self, is what was wanted?" asks another one of his wives.

"That is correct," says the writer.

"Who is benefited from this?" asks the Empress.

"At the beginning of time," begins the writer, "an assembly of Eternals received the office of Creator: they were to co-exist as being the creators of every *thing*. Not long after this assembly was formed, a prophecy concerning their overthrow entered into existence; it was said that one Sovereign would replace many Eternals as the Creator.

"As the centuries and millenniums passed, so did the *Select*. The dimensions gave birth to many Sovereigns believed to overthrow the Council of the Eternals, but none fulfilled the vision. Upon learning of their inevitable defeat, the Council created an examination to confirm the identity and dominion of the *Select*: they created a matrix for the Sovereign's; if they could escape the matrix, they could then reign as intended."

"So this is all a game?" says one of Azazel's wives.

"It is not a game," says the writer. "You were led to the Estate to understand that this is no game, but that there is no thing taken more seriously than that prophecy of *one* replacing the *many*."

"He has to release them," says one wife to the Empress. "He has to release every Sovereign that they've trapped."

"No!" yells the Empress. "That is, again, not the solution."

"Azazel cannot overthrow an assembly of Eternals alone," says another wife, causing the Empress to pause and think.

"She's right," says the writer. "As profound as Azazel is, the Eternals, should he attack them, will not let him live. He may be able to stop two or three by himself, but he cannot take on all six of them."

"Maybe not," says the Empress with a glimmer in her eye, "but Azazel with a writer can."

After feeling an uncomfortable pressure from the silence now filling up the room, and from the eyes of the women looking at him, "You're not serious," he says, staggering in his speech. "Writers belong to Eternals, and Azazel's office as Eternal is based upon his own efforts to awake."

"Join us," says the Empress, drawing nearer to him. "Aepharia is and will for ever be life's sole dimension. When Azazel awakes, he will kill whatever Eternal is in front of him, and if it is your Eternal that he kills, you will cease to exist. I know my husband; he kills the least and the greatest equally."

"The writer is attached to their Eternal," says one of Azazel's wives, "I once heard this and I believe that it is true."

"You will cease to exist once your *God* is killed," says another wife.

"You are correct," says the writer, "and if I had a stake in the affair, I would act for my self, but I already, being only an extension of the Eternal, cease to exist; my living or dying, depending upon the life and death of the Eternal, means nothing."

"And is that what you would have?" asks the Empress. "Would you only have an existence dependent upon the breath of an Eternal, or would you rather have your own breath, your own independence, your own right to live? Would you not rather live for your office, as opposed to having your office live for you?"

"We are offering you freedom, sir," says one of Azazel's wives.

"We are offering you a home," says the Empress.

Unable to think of why he should refuse their words, "Come," he, after a moment of deliberation, says.

He leads them to the laboratory where all six members of the Council of the Eternal are. The Empress and Azazel's wives see him in their midst, and in a tank-like chamber similar to the other Sovereigns at the Estate of the Eternals. Without saying anything, the writer vanishes, returning to his desk. The women, paying no mind to his missing presence, stealthily make their way into the room.

"Did you hear that?" asks one member of the Council after hearing an instrument fall to the floor.

"I did not," says another, "but his movements are becoming sharper and are happening more rapidly."

"Something is wrong," says a third, looking around.

Trusting that more noise will cause the group to break up and to go searching for the matter, the Empress, looking at one of his wives, signals to her to make more of a commotion. Upon doing so, all six of the members depart to find the sound's location. Seeing Azazel now alone, the Empress quietly walks towards Azazel, placing her palm on his chamber.

It's indestructible. Feeling around the chamber and banging on it, she is unable to use any of her abilities to rattle it. Watching Azazel twitch, her drops to the floor, wanting to save him but can do nothing to set him free.

But she isn't as careful as she should be. Her mind slipping into a wave of feeling, she is surprised by an Eternal, who has grabbed her by her neck. Now turned around, she sees that her companions are also in custody.

The Empress, sending a large volt of energy through the Eternal's hand, causes him to release his grip. Quickly releasing her, she sends a fire-lit punch into his chest, sending him stumbling backwards. Her attack slightly distracts the other Eternals, allowing Azazel's wives to perfect an attack of their own. Hereafter a battle between these women and the six Eternals begins.

The women defend themselves courageously, but it isn't enough. The Eternals have killed two of Azazel's wives; the other is on the brink of death, along with the Empress. And this outcome is exactly what the Empress wanted. Knowing their history, and that Azazel would kill or be killed for her, she knew that if he should sense her impending death, that he would awake to avenge her.

All she needed was to be close enough to him. All she needed was an opportunity for him to sense her. She knew that she could do nothing to physically liberate him, but if she could get close enough to touch his chamber, she knew that he would feel her presence, and that their invisible cord should vibrate to awaken him.

She was right. Azazel's movements were rapidly increasing and he was preparing for exiting both the chamber and that *other* realm, but the presence of the Empress made it happen a lot faster. Having one wife in one hand and the Empress in the other, and preparing to disintegrate them, a large boom shakes the room, moving everything and everyone out of order; Azazel, after the fog is settled, is found on his hands and knees, breathing deeply.

Catching his breath, Azazel stands to his feet and makes his way to the first Eternal in his sight. Lowering his hand to the ground, with his palm facing down, the ground under the Eternal in vision begins to heat up, eventually becoming a beam of light shooting from the ground and through to the ceiling, turning him to ash.

Azazel then does the same to the next Eternal he sees, then locking eyes on the third, he holds out his hand, bringing the Eternal's neck into his palm. Tightly gripping the Eternal's neck with his right hand, he places his left hand on the *God's* right shoulder, forcefully moving his right hand up and his left hand down, causing the Eternal's head and spine to separate from his body.

"Enough!" yells the fourth Eternal, stumbling to his feet and collecting himself after the boom.

After saying so, the Eternal sends an orb into Azazel's chest, paralyzing him. Standing over him to give the final blow to Azazel, the Eternal is hit in the back by a forceful beam. The Empress has sent out energy from her self and into the Eternal.

"Go!" she yells to Azazel who, understanding the release of the *Select* that must happen, quickly vanishes from the scene and appears at the Estate of the Eternals.

Standing outside of the Estate, he drops to one knee and places his palm onto the ground. The *force* of every trapped Sovereign within the estate travels through the ground and into Azazel's palm, assimilating with his inward person. Upon receiving their essence, Azazel, from his palm, shoots a line of fire through the ground and into the Estate, destroying it and every coma-ridden Sovereign within it. He then destroys the Estate's dimension.

Quickly returning back to the scene of action, and with the essence and force of Sovereigns flowing through him, he finds the Empress dead and two Eternals remaining; one of them is the one that sentenced him. Looking at them, Azazel, with his mind, causes them to kill one another. Upon their death, he walks over to each one of his wives and resurrects them. He, last of all, brings the Empress back to life. Exiting the Palace, Azazel executes the same judgment against the Palace and its dimension that he did for the Palace and dimension of the Estate.

Consolation

Order returned. With Azazel back in the Universe and Palace of Aepharia, the *plague* affecting its *beings* ceased. Passing, in triumph, through the entire Universe on a cloud, Azazel, his Empress, his wives, and his Council are celebrated by their creatures.

Azazel is the first prophesied Sovereign to successfully overcome the Primary Creator's design. This is that same Eternal Creator who, in the beginning, brought his script and its vision to life. He created the dimension with its elements, giving to the atmosphere's elements a character fulfilling a specific role. Now, after this dimension's many eons of generations, one has met and fulfilled the role given to him, becoming the dimension's sole Eternal.

The Jubilee of the dimension's family is beyond royal. As they, in absolute brightness, pass through the eastern, western, northern, and southern spheres of the Universe, cheers are heard. The ruling family of Aepharia lives, and with the *ghost* of many Sovereigns within their King, the *beings* of Aepharia know that the family's work isn't done.

Azazel, along with every *being* within the dimension, knows that both Heaven and the Underuniverse must now accept subjection under Aepharia, eventually passing away as individual Universes, amalgamating into Aepharia so that there may be only one dimension. This is his next labor, which should not be difficult, seeing as how every being, despite the Universe, understands that the Eternal is to graft the Universes into one, and under allegiance to himself.

But while this is known, it is not accepted. Heaven and the Underuniverse do not want to relinquish their identity to Aepharia. With Azazel conquering most of these Universes, and them uniting to conquer Aepharia, the dimension, in Azazel's absence, has become unbalanced.

In order to exterminate the "plague" of Aepharia and return balance back to the dimension, enemies have becomes acquaintances. The controversy is now a battle between Aepharia and the union of Heaven and the Underuniverse. Leading the way for Heaven, with Azazel having conquered most of its Sovereigns and their realms, is Anastasia; Azazel's father remains in the Underuniverse as its chief Sovereign, and must be overthrown.

Although surrounded by majestic allure and an impenetrable aura, Azazel may have a smile on his face, and he may be enjoying himself, but his mind is elsewhere. He understands that the work isn't finished, and feeling as though his absence was a waste of time, he is anxious to gather Heaven and the Underuniverse into Aepharia, completely erasing them from memory to create an entirely new history.

He is sorry that he must war with Anastasia and his father, the two people that actually gave him more love than anyone else. He could have ended their Universes sooner, but because of his affection for them, because of their memory, he intentionally refrained, and traversing through every region of Aepharia, he is inclined to procrastinate.

It was Anastasia's mother that helped care for Azazel when his mother found him. After bringing him to the Universe of Heaven, his mother did not immediately go to her parents, but went to her closest friend. There, with Azazel in her arms, they talked, his mother being afraid of her father's response to the child.

"Have you cleaned him?" asks Anastasia's future mother.

"I have," responds Azazel's mother, "he is fine."

"But how many times have you cleaned him?"

"Just once," says Azazel's mother.

"You have to make sure he does not have the scent of where he came from. You have to make sure that his smell is Heaven's essence."

Taking the child from the goddess, Anastasia's mother holds him in her arms, a luminescent brightness engulfing them.

"You have to do it this way," she says from within the light. "You have to make sure his aura is refreshed; this will ease your father's spirit when you present the child to him."

Returning the child, the baby glows in the arms of the goddess, sending warmth throughout her body.

"Stay with me," she says to the goddess. "Stay until you are ready to go."

"I couldn't impose," replies the goddess.

"Just stay here," she says to the goddess. "Eons have not yet separated us, and I know you, that you are ready for him. Stay and let me help. Leave whenever you will, but stay and let me help as I can."

The goddess stayed for a short while, adopting the motherly spirit of her friend. She would leave when her friend would become pregnant with Anastasia.

Azazel's mind, like the cloud he rode on, traveled through its own regions. There must be a way, knowing that he would pulverize the *beings* and the environment of Heaven, for him to spare not only Anastasia's life, but also the life of her mother and family. Wasting no time, and moving off of impulse, Azazel hastily vanishes from Aepharia and appears in Heaven, at the Estate of Anastasia's family.

She still lived with her family. Her family's Estate was famous in Heaven, being operated by aristocratic Sovereigns heavily involved with the direction of Heaven's government. Upon entering into the Estate, Azazel is greeted by Anastasia, who is surprised to see him.

"Come to finish your work?" she sarcastically says.

"Have you forgotten who I am?" he asks.

"Is Azazel never satisfied? When is it enough?" she says.

"I have not forgotten who you are," he says.

"Do you know that I led armies into Aepharia and we ruined your little child. Do you know how much it hurt me to do that? Do you know that with every dead *being*, I felt as though I was killing you? Do you know that you abandoned them as you abandoned me, and that I loved every minute of them suffering without you?" she responded, her eyes watering.

"I know," he replies, walking closer to her.

"Do you know the imbalance you've caused? Do you know that Aepharia repeatedly tried to conquer us, and that your Council is behind half of the deaths in my family, including the death of my father? Do you know the position you put me in? I hate you," she says, her head bowed, her face, due to her crying and uncontrollable breathing, disfigured.

"You know who I am," he says, making it to her, and taking her in his arms, holding her, the side of her face resting on his chest. "I can't control who I am to be; I can only be who I am."

"You are a criminal," she says.

"I only do what is written of me," he says, holding her tighter.

"What do you want!" she belches, pushing off of Azazel. "Do quickly whatever you are here to do."

"I've only come to talk, to see if you would live near my Estate, away from every other *being*. I'm here to let you know that Aepharia is yours, and that you and your Estate, with your family, can live wherever you want in Aepharia, but I prefer you and your Estate in your own section of Aepharia."

"And what about the rest of Heaven?" she asks. "Should I live while my Universe and its *beings* cease to exist?"

"I have no expectation Anastasia," he carefully says, "but intend only to offer this to you. If you will accept, I will not harm the *beings* of this Universe, but only the Universe itself. I know that Heaven will fight against my intention, but if you will accept, Heaven will see no war, but I will peacefully bring Heaven's remaining families into Aepharia. But Heaven will dissolve."

"I cannot let Heaven die," she says. "This is home."

"Heaven will not die," he reasons. "Heaven continues through its families. Heaven is only a Universe, and its existence is no longer needed. To Aepharia alone belongs existence."

After a period of deliberation, Anastasia finally consents. Azazel keeps his word, safely bringing the remaining families of Heaven into Aepharia and giving to Anastasia and her family the best sphere in Aepharia for their Estate.

Soon after re-locating Heaven's *beings* and its remaining Sovereigns with their families to Aepharia, Azazel, observing the Universe from a distance, closes his eyes, causing Heaven's evaporation to occur; even the *space* holding the Universe together dissolves. Vanishing from this scene, Azazel re-appears in the Underuniverse and at his father's throne.

Azazel presents the same offer that he presented to Anastasia to his father. His father declines; he prefers to pass away with the Universe and the *beings* that he created, and that faithfully served him. Azazel then does with the Underuniverse and it's realm as he did with Heaven, this time dissolving the Universe, and the *space* holding it, with its *beings*.

The vision is fulfilled; Aepharia is now the sole Universe of the dimension, and under the direction of the sole and only Eternal Sovereign of the dimension. Looking on his *world*, his Empress in his arms, his wives beside them both, and his council behind them, the promised reign of ages has begun, but the conquest of other dimensions, to have Aepharia as the only dimension in the Primary Eternal's Island Universe, awaits.

Note A: Zeus' Act Against Azazel

"Could you not tell that it wasn't me?" he said to her. "Are you not the mother of wisdom and prudence?"

"I understand," she said, wearing a look of shame, shock, and worry.

"I don't think you do," he quickly replied. "You of all the gods and titans should know the prophecy."[6]

"We cannot control fate," she said.

"We cannot control fate, but we can guide it. We can guide possibility. We may not be able to predict possibility, but we can assume control of the outcome to persuade the prophecy as we wish."

"Zeus, whatever you are proposing is contrary to reason."

"Is not my wife being unable to discern me from an imposter also contrary to reason?" He said in a tone of disappointment. "And yet it has happened."

"The prophecy is between us and no other," she said. "It is a son of ours who is to fulfill the vision."

"Do you think a vision cares about particulars? The prophecy concerns us, yes, but a vision is simply a depiction. I was seen in vision, but it does not mean that it was actually me."

---

6 See Hesiod's Theogony

"Zeus, I will not hurt this child," she said sharply.

"And you think you now have the right to judge? Where was your judgment when not I, but my depiction was with you? Do you think that you now have a say in what happens next?"

"So like your enemy, you too plan to rob me of my body?"

"It is not robbery. If we are now here having a discussion about this, then it is according to time and chance that I do what I now feel I must do. I will commit no act contrary to time and chance, but an act persuading the vision's time and chance in a new way."

"And what is now according to time and chance?" she asks.

"That our blood never has a record or remembrance of this in our history. We cannot risk this child gaining any sort of commendation in our realm. We cannot know if this child will fulfill the prophecy. If he does, the scribes of Thoth will change the fate of the realm."

"So you would rather preserve your legacy in the annals above letting this child discover his own?"

"It is not I, Metis, but time and chance."

"Your care for adoration from the lesser minds has never sat right with me," she said.

"Then so be it; let my flaws die with you but remain unknown forever."

Zeus, then, manipulating the laws of nature, of being, of essence, of time, and of chance, held out his right hand, his palm open and facing up. Soon enough his palm became bright; from Metis' abdomen flew small glowing elemental particles into his palm. A child, made out of the bright particles, then began to form within Zeus' hand. Zeus made his way to the outside of the palace and then hurled the child into the Cosmos, where the child, silent and sleeping, as if still in the womb, floated.

Soon enough the guards of the cosmos became aware of the child. Mystified about how the child ended up there, they consorted with Zeus, who, of all, may have knowledge about how this may have happened.

Zeus stated that he had no idea. Not only did he say that he had no idea, he advised the child to be sent to a realm, suggesting Heaven. The guards of the Cosmos then took Azazel and brought him to the Chief Mind and King of Heaven, where he was closely watched and trained in the wisdom, history, and power of the realms.

Note B: The Scars

Azazel received many scars as a youth, some when fighting, for example, Ammit, a goddess of Egypt whose body was part lion, hippopotamus, and lion. When the heart of an individual had been found unredeemable and impure, the judges of the Underuniverse sentenced that heart to be devoured by Ammit, preventing that person from continuing their journey into their divine solemnity.

One of Azazel's best friends, being a god, had been found unworthy of their divine status. Being found unworthy, he was sentenced to a trial, where his heart was found to be impure. His friend, Tharros, had his heart given to Ammit for devouring. As his heart was between her teeth, Azazel materialized, opened her jaws, took out Tharros' heart, flew into the fourth realm of Heaven, and, with his mind, removed Tharros from the scene of judgment and brought him to where he was.

Placing his friend's heart back within him, Tharros commented on the left side of Azazel's face, also pointing out his arms and his back. He had suffered an attack when wrestling the heart of out Ammit's mouth, walking away with a scar running down the left side of his face, and scars, due to attacks not just from Ammit, but from the courts' *beings*, along his arms and back. He had fended them all off to resurrect Tharros.

There are then times when Azazel, for certain purposes, and in dedication to some *thing*, would scar his own self. Azazel, as is told in the story, due to his current state of mind, gave himself a scar running down the left side of his face.

Note C: Bune

Knowledge of Bune's exact origin is unknown. Knowledge of the time in which Bune first appears in history is unknown. What can be said about Bune is that he, for his wisdom, and for his profound judgment, and for his cunning speech, was sent into a realm belonging only to him. As time passed, his realm developed according to his character, cementing his profession and reputation. He has been an advisor to major and to minor gods, including, for purposes of creation, and of the laws regulating both life and death, Ra and El. Having three heads, Bune's wisdom is drawn from three different yet similar natures, or from three similar dispositions ruling three very different natures.

With the head of a dog, he speaks from an empathetic yet prideful heart. Speaking by the head of a dog, his counsel is thoughtful, his tongue is unguarded, his beliefs are untrained, but his position revolves around the liberty behind loyalty to self and to others.

Having the head of a Gryphon, as the Gryphon is known to guard treasures and timeless possessions, being also depicted on ancient sanctuaries and tombs, and being seen as a divine guardian, Bune speaks from the perspective of guarding, securing, defending, fighting for and paying attention to what matters most, which is the personal and spiritual state of self. Having the head of a Gryphon, when he speaks, Bune cares to enlighten his hearer about their sacred duty to learn the principles and laws of life and of creation, encouraging and guiding them on their journey of discovering their hidden essence within the *Creator's* playground, which playground is their thoughts and feelings.

Bune's third and final head is that of a man. Having the head of a man, Bune's wisdom reaches into the conflict of being human. Having the head of a man, he speaks to encourage the discovery and the positive regeneration of the human condition. He believes that this positive regeneration can come only as what is discovered is put to death. Possessing a man's mind, he is able to advise on the ignorance and also the pleasure of the human nature, giving his student the opportunity to wisely choose which passion they would have.

Note D: The Wisdom of Bune

Reflecting on Azazel, Bune notes, "The biggest decision one can make is in deciding whether or not to continue living. We live this life thinking that it depends on us, as if we are its sufficiency. Yet the relationship our breath has with life is not one where one is dependent upon the other, but where neither our breath nor life can exist without the friction they give to one another.

"We think that life is a game or a personality consistently being coy with us. When we should let go of what we think and feel, we are oddly found tense, our frame tightening due to the unfamiliarity of the experience. And so we play the game, resisting life, and the vision given by the *life* of our life, because we believe the attention is fitting the case we hold against life for making us its victim.

"But are we really life's victim? Is it really knowledge of self we want, or is it confirmation about the understanding we already have about our self that we want?

"To let go of the desire to want information on *us* is to receive the understanding we desire. It is our desire to want information on our self that actually stops us from receiving it, causing us to stumble over ourselves when we should, for freely receiving the intended vision, let go of the desire to want knowledge of our self.

"Is this not a matter of faith? To have faith is to let go and not to cling. To have faith in something is to trust that you already have whatever you hope for and that no reminder, whether routine or in the form of adornment, is needed. If therefore knowledge of self should come, a letting go of the idea to retain knowledge of self should take place.

"Letting go of the idea to retain a knowledge self, there is faith that a hope for such knowledge will come, and it will. But to cling to the idea of retaining knowledge of any *thing* is to frustrate the effort for it, actually causing a greater gulf between that *thing* and us by our failure to simply capture without effort."

Note E: Bune's Take

Before major and minor deities were created and had their assignments engraved upon their characters, the Sovereign Creators held a council about the types of *divinities* they needed to create for their realm's sufficiency. The Creators got together to discuss the philosophy they would encode their created realm and *beings* with, along with the intention every created *thing* should possess and serve.

They wanted to create a realm given to creators, in which those creators should then create whatever should be created for creation. They consulted Bune to challenge their purpose for the realm, who advised them to create every thinking and feeling creature inwardly fractured. Doing so, he said, would make their experience authentic, giving them the opportunity to learn of that fracture to do something about it. "Think of the encoded error within their person, despite the dignity you assign them, and then the dignity they assign to one another, as being what they need to achieve an awareness allowing transcendence," suggested Bune.

The council of the Creators incorporated Bune's philosophy into the elements forming their realm. These elements formed a code of life. This code created the next Creators that should create the next Creators who should solidify the creation of the realm.

CPSIA information can be obtained
at www.ICGtesting.com
Printed in the USA
LVHW021520110522
718482LV00001B/110

9 781955 622547